OUT OF REACH

AND OTHER STORIES

Lloyd Rees

Published by
Llyfrau Cambria Books, Wales, United Kingdom.
*Cambria Books is an imprint of
Cambria Publishing.*
Discover our other books at: www.cambriabooks.co.uk

DEDICATION

As ever, I am indebted to my wife, Rachel, for her patience and support. I would also like to dedicate this volume to my grandsons Jasper and Harri, who do not know it fully but who helped me no end by making me smile and be happy, even as I catalogued the unhappy circumstances of the characters, all of whom are fictional, in this book.

Author's Note

It might be helpful, though the stories are all stand alone, to note that a common thread runs through them, and also that characters can reappear. I toyed with a number of choices for a title for this collection. 'Twenty Different Colours', 'Marked for Life' and 'The Sudden Intimacy of Strangers' were strong contenders, but ultimately 'Out of Reach' was chosen because I believe it most exactly describes the angst and loneliness of so many of the figures in this book. Having said that, I hope readers will understand my desire to show that there is also frequently humour to be found in the sorts of situation in which these characters find themselves.

Some of these stories have appeared in a range of publications, including New Welsh Review, The Bridport Anthology and Cambrensis.

CONTENTS

OUT OF REACH

It was not till the third day that the lodger began to panic. Linda had told her husband that there was something weird about him, but Robert had dismissed her concern with a lazy shrug.

'He's just quiet,' he said. 'But he hasn't missed any rent. You think everybody who wears glasses has a shifty look about them. He's alright.'

Linda had not been so easily reassured. Once, when she knew their lodger would definitely be out, she had offered to go up to empty his meter. 'It doesn't need it,' Robert sighed. She had taken the key anyway. She was back within five minutes but this was a couple of minutes too long. Robert looked up from his paper.

'You haven't been sniffing round in his room, have you?'

Linda blushed.

'Oh come on, that's not fair. He doesn't bother us.'

She sat down next to him and put her hand on his leg. 'That's the point,' she said. 'I just wanted to know what he does in there all the time. He hardly ever goes out.'

'He's a single man in a bedsitter. What do you think he does?'

Linda shrugged. 'Well, it's clean enough, I have to say. Nothing in there really, just a lot of papers on the table, that's all.'

Robert fought with his newspaper, in order to read the centre pages. He was not interested. After a while he said, 'Well, he's a student of some sort, apparently.'

There was no further mention of the topic until the man in the shop downstairs went away for a week's holiday. Robert and Linda had the flat that occupied the two floors above a vacuum cleaner repair shop. They had decided to let the top bedroom when Robert

1

had lost his job. Arthur, the vacuum cleaner man, had let them put a card in his window and the silent lodger had turned up and moved in within the week.

On the Tuesday after Arthur had closed up his shop and gone to Bournemouth, or wherever it was, Linda was startled by the appearance of their obviously distraught lodger at the lounge door. He was still in a dressing gown, though it was late morning. His hair looked like a child's drawing. He had plainly washed it and slept on it without drying it. He pushed at his glasses and gave a sort of snort before speaking.

'My letters,' he said.

Linda stared in incomprehension.

'My letters,' he gasped. 'They're in the shop downstairs. I can't get at them!'

She managed to get rid of him, though she didn't say how when she was relating this encounter to her husband that evening. Robert nodded. Yes, he had noticed an electricity bill for them through the glass door to the shop. There were a few letters in there.

'He's desperate,' Linda cried. 'You'll have to get them out.'

'How can I get them? The door's locked and we haven't got a key. Arthur won't be back till Saturday or Sunday. They'll just have to stay there till he gets back, that's all.'

Linda banged down his plate on the Formica kitchen table. 'You can't tell him that. Don't leave me to face him tomorrow. Why couldn't you come back earlier anyway? I was afraid he'd come down again. You've got to deal with it.'

Robert winced at the prospect of this irksome task, but when she refused to talk throughout their meal, and then raised the matter again as he went to switch the television on, he snapped. 'Alright,' he said. 'I'll speak to him. I'll see him in the morning.'

He was forestalled, however. There was a sharp rap at the door, just as the News was coming on.

'I need a tobacco tin. I don't smoke, you see.'

Robert looked at him properly for the first time. His hair was still wild and he hadn't shaved. It must have been something of a shock for Linda.

'What?'

'You must have a tobacco tin or something like that.'

He hovered on the threshold as Robert stepped back inside the lounge. Robert shrugged at Linda and opened a drawer where there was an old tin he kept elastic bands in.

He handed the tin to the lodger.

'Weights.' ⁱ

Robert misunderstood. He waited.

'I need weights,' the lodger insisted, his voice sticky and dry. 'Do you fish?'

Robert shook his head. He wanted to help. Or rather, he didn't want not to help, but the young man's monosyllabic nature was disturbing.

'Can you wait here a minute,' the man said. Robert obeyed. He didn't want to catch Linda's eye, so he stood in the doorway, his head resting on the arm that held the door open. Within a few seconds the lodger had reappeared. He was shaking the tobacco tin, holding it to his ear, testing it with a thumb.

'Water's no good,' he sighed. 'The tin leaks. Is this the best you've got?'

Robert ignored the question. 'What on earth do you want it for?' he said.

The man tufted. 'I need something heavy,' he said. 'to put in the tin.'

Robert looked around, but they were standing in the hallway. There was nothing but an upright vacuum cleaner in the way of anything heavy.

'Plasticene. Or play dough,' the lodger exclaimed.

'Blu-tack?'

'Yes, that might do it.'

Robert went back to the drawer where he had found the tin and brought out a new packet of the adhesive gum. The lodger was bounding back down the stairs, having raced up to get rid of the water. He seized the adhesive, rolled it into a sausage and pressed it into the tin. He carefully rolled a thin strip around the edge of the tin and pressed the ill-fitting lid back on.

'Not bad. Sellotape to make sure though.'

Robert wanted to point out that he didn't run an office supplies outlet, but he obediently fetched some tape. The lodger wrapped a long strip round the tin and weighed it in his hand.

'Fine,' he said. Then he took out a piece of string from his pocket and held it against the lid. 'More tape,' he demanded. Robert held it out and the lodger bit off another long strip. Robert watched, intrigued, as the string was attached.

'Just need a rod now. Hold that.'

Robert took the tin and felt a tackiness on the underside. The man had pressed on some adhesive tabs. He must have been doing this as he ran from his own room back down the stairs. Robert realised the madness. Late night fishing for letters, through the letterbox of a locked door. He said nothing, however, when the man returned with a piece of white plastic tubing. It looked like part of a frame from a child's playhouse. Robert couldn't imagine where he could have found it. He watched as a knot was expertly and quickly tied and he followed him downstairs to the glass door, where a small heap of letters lay temptingly in view.

Two men in a darkened shop doorway, Robert thought. If a policeman passes, I'll just say I found him inserting this tin through the letterbox and I stopped to see what he was doing. Much the same as you, officer.

'That's yours on top,' the lodger said.

Robert smiled thinly. It was a bill. There would be a reminder in due course anyway, and this could take hours. He remembered playing a machine at the fairground where you tried to seize hold of a shiny metal cylinder with a packet of ten cigarettes perched in cotton wool on it. There you used a metallic grab that invariably slipped off the prize and deposited air into the win chute. Clearly the lodger had never been to a fairground, or was possessed of more patience. He lowered the sticky tin down through the letterbox and waited as it spun, then he eased it on to the manila envelope. He tried to drop it down heavily to make it stick, but the first three or four times the reeled up nothing more than a tin of blu-tack. Then it worked.

He eased back the plastic tube then seized the string and delicately reined in an electricity bill to within an inch of the letterbox. Agonisingly, the friction against the door caused the letter to dislodge and flutter back down to the floor.

'Do you mind if I go back for that one later?' the fisherman said, desperation glinting in his otherwise darkened face. Robert shrugged. He was hooked on the man's strength of purpose now; he was almost enjoying himself. The lodger had not waited for an answer but had turned back to his task. The second time he was successful, slipping two fingers through the spring-loaded letterbox and working his rod hand so carefully, an operation which took several minutes. The third time the tackiness of the adhesive labels on the base of the tin was no longer strong enough, and the tin had to be withdrawn and re-labelled.

Then, over the space of about forty minutes, six letters were delicately retrieved. The electricity bill lay almost within reach but several casts failed to land it.

'Do you specially want that one? the lodger said. Then, 'I've got one here for you. Looks like it's a council tax one. And there's one here for the shop.' He pushed the letter back through the opening and flung it as far into the shop as he could.

Robert said, 'I don't specially need it, but here, give me a go.' He twisted the tin and thrust the tube back and fore until he finally managed to land it on the cellophane window of the envelope. The lodger did not take his eye off the operation, despite the fact that he had a small wad of envelopes of his own in his hand. Robert

5

managed to raise the bill till one corner was resting on the frame of the letterbox.

'This is the awkward bit,' his friend advised him.

Robert got two fingertips to the envelope and pulled it, crumpled, through the slot.

'Got it!'

'Well done. '

'That was a good idea.' Robert paused. The lodger had of course said his Christian name when he first came to the house, but Robert had never had cause to use it and he was embarrassed for a moment as it eluded him.

'Simon.'

'Yes, sorry. I'm Robert.'

'I know,'

They stood for another few seconds, looking down at their haul of letters.

'Better go back up then,' Robert said at last.

The man nodded.

Linda was in bed, but awake, when Robert re-entered the flat. She moved her swollen body across to her side of the bed as if it was someone else's body, or an inanimate thing, and Robert slid between the rough sheets.

'It's cold,' he said.

'You'll warm up,' she murmured. He did not reply. 'What was all that business with the Sellotape and the blu-tack? That man's weird. I told you he was.'

'He's alright. I'll tell you in the morning. I'm tired now.'

She did not pursue the matter and presently her breathing slowed and her body lurched in a last spasm before deep sleep. He listened to the traffic outside. The house was a hundred yards from a set of traffic lights so there would be a lull for a while, then a burst of cars, invariably changing into third as they roared past. He had got used to this pattern of noise since they had moved in, but he could not blot it out tonight as he lay wide-eyed staring at the ceiling. He was suddenly bitterly alone.

Upstairs Simon was at his table with four identical slim white envelopes in front of him. He would be smiling now, devouring words slowly like a beautiful meal. A floor below, in an unlovely bedroom with an unopened council tax demand and an electricity bill on the bedside table, Robert lay stiff as a stained handkerchief. Out of reach.

TWENTY DIFFERENT COLOURS

I was at a loose end. In the four months I'd been in Northampton I'd only met one person I could get on with, and that was one of the other drivers, Dave. I'd had a drink with him a few times after work and once we'd had a takeaway back at his flat. He was pretty tied up with this girlfriend over in Cambridge though. To tell the truth we weren't that matey, I suppose. I mean, I couldn't ring him to go out for a drink; it was just if we happened to be coming off work at the same time we might call in for one before going home. All the same, I went round to his flat this one Friday evening. I just couldn't stay in on my own again.

There was no answer when I rang. I was fairly sure it was the bottom bell, but there were two flats on each floor, so I tried to convince myself I could be mistaken when no one answered. I stared at that plain blue door willing him to come and open it, and when he didn't, I couldn't stop myself, I rang all the other bells, my hand on the buttons for too long. It was the awfulness of the thought of trudging back through the rain- slimed streets to my bedsit that made me do it.

It seemed like everybody had cleared off for the weekend. No one answered. Then, just as I was turning away, I heard a sort of flopping sound coming down the corridor. I steeled myself for some old guy in carpet slippers, who'd glower at me and send me packing with a flea in my ear for disturbing him from his early evening nap. But it was a woman.

'Oh, hello,' she said. She had slippers on, but she was quite young, and sort of pretty, though a bit made-up, and made-up badly somehow, as if she'd been trying on different shades of the stuff.

'Um, sorry, I must have rung the wrong bell,' I said. 'I was looking for Dave.'

8

'Oh, Dave. He's gone out. I think he has anyway.' She wiped the corner of her eye with a knuckle and looked at me. 'D'you want to come in and check?' she said.

I had a funny feeling, but there was nowhere else I was going. 'Yeah,' I said. 'He might have his stereo on or something,' It wasn't likely. We were standing a few feet away from his door and there was no sound coming from his flat. 'Best to check, you're right.'

She stood right next to me as I banged on the plywood door. It was obvious he wasn't in. I'd already told myself he must be in Cambridge, but I had to go through with the charade now. The woman was wearing a housecoat thing, and she kept pulling it together in front with her fist, which was strange because I'd already seen she was wearing a jumper underneath, and she was wearing jeans too.

'No good,' I said.

'Do you want to wait?' she said.

I looked at her.

'You can have a cup of coffee and give him a few minutes if you like. Perhaps he's just popped out.'

I didn't know what to say.

'My flat's the back one,' she said.

I followed her down the dingy corridor to an identical plywood covered door, and then into her living room. The first thing to strike me was this huge parrot she had in a cage hanging from a hook in the ceiling. The cage took up most of the window.

'That's a colourful bird,' I said. 'What's she called then?'

'That's Henry,' she said. She looked down at herself and seemed surprised that she had this tatty nylon housecoat on, and she ran off to another room. She came back a few seconds later in her jumper and jeans.

'Well, I'm Mick,' I said. 'Nice to meet you, Henry.' The bloody bird turned round and bobbed his arse feathers at me for my trouble.

'I'm Sandra,' the girl said. 'Ignore Henry, he gets offended when

9

I have company, he's always like that.'

I stayed standing while she went into a little kitchenette - it was more of an alcove off the living room really - to make some coffee. Then I sat down on one end of a long settee that took up most of the space in the middle of the room. She brought the coffees back and stood in front of me by the gas fire in the grate holding her cup and twiddling a bit of her hair, like she used to have it longer and was wondering where it had all gone. She asked me how long I'd known Dave and said she hadn't seen me calling round before. I had to admit I'd called on the off chance, more than anything. I asked her how long she'd been in her flat. Stuff like that, designed to last the five minutes it takes to get a cup of coffee down without burning your lips.

Then she seemed to relax all of a sudden and it put me more at ease. She started pointing out these photos on the mantelpiece and a big, expensively framed one on the wall. They were all of her, and her hair was a million different lengths in them. Twenty different colours too. She'd been an air hostess, she told me. Travelled. Travelled everywhere. And ended up here, I thought, as I looked for somewhere to put my cup down.

'Look, I'm sorry I haven't got anything else for us to drink,' she said. 'I sometimes have a bottle of wine here, but I'm right out tonight.'

I'd already noticed a couple of empty bottles in a corner of the room and there was another one on the table by the window, just underneath the parrot's cage, with wax dribbles round the top but no candle in it.

'I should have brought a bottle,' I said with a laugh.

She joined in laughing. We were both finding it funny that, despite never intending to come here, I was rebuking myself for not having a bottle of wine about my person. Just in case I stumbled into someone with nothing but a parrot, some empties and a few photographs to her name.

'I could go and get one,' I said, suddenly tense with all that the offer presupposed.

'The off licence is a couple of miles away,' she said. She spoke as if the distance was a special grievance to her. 'Um, d'you want to borrow my car? I'd go myself but ...'

'Well, I'm afraid I came here on foot ...'

She turned round and picked up a bunch of keys off the mantelpiece behind her and she tossed them onto the settee next to me. I noticed all the keys had these different coloured rubber things you put over the top to identify which one's which. This careful labelling seemed an odd clash with the disorganised state of the room, the scruffy housecoat and her messy make-up. She told me her car was the blue one on the opposite side of the street and said where the off licence was, and I rushed out. I didn't want her to change her mind or start yelling 'Stop thief!' down the corridor and me be caught disappearing with a stranger's keys and no believable explanation.

I was back in less than fifteen minutes clutching a bottle of Valpolicella. She'd changed out of her jumper into a faded denim shirt, but she still had the same jeans on. I put her keys back in the exact position on the mantelpiece, which was something I thought she'd appreciate. Then we started in on the wine. Before the bottle was halfway down, I'd heard all about the succession of blokes who'd done their level best to wreck her life. Well, I say succession, there were three main ones and a few other more shadowy characters. I was surprised in some ways. I'd put her at about twenty-eight, nine, but she seemed to have packed a lot in, if I was right about that.

I mentioned Allison, and how I'd decided to start up afresh in this new town, but I didn't say too much. I thought it'd spoil the moment, or rather, spoil the moment I was fully expecting to arrive any time now.

In the event I never had to wonder how I was going to make a move because I didn't have to. 'D'you want to come into the other room?' she said. I threw down my last half inch of Valpolicella and stood up to try and kiss her, make it more my idea, so to speak. She

11

avoided my outstretched arms and just caught the tips of my fingers. She led me round the edge of the settee like we were in some Indian or Chinese dance or something. It was that slow and sort of stylised. I felt a bit of a fool, to tell the truth, not least because I was holding the empty wine bottle in my other hand. She took it off me and put it down in the corner with the other empties, then swirled over to me again like a sort of more staggering Jayne Torvill. All of this wasn't making me exactly comfortable, but I was thinking at least I was having an eventful evening. More eventful than if Dave had been home and we'd gone for a pint somewhere anyway.

She started taking her clothes off as soon as we were in her bedroom. I went round the other side of the bed and prised off my shoes by wedging each heel in turn under a big brown wardrobe and sort of stumbling forward. I was trying to catch up and synchronise our undressing, but I kept fumbling at my buttons, while she had her denim shirt off in a moment. It had poppers rather than buttons, I realised. She took off her bra more slowly, as if in time to some sleazy music only she could hear. It was quite dark, the only light coming from the lamp in the other room, but I saw her skin shimmering and pale and I was transfixed by the shock of her dark nipples against the whiteness of her flesh. She pulled down her jeans in one and dived under the sheets while I was still struggling with my last shirt button. This left me having to get my own jeans off clumsily, knowing I was being watched. I might have even blushed there in the dark. Certainly, the erection I'd started to get began to collapse, which made me hurry all the more. I slipped into the bed and felt the coldness of the sheets almost like a blow. She put her hand on my leg and that was freezing too.

'Love me,' she said.

I didn't know whether to respond to this as a question or a demand, so I didn't say anything. I kissed the top of her head, because she was snuggled into me, and it was all I could reach. Then we kissed properly, and without saying anything we managed to make love. It was a quick, bittersweet, sharp experience for me. She didn't comment on the brevity or throw her arm dramatically round her head and stare up at the ceiling or anything. In fact, as far as I could tell, she was asleep within a few minutes, and it was me actually who was left gazing up at the ceiling. I can see it now; it had those awful polystyrene ceiling tiles people used to have. There was a crack in one.

I don't know what time I got up. I spent ages doing it, like a parent who's got into bed with a distressed kid and wants desperately to sneak back to his own bed, but who's terrified of waking the poor kid. My clothes were in a heap at the side of the bed, my jeans inside out and one of the socks caught up in a leg, as always seems to happen, so I picked up the whole bundle and tiptoed into the room next door. I knew we didn't owe each other anything, but I still felt guilty and afraid she'd wake up. As I'd been edging out of the bed I'd looked at her face and it was big and blank with sleep, but I could see at close-up her smeared mascara and the faulty line of her lip gloss. I'm glad she didn't get the chance to study my face at such close quarters, was all I could think.

As I was dressing by the fire, though it was out, of course, I had another chance to look at the photos of her when she was younger, and a lot happier, by the look of it. There was such hope and brightness in her expression in all of them except for the big, heavily framed photo. I went up close to that one. Before I could really decide what it was that made her look sadder here, however, there was a noise which nearly made me jump out of my skin. It was the parrot squawking at me. I pulled my shirt together - I'd just thrown it on but I hadn't buttoned it up yet - as if it was my nudity it was complaining about. Then I went up to his cage and glared at him.

I was daring him to squawk again, and he was looking back at me massively unimpressed. It wasn't much of a stand-off. Then I found myself starting to inspect all his colours. There was every colour you could think of in that plumage - the most passionate reds, the most golden yellows, blues like you only expect to see scuba diving off Barbados or somewhere. I wanted him to utter something again, a word maybe. I tried a whispered 'Pretty Polly', then 'Pretty Henry' as I remembered his name. Nothing. He had nothing to say, or perhaps something to say, but nothing he was going to say to me. Not tonight anyway. I give his cage a nudge, but he hung on to his gently swinging perch with total indifference.

From the bedroom I heard a groan. I froze, hanging on to the cage in mid swing, although it wasn't creaking or making any noise. I listened hard, but it was the groan of someone turning over in bed, not anything more disturbing. I put my finger to my lips to gesture Henry to be silenter than he already was. Then I finished getting dressed and slipped my shoes on. At the doorway I turned back, and the parrot was lifting its beak up at me as if in preparation for the loudest squawk it'd ever made. The noise reverberated after me as I clicked the door shut. Ever since that day I've thought about it and I know it was a word, not just a squawk. I always try and convince myself I don't know what that one, terrible word was. But I can still hear it.

MARKED FOR LIFE

I was never what you'd call really handsome. I used to think I had pleasant features, charming in a way perhaps, but I knew I was no looker, right from the start. You compensate for these things though. I mean, I don't look like some guys, the ones with freckles like someone has spilled coffee granules all over their face or ginger hair like their head was some old busted settee. I'm just sort of ordinary. Apart from the stigmata, as you might say.

You see, there's two things about me. The first thing is, I bruise easy, and I seem to stay bruised. Every little dent, dint, collision, contusion, bang, graze and tumble leaves me marked for life. The second thing's to do with my appearance. I don't mean just my face, I already mentioned that. No, my walk, my stance, my hair - whatever style I choose, oddly enough - everything about the way I strike people reminds them of somebody else. My voice. My laugh. Someone just said the other day my footstep reminded her of her husband. I mean, footstep! Perhaps we both get our shoes from Marks and Sparks, I said. No, she said, don't be silly, you've got a special way of walking into a room, you should have been a dancer. Only my husband can walk into a room like that, she said. I had this impression it was because it was her bedroom I was walking into. Perhaps it's only me and him that get to shuffle in there, I was naturally enough thinking. Anyway, you get the point, it's an example of me reminding people of other people for all these different reasons. Quite frankly, I don't know whether to be flattered or insulted; it's all very well one day being told you smell like Clint Eastwood, but when you stop and analyse it you start to wonder what this woman means. She's certainly never met Clint Eastwood, so it probably means I smell of horseshit. Anyway, the next day someone says you've got the same sort of nervous half-smile as Woody Allen. It's not much wonder, if people are saying you've got a funny walk, and you smell like the man with no name.

Well, you're probably getting the picture by now, I am a little partial to a little bit of a fling. I'm not saying I'm a raving sex maniac or anything, it's just that I seem to have had my share of good fortune. Well, good fortune in one sense.

I was in the bath this morning and I got to examining my body, as you do from time to time, especially as you get to, well, thirty or so. I know, you also do it a fair bit when you're fourteen or fifteen, but somehow, I don't know how, the time just rushes by in between and you don't get a chance to give yourself a good looking over, so to speak. Anyway, as I say, I was having a nice contemplative bath, the water was getting a bit tepid and my hands were getting those massive crinkly fingerprints, and I couldn't help noticing the scar on my stomach again. I thought it would disappear, but it hasn't. It just goes a funny aubergine colour when I'm steeped in water too long. Honestly, I feel like a teabag, or a piece of litmus paper sometimes. But before I could begin to think about the woman who did that I was distracted by the mark on my leg. There's absolutely no chance of that kick mark ever going away. It's a funny little brown hollow right in the middle of my shin. Hard to think that she did that with her normal pointed shoe, not a steel toe capped workman's boot. I felt like I was some sort of 'Try Your Strength' machine they used to have at fairgrounds.

I've got that scar on my abdomen from a knife wound but it's a bit like a caesarean, below the waist, so no one much sees it. Worse is the scar down the back of my calf, but that's from when I came off my bike, so it doesn't count. The other stuff is fairly minor really, though my thumbnail is black and never grew back properly after that Australian girl tried to electrocute me with a table lamp, and I've got a tiny scar above my left eye from when the Ford Escort went into a parked van. That was Shirley losing her shit at me about something.

It was Mandy who did the mark on my shin. I don't really know why I married her. Not many blokes of my acquaintance do know how their wedding comes about. Seems like you're in a bit of a daze for a while and then when you come round preparations are too far advanced to call it off. Some insurance salesman had me much the same way once. I'd been having a bit of a kip on the settee and there was this knock on the door, so I stumbled up and let him in. I couldn't have been properly awake because I remember thinking, if I just sign whatever it is he's got here he'll go away, and I can get back to sleep. Tenacious creatures, insurance salesmen. Like young brides-to-be. But I had to cancel Mandy's policy before too long, I have to say. That was on the cards from the moment she started comparing me to her first husband.

Now I don't mind a drink. Nothing spectacular, just a few bevvies with my mates once or twice a week. And a game of snooker now and again. Well, she starts in on me that I'm out seven nights a week. That was a downright fib.

'Just like Derek,' she'd say. 'Can't stay in like a normal married man.'

I told her. I said, 'I don't mind staying in now and again, Mand, but occasionally I have to have a pint with the thirty of forty other abnormal married men down the local.'.

So she broke my snooker cue. She wasn't big. Average, you'd have to say, average height, and quite slim with it. But she snapped that cue right across her knee like it was a twig. Then she threw one half of it across the room like I was some sort of retriever. I said, 'That's not on, Amanda.' And I walked out.

I didn't walk out, walk out. I just caught the bus into town, because I knew I'd have a few beers, and drink driving's one thing I don't do. I went to a sports shop and bought myself a nice new cue and went for a game of snooker. I was going to go home again. But she turned up in the car outside the club. I was coming out after a quick couple of frames and just going to have a quick pint or two in the pub when I saw her striding down the street at me. I sort of shrugged my shoulders, held up my new cue to show her I didn't harbour a grudge, you know, and the next thing she'd taken a run at me and tried to kick my leg off at the knee. The cue and me just clattered to the ground. Luckily, the cue was unharmed this time, but

17

I did seriously think my leg was a goner for a second or two. Do you know what it's like when a person breathes with every inch of their body? I was going to say, she stood there shaking with rage, but that doesn't describe it at all. It was like she was a massive pile of snakes all hissing and spitting and breathing in and out very fast at the same time. Quite a sight.

'You remind me of my husband!' she said. I suppose she hadn't quite got used to me being her new husband. Then she walked off. I just lay on the pavement expecting to see shards of splintered bone sticking out of my trouser leg and a damp red patch spreading on the ground. I had serious trouble getting on the bus, in point of fact. But there was no blood, no breakage I'm aware of. Just a dent. I mean, I'm marked, but I can't say, 'Oh, that's where I broke my leg once.' I have to pretend it's a forceps mark from when I was dragged screaming out of the womb. Anyway, I got home eventually, had to sit on the lower deck of the bus too, and I hate that. Got home and she'd buggered clean off. I'd had a good half hour to rehearse my speech and there was no one to make it to, just a note on the TV screen that said 'I CAN'T STAND IT ANY MORE, AMANDA.' Just what I wanted to write, apart from the comma.

Anyway, she divorced me for mental cruelty. I could have gone to court, could have gone on crutches now I think about it, and shown them all about cruelty. Sod it, I thought. I pleaded guilty by post.

Then I found myself on the loose again, so to speak. But within a few months I was sitting in Casualty holding my nose on with a red wet hanky. Now Christine, she was a volatile type of woman. Red hair and big eyes. I hadn't considered she was given to violence on Mandy's scale though. Turned out she wasn't averse to attacking a man's olfactory organ when it came down to it, I now see. And why did she bust my hooter? It's funny really, she smacked my head against the steering wheel of the car because I'd been seeing Maureen. Little was she to realise, Maureen was going to smack it back into shape, more or less, before the week was out. Squash racket, she used. I tell you; they didn't know what to think at Casualty.

The thing is, it was a bit of a rebound. Not the racket, now, the relationship, I mean. It was only a day or two after the decree nisi that I bumped into Christine, and I thought she was the most marvellous thing on two legs I'd ever seen. She was serving in this wine bar and somehow I got talking to her, you know how you do, and next thing I was back at her place most nights. I know, you're not supposed to break that magical but unreal bond between barmaid and customer, but in Christine's case I had to make an exception.

Trouble was, she started saying things like, 'Shall I give up working evenings? We could see more of each other then,' I thought, hang on, I'm barely an outpatient from my last marriage and she's already moving her clothes out of one of the wardrobes for me. So I knew it was time to put the brakes on, and accordingly I started not turning up. First of all, I said it was to do with work; later on I just said, 'It's more fun if it's spontaneous. You know now I really want to be with you when I come round; it's not just me coming round out of a sense of duty.' I mean, I never thought this stuff would work, but it's amazing what people will let themselves believe sometimes. She agreed. She said, 'You're right, a man's got to be free to decide what he really wants.' I didn't know if she was taking the mickey when she said this, but it suited the occasion. Because frequently the occasion was Maureen.

Maureen was married. Oddly enough, despite this she liked to play house. I mean, her old man was often away on important courses and such, so she obviously didn't get enough of being the housewife. Don't get me wrong, but all women like that, don't they? So what used to happen was, I'd go round to her place and she'd make me a meal, then we'd watch TV, then we'd go up to bed. From then on it was a bit different from being married, of course. It was more like we were seventeen and we had the house to ourselves because her parents had gone out. In point of fact, we never had the house to ourselves because I used to go round there late, after she'd put her kids to bed. She was a devious woman, was Maureen, but sexy. Dead skinny she was, but warm and sticky, like candyfloss. Quite the opposite from Christine really, who was on the large side, but soft and loving. And as open as a village pub, if truth be told. But she had a dormant violent side too, in the event.

As luck would have it, Christine spotted me the one time I ever appeared in daylight with Maureen. I knew it would be a mistake, but I foolishly let Maureen persuade me to go shopping with her. Her husband was away in America, so I knew the only danger was the rest of the malicious world sniping, sneering, and snivelling jealously at my good fortune, but I didn't really think I'd be that unlucky as to be spotted by Christine herself.

You know how it is: you're pushing the trolley, a little bored but not too much, and you think you see somebody you know just disappearing behind the next aisle. I didn't realise who it was, of course, I just had this faint notion that there was somebody always behind the tins of asparagus or the rows of rum babas. I never used to get the feeling, oddly enough, when Joyce's nerdy little husband had that private detective following me. I did, of course, spot him (her husband, I mean) following me in their stupid Renault that time. That was so typical. He was that paranoid, he was trailing his own private detective to see if he was getting value for money. But I digress.

Maureen got all the stuff she wanted. I wasn't all that interested because most of the grub wasn't for me, it was for her husband, but I did have my eyes on some fresh salmon she'd put in the trolley. Probably it was concentrating on that that made me miss Christine lurking behind the Italian wines while I was hanging around at the checkout. I never got nearer to that salmon than that salivating, needless to say.

It all seemed to happen so quickly. I'd driven Maureen home, dumped the food in the kitchen, and we were just starting to get amorous in the front hallway when there was the sound of the BMW in the drive. Maureen froze. I nearly wet myself. Her husband wasn't due home till late that night and here we were, miraculously still dressed, but definitely in a tricky situation, entwined in her hallway at three o' clock in the afternoon. This sort of situation calls for quick thinking but the best I could come up with was that I was the delivery boy from the supermarket. There were several things that were a bit suspect though:

(a) I was thirty-five at the time.

(b) Where was my bike?

(c) Since when did M&S actually send round someone to put your stuff in the freezer for you?

Maureen was no help. She hotfooted it into the bathroom. I was left to my own deviousness. Later she told me she was going to deny all knowledge of me and claim I was a burglar or a rapist.

Of course, the one thing that saved me was the BMW. It was brand new, more or less, and he wasn't out of the habit of putting it in the garage. We both stood there frozen, as I said, as he pulled up and got out. Then the next thing Maureen was bolting the bathroom door. But then the guy walks past the front door and I hear the garage door opening. It was crazy, but I opened the front door and just walked out on to the front lawn. I knew I'd never make it down the drive, so I ducked to my right and vaulted clean over this low privet hedge and landed in their next-door neighbour's flower border. I don't suppose I could ever clear it again without tearing myself to ribbons or ending up sprawled across it like a piece of washing, but I found myself lying in a bed of chrysanthemums uninjured, apart from my dignity. Of course, there was worse to come, but I didn't know this because I didn't know that Christine was watching this piece of suburban drama from the passenger seat of my car. I'd parked opposite because I hadn't been worried about Maureen's husband getting back from Houston or Dallas, or wherever it was, this early. I didn't even see Christine was sitting there though till I'd slipped into the driver's seat. Cool as you like.

She just said, 'You've got mud on your knees.'

There's only a set number of traumas you can take in the space of three minutes, and in my case it's not two. I couldn't even begin to think of a lie. After the opening tirade of bitterness though, my heart slowed down to about a hundred and forty and, very convincingly, I like to think, I begin to tell her that Maureen was an old friend of my former wife's that I'd bumped into carrying all these heavy bags of shopping. I'd simply offered her a lift home. Her husband was a paranoid maniac who would have killed her on sight if she'd so much as recognised that there were other men in existence on the planet, let alone allowed herself to be given a lift by one. Hence my urgency to depart the place rather sharpish.

She simply said, 'How many bags of shopping did she have then?'

I should have known this was a trick question.

'Five,' I lied.

'Then how come you only had two bags leaving Marks and Spencers and you only took two bags into her house?'

This was uttered at some decibels, so my ears were ringing even before she grabbed my head and smashed it against the steering wheel. You see, I had an old Triumph Herald at the time with the horn in the middle of the wheel. It was a good car, that. Red and white two-tone. Bit like my face after, as a matter of fact. Two things happened at the same time. She broke my nose, but she also broke the horn. The button just bounced up on a spring while I promptly bled all over the steering wheel and, incidentally, on to my muddied trousers. I mean, the blood was bad, but the blaring horn was almost worse. It did shut Christine up though. I didn't say anything, I just tried to ram the spring and the button back into place, but it was difficult because I was also trying to hold my head back to stop the bleeding. Apparently, quite a few people observed the incident. Even Maureen and her husband came to their front door to see what all the racket was about. If you care to date these things, it has to be said that it was at this time that I began to realise that there was little future left in my relationship with Christine. But, ever the gentleman, I drove her home as soon as I'd fixed the horn.

The squash racket episode was scarcely a week later. Now, I don't want to be controversial, but it's got to be said, women are fickle. And none more so than Maureen. I'd naturally felt it was time to lie doggo after this near sighting by her husband, so I didn't go round for a few days, and I didn't call her up either. Actually, I was a shade embarrassed about being beaten up by a woman outside her house too, to tell you the perfect truth. Maureen, in the meantime, had taken up with a past lover of hers. Her husband had gone away again, saying that he was on a course for a week, but in fact, because he was suspicious of what she was getting up to, he'd sneaked back after a couple of days and very nearly caught her with this guy. He said he'd just returned because there were some important papers in the house that he needed, but then she more or less got him to confess that he'd come back to prowl about and catch her out. In *flagrante delicto*, I think was the term she said he used. Posh bastard. Anyway, in righteous indignation, she'd packed him back off to his course, then she sat back to think about how she was pushing her luck a bit.

Now, because I hadn't rung, and presumably because she'd seen me getting a simple fracture at the hands of another woman whilst parked outside her house, I simply wasn't in her thoughts the night I called round. My own fault, I suppose, for being a little cowardly, but I didn't just walk up and ring the bell. There was no BMW in sight and the garage door was open, but I'd been known to park well away from the house myself, so I wasn't going to fall for a simple trick like that. So I crept round the house and peeked into all the downstairs windows first, to look for signs of a husband rocking slowly with a 12 bore across his knees. I caught sight of Maureen once, disappearing into the kitchen, but there was no one else in evidence and the kids were obviously in bed at this time of night. I'd just tried the back door but thought better of it and was going back round to the front of the house when she came flying out brandishing what I later realised was a squash racket.

When I was sitting in the kitchen a few minutes later wearing a cold, wet flannel over my nose, Maureen explained that she'd planned to teach her husband a final lesson for snooping on her. Just as she'd done to me, she was going to break a squash racket on his head and pretend that she'd thought it was a burglar. It served him right for behaving like one, or worse, a Peeping Tom. It seems like this burglar theory had stuck in her mind. In a bunged-up sort of way I quietly complained about her aim, saying I almost would have

23

preferred a lump on the back of my head and possible unconsciousness to yet more blood and a seriously impaired sense of smell. Needless to say, my heart wasn't in it that night and I decided not to stay.

So, as I say, I ended up in Casualty again. Just to be on the safe side, and also, I've got to be frank, because I'd taken a bit of a fancy to a little nurse they had there. She said I reminded her of Jack Palance, and she liked a man with a lived-in look. I have to admit I nearly backed off for a minute when she started saying I reminded her of somebody. It's funny really - they start off thinking I'm just like someone else, then they get to like me because I'm me. More probably they see the raw materials that they think they might be able to mould into a me that they would like. Then they end up attacking me because they think I'm their husband. Like I'm being confused for somebody else, but really I'm being confused for me. Do you get what I'm saying?

You don't mind me going on like this, do you? No, the reason I ask is, some girls don't appreciate you talking about your previous experiences. I know I couldn't talk like this to my present wife. But you, you're different ...

THE HAMMER

Terry always maintained he should have been a scaffolder.

'A steeplejack,' I said, that time we were coming back from the pub. We'd been veering all over the pavement, laughing and singing, when he saw the scaffolding by the unfinished block of flats they were putting up on the bit of waste ground near there.

'I just climbed up scaffolding, you fool,' he said.

'Yes, but any fool can do that. You flew up,' I said.

He claimed it was because he was drunk. I told him he would have fallen off if that had been the case. No, he had a talent. He thought for a moment.

'You're right,' he said. 'A mountaineer I should have been then.' He was tucking his shirt back in. 'Yeah, it feels good with the wind in your ears.'

'How much wind is there twenty feet up then?' I said.

He looked up. 'It's different up there. Twenty feet, two hundred feet. Any height.'

I had always thought he just enjoyed the climbing, the challenge, that being at the top wasn't the point. I said this, but he shrugged.

'I don't know what it is really.'

We started walking again.

'Sometimes I get the ladders out and tell Mo I'm going to check the aerial, or the tiles. I just enjoy being up there.'

There was a time when I'd asked him to come round and put a slate back on my roof. I'm none too good with heights myself, especially when the ladder starts to bend as you go up. That stops me dead. I can creep up the last few rungs, my face about an inch from the ladder and my knuckles white as sliced bread, but I've only done that to paint the eaves. The idea of stepping off a ladder on to a pitched roof churns my stomach.

He came round that time within half an hour. He ran up the ladder and clambered up those slates all in one movement. Then he sat astride the ridge tiles and made me crawl up the ladder behind him to pass him his tools. I couldn't get all the way up there to pass them to him, of course, so I lobbed them up carefully. He caught them almost absent-mindedly.

'Good view you got,' he said. 'These timbers are like Weetabix though.'

I reluctantly agreed. 'Next year,' I said. 'As long as it gets us through one more winter.'

He didn't have a roof ladder with him, but he was able to reach the loose slate by wriggling along the ridge tiles to the part where the gable juts out. He swung his legs over so that they hung down the lead valley on one side, then he reached over the other side and started manoeuvring the slate back into position. He looked like something from an old cowboy film: the victim of a shoot-out being brought back to town slung over his saddle. He delicately worked a strip of lead between two slates and fastened it with slow, upside-down hammer strokes. His strange blend of awkwardness and graceful ease as he carried out the task reminded me of a diver working on an underwater wreck. He paused for a moment.

'Anything the matter?' I cried. He didn't say anything for a few seconds. He looked as limp as an antimacassar.

'There's something sticking in my ribs. I'm just having a breather.'

'Would it be easier if I went and borrowed a roof ladder?' I said. 'You look bloody uncomfortable like that.'

'I am uncomfortable. Nearly finished though.' He swam forward one stroke with his left arm and bent the lead hanger over the bottom of the tile, but as he did so he let slip the hammer he was holding in his other hand.

'Let it go,' he cried.

I ducked, expecting to be clouted in the face and sent reeling back into space, but the hammer merely clattered down the slates and came to rest in the troughing. When I peered over the fascia again he was swinging himself back into a straddled sitting position.

'Do you need the hammer?' I said.

He shook his head, a strange expression I'd never seen before on his face.

'Aren't you coming down now then?'

'In a minute. Why don't you come up? It's a powerful feeling up here.'

I thanked him for the offer but suggested I'd be better occupied going back down to make coffee or getting a couple of cans from the fridge. He nodded and said he'd be down in a while.

'How will you get back down?' I asked. 'Won't you slip, coming backwards?'

'I'll trust my luck,' he said, 'Actually though it is a lot harder coming down than going up.'

'Shall I try and get that roof ladder then?'

'No,' he said. 'I'll have a cigarette, then I'll just slide down slowly. As long as you don't panic, you don't hurt yourself.'

I lowered myself gingerly back down the ladder, panicking all the while that a sudden gust of wind would nudge me into an awful slow-motion dive through the air. By the time I came out of the house again with two cans of lager, Terry was speeding down the ladder. He grinned at me with three galvanised nails sticking out of his mouth, He looked like a cat that had eaten a metal bird.

'It's just a state of mind, you know,' he said.

That was about four months ago. In fact, it must have been a couple of days before he was told about his illness. I didn't know about it for quite a while though. He had already lost a lot of weight when I next saw him and his face had taken on a grey colour which emphasised how thin his cheeks had become. It's impossible to know what to say. We talked about other things and I reminded him I still owed him for repairing my roof. He waved his hand slackly at this, then he chuckled at the memory of me diving out of sight when the hammer had slid towards my face.

'I told you I was no good up a ladder,' I said.

He smiled wanly. 'Don't expect I'll do a lot more running around on people's roofs, or up scaffolding. Remember that time I climbed up that scaffolding outside the pub?' His smile faded. 'It's a bit of a blow, you know.'

The understatement silenced me.

'Shame though,' he added. 'I wish I was at the top of a building now, the wind biting into my cheeks, instead of something else gnawing at me, from inside.'

'Don't talk like that,' I said. 'You'll be alright. There's radiotherapy and all sorts these days.'

'Yeah,' he sighed. 'Another wall to climb is all it is. I can do it. It's just that sometimes I want to let go, leap off the ledge, so to speak.'

That was the worst time, or rather, the time he was lowest about what was happening to him. The next time I went round he was a lot more cheerful, though his condition looked to me as if it had deteriorated even in the space of a week or so. He had been making his own wine and our conversation was punctuated by a monotonous plopping as the air bubbles escaped through the funny shaped plastic tubes on the demijohns. It was like we were under water. The rest of the house was quiet, and I had an eerie feeling, as if I was in someone's deserted laboratory.

'Taken up a new hobby, I see,' I said, rather lamely.

He smiled. 'Yes. It's okay. I can't drink the stuff of course.' He rubbed his abdomen. 'Nothing stays down.'

My last sight of him was as I was leaving. He opened the door for me and turned to go upstairs to the bathroom. I saw him climbing those stairs, one by one, his white knuckles gripping onto the banister as if the house was rolling in a storm. I stood by the door for over a minute. In that time he had scarcely got halfway up the first flight. I felt a slow hammer in my chest like someone was nailing lead to my own crumbling joists.

STRANGERS

We were on our usual walk when my four-year-old son went up to a stranger. He said, 'Are you a stranger?' Somebody laughed and my wife grabbed the boy's hand, mumbling an apologetic pleasantry, but the man gazed off into himself. He was touched by the frankness of a four-year-old perhaps; touched perhaps too by the awfulness of some truth about himself.

I looked at him longer than you should. He was a lean, sandy haired man in the off duty jeans and sweatshirt of most weekend men in their thirties. He wore white training shoes that were newish but not an expensive name brand. His face was scored by the grimace lines of a man who had hoped to be something one day. The day looked close now and importance had evaded him. I dropped my gaze as the outreach of his eyes hardened back into a normal expression. Then I tightened my grip on my son's hand and we walked on. I half listened to another explanation from my wife of the dangers of talking to strange men. After a while we all fell quiet.

Tomorrow, I thought. Tomorrow I will set my life in order. I will write to those relatives who keep hinting that they would like to visit. They haven't seen Max since he was a baby. The time swirls past. Time. Big as a meadow, unchartable, scarcely worth thinking about when I was Max's age; now shrunk, pre-shrunk, into ten- or twenty-minute capsules. Ten minutes for making love, twenty minutes to drive to the newsagent's and back. I never knew I'd deal out my life's hand like this. But still, twenty minutes to write that letter, I could afford that. This time I wouldn't start: 'Sorry I haven't written, but I've been rushed off my feet ... ' I'd start with talking rather than excusing. 'I was sitting by the window looking out at the grass furtively growing and I thought, before it grows a fraction of a millimetre more, I'd write to you ...'

Then I'll get the cricket stumps from the shed, push them into that lush patch at the end of the garden. I'll go up to Max with his size two bat and proffer it wordlessly. I'll be spinning a tennis ball temptingly from hand to hand. 'You and me? One on one?' I'll say. We will sidle conspiratorially out of the kitchen door before Sunday's chores can waylay us. When we are hailed and hauled back in I'll talk to Jenny about the good old days. I'll make fresh coffee. She'll want to know what is wrong, but I'll tell her I just don't feel a compulsive need to read the Sunday newspapers - just so many strangers' lives, tragedies, remarriages. I just want to enjoy some time with my family. I'll point out that we're growing apart. Nothing dramatic, just a slow inevitable drift. But we don't need to drift, we can arrest it, take time to get to know each other again. She'll think I want to make love. Or perhaps that I'm having an affair. She'll think that I want to make love to be shriven somehow. I'll explain about the stranger, but that will make her digress into talk of Max and how he is too earnest for his own good, Max will interrupt us, wanting lunch, or another breakfast, and I'll offer to make it this time. Maybe that will compound my obvious guilt in Jenny's eyes.

I was in a pub the other day. I happened to be driving to Hereford and I stopped in a little village I'd never passed before. The pub was pretty empty but there was one surly man on the bar stool arguing with the frazzled barmaid about the ending of a film they'd both seen. I'd seen it too and I remembered better than either of them. I don't normally enter other people's conversations. but this time I thought it might help out.

'It was Mr Pink who shot him,' I said.

They both spun round. The barmaid said, 'Oh, you've seen it too, have you?'

The man barely suppressed a snarl. He grabbed his glass of cider like he wanted to throttle it. I took my drink to a table at the other end of the bar, but I overheard them agreeing: it was sickening how the village was overrun by strangers in the summer. At least, I thought, the altercation is resolved, or moved on to the evener ground of parochial xenophobia. I thought about this. I never taught

Max that you should despise strangers; merely to be suspicious if they came at you with blandishments. I didn't use these words, naturally.

And now, the blandishments I plan for my wife. Perhaps I'll go and get the newspapers as I always do. Maybe I'll go over to that farm shop - another five minutes' drive - and buy a bunch of flowers. I'll say: 'A whim, a mere whim. An impulse, like the advert on TV. But you know me. I'm not a stranger. I'm the man you married.'

She married less of a stranger than I am now, if truth be told. And I don't suppose I know who she is any more either.

Perhaps I should just talk. Tomorrow I'll talk. I'll approach these intimate strangers who share my table, my bed and my one-time dreams and I'll chat to them. 'Hello,' I'll say, 'Remember me?'

I only hope they don't look at me with those far off eyes, or worse, with a kind of alarm as they tighten their grip on each other's hand.

FIVE MEN SMILING

'We'll go to the Board Room,' the Principal said cheerily, 'Where we go to be bored.'

The five men, in suits and haircuts, smiled uproariously, their hands throttling each other behind their backs. All five seemed to have somehow acquired extra limbs that morning. Crossing and re-crossing their legs as they sat waiting for the proceedings to begin, they resembled nothing so much as a French plait competition in slow motion. Indeed, an alarming Vishnu-like manifestation of apparently extra arms had enabled them to pat their side pockets, rest hands on knees and pick at cuticles all at the same time. So, at last, it was good to be on one's feet, albeit huddled together like a polite rolling maul, following the Principal as he breezed across the courtyard. They tacked behind him, unsure of direction but determined in their stride.

The boardroom was an elegantly plain room dominated by a long conference table. This had been converted to a dining table and was set for ten. Cheap but shining glasses were ruffed with white paper napkins so that they looked like pageboys' throats. The tablemats had pictures of Welsh castles and enough reading matter for the first few seconds until polite conversation could begin.

'Come far?' one said. Another nodded,

'From York, actually.'

This was of great interest but uncommentable upon.

Further down the table a man in a suit which was slightly lighter grey than regulation charcoal was admiring the view.

The Principal practised a grin. 'They say if you can see the bay from here, it's going to rain. If you can't see it, it is raining'

More joy and hand throttling, this time on laps or on the tablecloth before them.

'Tony Symes and our two Vice Principals will be joining us in a minute,' the Principal said, 'Ah, Mary!'

A slim, confident woman in a blue plaited skirt and a cream silk blouse had appeared.

'Have you seen Tony or Alan around?'

'They'll be here in a moment. Alan's just sorting out the WBA stuff.'

The nearest interviewee's eyes closed in a moment of intense personal grief. WBA were a football team, but otherwise the initials meant nothing to him. Would this be the first question?

'Good. Can I introduce Mary Shilling, our Head of Student Affairs, to everyone?' He attempted the candidates' first names and only had to be prompted once. Mary Shilling smiled as if she had heard it before and said something quietly to the Principal.

'Fine, fine, of course, of course,' he murmured.

This did not seem to gratify her much. She sat down in the seat next to him and rearranged her cutlery. The man opposite her smiled weakly.

'That's a provocative job title,' he quipped.

She widened her lips by a millimetre to indicate that she understood he intended something humorous here.

'We had a woman in my last place who had the glorious title of Staff/Student Liaison Co-ordinator,' he persisted. 'You'd think from that that there was no liaison between staff and students, wouldn't you?'

Mary Shilling tried ungluing her lips again. 'Sounds a little tautologous,' she said.

The man hadn't thought of this before. He gave her a watery look then concentrated deeply on the water in the glass before him.

At this point Val, the canteen manager, came in and hailed the Principal. 'Lovely morning Mr D. We've got lamb, chicken or fish, but I'd recommend the chicken. It's a chicken stew.'

Mary Shilling drummed her fingers till she caught Val's eye. 'I'll have a salad.'

'Ham, my love?'

'Cheese.'

The men in suits waited for their prospective employer to order first, but were then thrown into confusion when he slowly pronounced he would risk the fish. Whom to please? The lightest grey suit confidently opted for the fish and wondered aloud what accompaniment there might be,

'Boiled or chips.' Val pursed her lips. 'There's only four chicken left, mind.'

During this exchange two men in suit trousers but with their jackets removed had joined the table. One called the other Alan; a Vice-Principal therefore. The other was older and wore the stern, realistic expression of a man who dealt with money. His crimped iron-grey hair spoke of economies and cutbacks also. Clearly the other Vice-Principal. The two men had immediately begun indulging in some speculation about the canteen's poultry-ordering principles upon taking their seats:

'Perhaps they thought we'd be down to the short shortlist already.'

'I wonder if it's just one chicken, quartered, or four quarters from separate chickens.'

'I'll have one leg if you'll have the other. Do you care if it's a right or a left?'

Another candidate had raised a forefinger roughly to the level of his handkerchief pocket.

'I'll have one of the chicken stews if nobody else ...

'That's three,' Val said without expression.

'Could I have that with a salad?'

She frowned.

Nobody dared risk the opprobrium of the rest of the table by going for the remaining chicken quarter. Two men instantly overcame their lifelong antipathy to it and ordered fish, in order to be indistinguishable from the young man they felt had taken up the running. The last two gloomily opted for a small burnt lamb chop with half-boiled potatoes and cabbage that looked dyed. By this time the last seat had been taken up by Tony Symes, role unknown, who hastily declared that Val could choose for him.

'Well,' she said without irony, 'I'd avoid the lamb.'

'Whatever.'

'Chicken then.' She did not wait for his approval. Anyway, he had involved himself hugger mugger in conversation, sotto voce, with Mary Shilling.

With these preliminaries over, the talk began in earnest. It revolved around the price of houses in the area. the prospects of a fine summer, and the exigencies of rail and car travel. It was conducted quite vivaciously, considering the predictability of views on these subjects, and no one felt that he had made any serious gaffe till the meal was nearly over. The sweet course was largely avoided, to indicate moderation, but whether coffee should be taken black or white after lunch was obviously a trickier decision. One man ordered white, then murmured something inaudible to himself as Val moved up the table. Everyone else ordered black. Then there was mortification as the Principal spoke.

'No coffee for me, if you please. I want to be alert for this afternoon's proceedings, but I don't want to be kept awake all afternoon.'

There was an alarmingly long pause before the obligatory chuckles and smiles of relief.

Enough time was allowed before the afternoon's interviewing session for the candidates to acquaint themselves with the building, but only one man wandered off. The rest were content with having pinpointed the exact location of the toilets and they now arranged themselves discreetly in a corner of a common room to await their ordeal. There was some more desultory conversation, but the urgency of talk had been deflated now that the Principal and his hierarchy had disappeared.

One man, who had sat furthest away in the loose circle of easy chairs, took out a hardback book from his slim briefcase. He was still staring blankly at the first page when he was interrupted by the man who had gone for the chicken.

'Looks interesting,' he said, nodding at the slim volume. It had in fact a dull blue binding with dull red lettering.

'Yes.'

'Not a textbook, I take it?'

'No.'

'Who's it by?'

'Raymond Carver actually.'

'Oh, the actor chap.'

The young man could not help looking baffled at this.

'You know, that American who plays the detective in that old TV series.'

'I think perhaps you are thinking of Raymond Burr.'

'Burr? No, no, Carver, I'm sure. He was in a wheelchair.'

The young man shrugged. 'I'm not aware that Carver ever did any TV work. This is a book of poems mostly.'

'Really? What's it called?'

'*A New Path to the Waterfall*. It's about someone facing his destiny.'

'Oh, like us then!'

'Well, in a way I suppose.' He returned to the page he had not started reading, having held his slightly quizzical look long enough to establish that the conversation did not need to be continued.

The other two men were talking quietly but they stopped when the fifth man, the white coffee drinker, returned from his circumambulations. Then, because it might seem that they had been talking about him, one of them asked if he had seen anything interesting.

'Not really. Place is a bit of a dump as far as I can see.' He declined to expand on this, despite the interested expressions on the faces of the other men. The silence that ensued was not broken until the crimped Vice Principal entered the room.

'Right, gentlemen. I don't know if the Principal actually mentioned my name to you, but I'm Peters. So, the form for this afternoon is that we are going to interview you in alphabetical order, that's the usual thing.'

One candidate, Mr Young, looked glumly down at his knees.

'It's all very informal. There'll be a small panel consisting of the Principal, myself, the other Vice Principal, Alan Stokes, a couple of governors and the Dean of Faculty, of course. We'll just ask you a couple of things about yourself, usual sort of thing, nothing to get nervous about, and we'll hopefully arrive at a decision by the end of the afternoon.'

He glanced about him to indicate that there should be no need for questions, then turned away. 'If you would follow me then. You'll be asked to wait in the Interview Room. We'll be interviewing in the Committee Room, you see.'

The suits rose as one, fastened their bottom jacket buttons, then unfastened them and followed him out.

The Interview Room was slightly smaller than the Board Room but had a similar conference table, set this time with blotting pads and pencils. Mary Shilling stood by a window but turned to smile curtly as the men came in. The five men were aware of how incongruous they must seem, bunched at one end of the room, tightly pressed to the door, no one wanting to be first to take his place by the table.

Mary Shilling motioned them to sit down and did so herself, choosing a seat in the middle.

'Did you find lunch satisfactory?' she said. It seemed an oddly worded question.

'The chicken looked good,' said one of the lamb chops. The fish men nodded in firm agreement. Clearly, anything would have been better than their piece of rubberised cod.

'I wasn't mad about the lamb, to tell the candid truth,' said the other burned chop man. 'Was that a typical menu, by the way?'

'Oh goodness me, no, that was special.'

A pause.

'Has anyone any idea when they'll be starting?' This was from the confident young man, who seemed to be leaking confidence badly now.

'Somebody said something about two o'clock, I believe.'

'It's gone that now.'

'It flies when you're in there; it's just the time out here that seems to drag.'

Mary Shilling looked in astonishment at the man who had uttered this platitude. 'They'll probably start before long, don't worry,' she sighed.

The youngest man heard this and felt weak. 'They!' This must mean Mary Shilling was an interviewee. An internal candidate! He looked at the other men to check if they had made this enormous realisation. Worse, she was a woman. Someone distinguishable from them because, if nothing else, she was not wearing a mid-grey suit. The others were looking across the table and out of the windows or surreptitiously wiping the sweat from their hands in their handkerchiefs. They all knew, obviously.

The door opened and Peters barked the first name: 'Mr Adams, please.' His voice had the hard, friendly edge of a dentist's receptionist. With the exception of Mary Shilling, the others stared at their watches and tried to work out how long it would be till they were called. One of the lamb chops actually pressed the stopwatch function on his complicated digital timepiece. Perhaps he hoped to make his own interview outlast, if not outperform, that of his rivals.

Twenty minutes later the man called Barrow was summoned. He stabbed his foot quite violently against the table in his haste to meet his destiny and he had to limp out of the room. Mr Newlands, Mr Parks and Mr Young smiled at each other. Mary Shilling had resumed her position at the window.

Eighteen minutes and forty five seconds later, the stop watch man shuffled out, anxiously setting his digital display. He lasted ten minutes. Mr Parks, on his way out, made a great show of unbuttoning his jacket again and nearly walked into the door as he wished the remaining two candidates good luck. Some hours later, as it seemed to the last man, Mary Shilling was asked to step into the Committee Room. She said something to the Vice Principal as she went out and there was a loud burst of laughter in the corridor. It caused Mr Young great sorrow.

When he was eventually led into the Committee Room his eyes took in a horseshoe of faces, but they failed to send any message to his brain about the identity of their owners. The face in the centre was addressing him. He slumped into the seat facing all these faces and tried hard to concentrate on what was being said. The interview lasted some seconds, or some hours, it was impossible to tell. There was quite a lot said, some of it from his own mouth, though by an exciting new means that did not involve any connection between tongue and brain. At one point there had been someone talking and he had been listening carefully, trying to follow the train of thought, when he had examined all the faces in front of him. They were all intent and motionless. Not one open mouth. Then who was it who was talking?

When he came out of the room he tried to remember the questions he had been asked and the answers he had given. There was nothing there though. A mind sucked clean of any sense of reality investigated itself vacuously.

The room he was taken into in order to await the panel's decision was someone's study. Of the five rooms he had wasted his time in this day it was the first to show any signs of a real person ever having been there before. There was a picture of a pretty woman on the desk and a Gary Larson cartoon on the opposite wall. Six chairs had been squeezed into this tiny office and he took the vacant one. The other candidates were all there, different men now. Mary Shilling still wore an air of complacency

'How did it go?' one of the men asked.

He shrugged. Like a dog being asked about nuclear physics, he showed keen attention. but not the slightest comprehension.

The final waiting period took them up to six o' clock. Then Peters came in and talked about the quality of the candidates and the difficulty of arriving at a final decision. No one paid any heed until at last he mentioned a name. Then he walked back to the Committee Room, followed by the successful candidate.

The five men in their grey suits smiled their umpteenth smile of the day, this time their faces emptied of uproar or joy.

I DRAWED YOU AND ME

You are flicking through a book or a magazine and you come to this page. This story. Why would you stop? Because of the title perhaps? Perhaps not, you've read stuff about kids and parents before. Too much stuff like that, though usually they start with a bit of description.

Max pushed the open exercise book across the kitchen table and tugged at his father's arm, which was pulled round in front of him as if he were afraid someone might copy what he had. What he had was an empty plate and a chocolate biscuit wrapper.

'Look! I've drawed you and me...'

Yeah yeah. A desolate father, a disingenuous kid, a kitchen table out of Kramer Versus Kramer. No, that wouldn't do it. Perhaps because you like the typography. People say it's less boring if the paragraphs are short. People who read The Sun and/or The Bible, I guess. No, if you get this far it's not because of a love of brevity, though you might just be tempted to thumb the next page or so to see if this is merely some dumb article or prose poem or parable. Maybe, if it's only a couple of pages long you can at least say you read one by that guy once, and not be lying. Or do you want to be part of the process perhaps? Fine. We'll do it together. We'll stick with Max and the drawing because we've got to now, but we'll go back and insinuate a little.

The TV was on mute and he was turned away from the screen but he occasionally caught its incandescent flickerings reflected in the glass of the patio doors. Max was sprawled at his feet like a dog, crayoning on a page torn from a Dot to Dot book, his arm shielding his endeavours as if he feared plagiarism …

So. You think the self-protection motif should apply to the boy too? And what about this middle-class domesticity? All middle-class fiction is about marriage, responsibility and the loss of identity;

that's why the third person pronoun rather than a name, eh? Oh, and property of course. I note there's a patio already. It looks like this one is heading fast for that slip road into the suburbs and the old lack of understanding between parents and children. I'll give it one more paragraph.

Max looked up once, then back down at his spidery drawing. Then he looked back up at his father, who attempted an unsuccessful smile. The boy regarded him seriously...

Regarded? In my dictionary it says 'regard' is now largely taken to mean 'consider' rather than 'look at'. I know, this is a story, people can regard each other just to make a change from looking at each other. But 'spidery"? Skeletal would be better, I would have thought. And what's he wearing? Has he got blond curly wisps of hair, or an expression like a cleric, a man warned, a somnambulist? Are we supposed to like him? Is the rain beating a silent tattoo on the triple glazing? Alright, I'll be patient. The kid has just pointed his eyes at the man.

His father had not moved. He sat with one hand dug into the side of his face, the elbow wedged hard into the arm of the settee.

Can't we have some clues? A discarded novel with an appropriate title like, ha ha, *The Outsider* or *Notes from Underground?* We could even curdle the milk in his mug of untouched coffee. 'The cup of coffee before him had started to form a skin as bland and impenetrable as the expression on a typist's face.' Nope. However opaque the drink, the image is as clear as tonic water.

He became aware of a sound outside. A voice and a car door slamming. The boy did not look up and follow his father's gaze out through the bay window to the gravel drive outside. There was nothing there, it was a neighbour taking her aged mother to church. The rasp and crash of an ancient Ford's exhausted synchromesh confirmed the unassailable fact.

Can I just say that I'd really appreciate it if some of the nouns could be un-premodified, for a change? Couldn't the bay window just be a window? The mother not necessarily aged, the Ford perhaps of indeterminate age, and the fact just a fact. How assailable are facts

43

anyway?

It was Sunday ...

Oh yippee. Everyone out there got the picture now? Estranged father, weekend parent, remorse digging into the side of his face like a clenched fist, like toothache on the outside. He can't even look at reality as reflected in the artifice of a TV screen, he has to look at the REFLECTION of a TV screen in a patio window!

He wanted to speak, to say something, to cry out loud, to howl his self-loathing at the moon, or the ceiling light. Or, though he restrained himself of course, at Max. The boy was engrossed in a pattern of thick purple lines executed by dragging the side of his crayon down the page. His father watched in silence as the boy proceeded to force crayons between his plump fingers and rub his clenched hand over what he had drawn. He scarified the page in this way for a few seconds, then dropped the crayons to regard his handiwork.

Well, that's better. Regard is okay there. And scarified is good. The fingernails down the face, the fork across the plate, the lawn rake wrenching out the weeds of an untended life. But PLUMP fingers? Make the language do the work!

Max paused, rolled over on one side to insert a hand down past his waistband, and winced as his fingers worked at some itch. Though his father was gazing at him again he was unselfconscious about it. He even sniffed at his fingers when they reappeared.

Well well. You thought about 'groin', didn't you? Or even worse, 'loins'. Still, an itch in this particular area, whatever you choose to call it, is pretty obvious, don't you think? I think we'd better steer clear of the symbolism for a while and get somebody to say something. We're beginning to drift a little, we need a drop of dialogue to colour the water, if not change it to wine.

'Don't scratch, Max.' The words came out too loud ...

Oh, the sickening banality! This is putrid! This is an empty can someone's forgotten to throw in the bin!...

... but Max did not answer. His attention was directed at the

44

window. The wind outside was shoulder-charging the glass and it looked like it was bending. It whipped round to arm-wrestle a tree in the blackness beyond, then spun back to kick once more at the window pane.

But some Kung Fu Northerly engaging in a metaphorical squabble with the house does not equal inner turmoil. You've got a taciturn (and still nameless) guy with nothing to identify him but a child of indeterminate age and a testicular itch, a living room with a TV and patio doors, plus said child with his Dot to Dot book. It's not Tolstoy, is it? Can we try being the boy for a bit?

Max imagined himself on the Common, blown along by this tremendous wind. It would scoop him up by the hood of his duffel coat and skim him across the grass like a pebble across water. He regarded his father once again. A handsome man, but tired- looking. He'd do something nice for him: a nice drawing. It could be a present. Even grownups like presents. He would draw the two of them out on a walk in the country. Green, first of all, and some brown for the trees. But how do you draw the wind?

I was thinking about 'scarified'. I don't like the look of the word. It looks like it means 'scared' and 'horrified'. Shouldn't we have him scarifying like something? Like a cat dragging its claws down a curtain, say, to suggest the languor and the menace at the same time?

He tried some squiggly lines, but then it looked like clouds benignly sitting there on a windless day. He crossed them out and they remained stubbornly static, though transformed now to rain clouds. He decided to draw two figures, one small with chicken-feet hands that stuck out at right angles to his body, one larger, with a hat. His father never wore a hat, but that didn't matter. Symbolism was all. And cliché, of course. For this reason he decided to include the sun in the top left-hand corner, its spoke-like rays contradicting the low cloud bank. Then a brain wave. Two brainwaves. An ocean of cerebral activity. He drew six or seven tree trunks at a 45 degree angle, their ice cream foliage twisted to the left. Then he made his father's hat into an extravagant hairstyle and drew in a new hat an inch above and to the left. Stasis and kinesis. A hat in mid-air, frozen

45

but aloft, an arm reaching out, but never to clutch.

Oh yes. STASIS, the boy thought. What insight into a four year old's mind! Little did the callow infant realise that the word signifies stagnation of the blood. KINESIS, he opined, making one of those mental peregrinations into the classical languages so beloved of the pre-school child. He hasn't been reading Theodore Roethke, by any chance? I only ask because if the lack of finite verbs in the boy's interior monologue, Perhaps Sunny Stories is serialising 'The Mental Adventures of Molly Bloom'? Still, there's something to look at, at last. Something to REGARD. Better than all that nervous jostling for tense atmosphere. Do go on.

He quickly coloured in the sky and the grass impressionistically and jumped up.

Hang on! What about the dots? This is not a blank sheet of paper, it already had the outline of a picture in dots. He's drawn over it, admittedly, but we're still bound to see the pre-imposed pattern.

He stared at the picture for a moment, deciding that the dots and numbers could be crows circling the two figures, and he thrust the work on to his father' lap.

'I've drawed you and me,' he said, with a delicate blend of pride and unconcern in his voice. His father scrutinised it seriously.

'Your hat's come off because of the wind. That's the wind.' He screwed up his face as he pointed to the black scribbles. 'It's a sort of story really. That's me, that's you, and we're on the Common, out for a walk.'

'What are these dots and things, are they the words of the story?'

The boy looked pleased. Then, 'No, they're punctuation marks. The story hasn't started yet, it's just at the beginning ...'

I don't want to play anymore. It's getting like a proper story: characters doing things, talking, relating ...

The man smiled. 'So there's no story really then.

The boy shrugged. 'No. Do you want one?'

A pause.

'No, not now,' he said.

FOOTLOOSE AND TWENTY-THREE

At one table four girls were shrieking with raucous delight at their own jokes. The one called Ronnie was now laughing loudest. She was the newest recruit to this fighting team and had not quite hit the right tone with her own attempts at humour, but she found the others hysterically funny. Her blood red lips opened to reveal a keyboard of even teeth and a hiccoughing laugh clattered out like a high pitched road drill. Alison and Kate, the two who had been at school together, worked deftly in unison to stoke this hysteria.

'And that was the exact spot I threw up next to Mr Wotsit ...'

'We were being so refained ...'

Another hiccough from Ronnie, and a quick dab at the corner of her mouth, where a driblet of rum and coke was fighting its way back out.

'Banned! That little waiter with the bald spot was screaming at us in Gujarati ...'

'Or Punjabi, it's so hard to tell when you're as pissed as a pig.'

Alison, bright eyed and spiky blonde, was darting at crisps and anecdotal detail with equal accuracy.

Zoe, the fourth girl and flatmate to the other three, was content to smile and give her vodka and lime an occasional twirl. Ronnie recovered enough breath to interject.

'Wasn't that the time you were telling me about, when the guy started to argue with the waiter?'

Kate downed her rum as if washing down a pill and yowled at the same time. Her turn, her turn: 'That was our teacher, Mr...' She clicked her fingers to count off the syllables of the name, for he only survived metrically in her racing memory. 'One of the lads... Simon, was it? ... was crawling round all fours begging at the tables for poppadoms. There was proper people in there, you know, couples and old timers and that, but even they were thinking what a grin, but the waiters didn't seem to appreciate.'

Alison was trying to dog her conversationally and she now seized the stick from her mouth: 'I'll have what he's having, I said, but they were a bit slow on the uptake...'

'Except when it came to the bill.' Alison had retrieved the chewed baton. 'Swept that away before we could even think about a tip.'

Zoe was smiling. She had dined in Indian restaurants herself, though perhaps not so noisily. Ronnie was coughing alarmingly. Then all smiles and coughs stopped together.

A man, carbuncular and about thirty-five, was approaching. In his hands he held twin bottles of Moet and Chandon. It was an expensive tightrope walk over to their table, and they watched enthralled.

'Wun drink girls?'

A miraculous space had appeared on the corner seat next to Kate, but Alison was the first to respond verbally:

'Don't mine fie do,' she slurred in imitation. Zoe and Ronnie were caught trying to demolish their glasses, so Alison was able to continue: 'And worrawe celebrating?'

'My divorce,' the man said immaculately.

Two smiles, a knowing look and a howl from Alison.

'When was that then?'

'June the sixth last year.'

Simultaneous laughter, not all of it forced.

'A man after my own drink,' Kate cried, sliding further over on her seat. The man leaned instead into Alison's chair, bruised his shin, and shakily poured out champagne into the glasses thrust at him.

'Nice to know you all,' he said.

'This is Zoe, Ronnie, Al, and I'm Kate, as in Kiss Me Kate.'

'Thazz very nice view,' he slurred, 'But I'd better not for the moment, I may need to throw up shortly.'

There was that pause that you hate, then Alison spoke up again.

49

'What's your name then?'

The man brightened. 'Ga...' He did various things with his face muscles then he tried again: 'Gary.'

'Well, here's to you and your ex-wife, Ga,'

'Nice to know you, Gary.' Zoe was not going to be left out.

'Must have been a hell of a marriage, Gary.' Alison pushed a hand through her spiky hair but sounded serious as she said this.

Gary shook his head in different directions attempting what he must have been hoping were the paralinguistics of agreement, then he took a step backwards.

'No need to go just yet,' Kate cried, a little too sharply. 'There's plenty more where this came from!'

Gary collapsed forward again and subsided onto her seat.

'I'm thirty six,' he began. Then he seemed to decide that this was explanation enough.

The girls nodded and drank quickly.

'What was the war like then?' Alison said. The joke didn't quite work because he had closed his eyes. She started again as he blearily opened them. 'I was saying, it's nice to er ...'

'I'm looking for summon to love,' Gary started to say.

'And you've come to the right place, darling.' Kate's voice was as soothing as a dentist's. 'But we're on a pretty tight schedule.'

Gary's face lit up. 'I'm pretty tight myself.' He chuckled, but avoided spilling.

Zoe was ready to go. There was only a third of a bottle left of the champagne. Ronnie was ready for somewhere more exciting too.

'I guess I'd bedder leave you lone. Boyfriends be here in a minute, eh?'

Alison smiled her carefree smile. 'Good on you, Gaz. You're a real man. A diamond, in fact.'

'But I'd like to leave you this bottle,' Gary took one last gulp from it, 'as a token of my extreme.'

Alison winked loudly at Kate and pushed back along the seat.

'Thanks.'

He headed back towards the bar, side-stepping invisible chairs and patrons.

'Well, that was a bonus anyway,' Kate said.

'What a pathetic character, Zoe said.

Ronnie offered the twenty-three-year old's wisdom that older men were all just sad cases.

Alison demurred: 'I won't have a word said against my mate Gazza. Anyway, you said you had a crush on one of your teachers. He was an older man, wasn't he?'

Ronnie had no time for a self-justification for the question had reminded Kate of the conversation that the champagne moment had interrupted.

'What *was* that teacher's name? Mr Wotsit, I mean. Wasn't it Bill Something?'

'Bill Bottoms!' Alison laughed loudly at her own joke. 'That would have been a good name for him anyway.'

Ronnie was poking around in the plastic ashtray at the remnants of the kitty. 'One more in here, girls?'

'My shout,' Alison shouted, but she did not move from her seat.

'Go on then,' Kate said accusingly.

'That was it, my shout. Do you want a shout, Zoe?'

Zoe smiled.

'Come on girls. Chuck a few quid in and we'll have one more here. Then we can move on.'

Zoe pecked at her handbag, whilst Alison tried the awkward manoeuvre of sliding her hand into her tight jeans pocket. Eventually all four girls produced the required contribution.

'Still your shout, Al,' Kate said.

Alison did a three-foot sigh. 'Humph. Just because I'm the tallest.'

'No, it's not that. But you are the loudest. You could try ordering from here actually.'

'Bitch,'

Zoe was not quite sure how serious this altercation might turn out. She hastily returned to the earlier topic. 'What was this trip you were on, anyway? How come the teachers let you get so drunk?'

Alison gestured to Kate that she could do this one and got up to get in the next round.

'We-ell, if you can imagine eighteen sixth formers on a weekend trip to see *Hamlet* in London and two teachers trying to hold us back from the pub ... it must have been like stopping water running downhill.' She acted it out by diving to her right and holding out a hand, then lifting one leg to hold back another student tributary. She blew back a fringe of hair and dived to her right. Mr Thingummy, Bill Bottoms or whatever his name was, gave up and came with us to the pub, and to the curry house after.'

Ronnie and Zoe beamed pleasantly, but Kate seemed to be working hard at her routine. She swivelled her eyes inwards so that they could examine each other. 'And we all got pissed as farts.'

Zoe's attention was wandering to the cigarette machine, where two young men who had just entered were now standing. They were apparently undecided over which brand of identical cigarettes they should buy. Kate stopped talking to scrutinise the new talent. The pause was interrupted by Alison banging down three glasses which she had hurried over from the bar. She followed their eyes and said, too loudly, 'Leisure complexes,'

Ronnie did not understand.

'Fitness centres. Something to work out on. Geddit?'

Ronnie, dragging hard on her mild cigarette, coughed.

Kate gave an intentional shudder. 'Bum like a camel in a sandstorm.'

'Bum on you, love,' Alison aimed this at the boys' backs, but one of them, a blond haired, dark eye lashed looker, turned to face the girls just as she said it. He turned back and whispered something to his friend, who self-consciously screwed up the cellophane from his cigarette packet and tried to flick it into a bin a few feet away. It lobbed up and descended in a pitiful parabola a foot short.

'Aw, come on, girls,' Ronnie complained. 'They're just kids.'

'If they're big enough to be out on their own, they're big enough for me,' Kate said.

Alison began to sing quietly: 'Whatever Lola wants, Lola gets.' She gave a snorting laugh and went back to the bar for the other drink.

The boys had talked it over long enough and approached their table now. They stopped short and sat down at the next table meaningfully. As a result, Zoe, on the margins of the conversation so far, became the central member of the extended group.

'Hi,' said the blond. His friend, a small, dark Italian-looking boy, was about nineteen. He simply smiled and poured lager into the side of his mouth. Zoe recrossed her legs.

'Nice in here, innit?' Kate drawled.

Alison spoke up: 'You'll have to excuse my friend - she's a bit tipsy because she's celebrating her divorce.'

The blond boy's smile widened. 'When was that then?'

Two voices replied in unison: 'June 6th last year!' Everyone laughed, some loudly, others more nervously. The elder of the boys moved his body round to face Zoe more directly, which partly shut out his friend. He said something too quiet for the rest of the company and Ronnie decided to resurrect the London conversation. Alison batted the question nonchalantly down to the area between cover and cover point. It Was Kate's turn to jiggle her drink.

Ronnie sighed. It was boring in here. Zoe was talking animatedly and laughing a lot. The other boy looked wistfully at the jukebox. He decided to risk a remark: 'Anybody want any sounds?'

Ronnie responded first this time: 'Put that Witness Houston one back on, that'd be good.'

'Anybody else want anything?'

53

'See if they've got 'And They Call It Puppy Love', Kate smiled sweetly.

'No, let's have 'The Wanderer',' Alison said. She and Kate glanced at each other and burst into song simultaneously: 'I'm the kinda girl who can never settle down ...'

The boy grimaced and headed off towards the jukebox. He did not return for some time, and then only to point meaningfully at his friend's glass. The blond boy threw the contents back and passed it to him wordlessly. Only some twenty minutes later, when he got up to get drinks, did Zoe return to the girls' conversation.

'You're pretty engrossed, Zoe.'

'Aw, Zoe, drink up and let's get out of here. He's a creep.'

'I'll just have this drink he's getting me.' Zoe said, 'Then I'm ready.'

Kate tutted. Alison shrugged. Ronnie flicked her cigarette ash wildly across the table towards the ashtray.

The evening had reached its mid-point. The pub was quite full, and being an estate pub, full of people who knew each other, so there was à loud hum of talk which partly absorbed the jukebox decibels. Most of the customers were in their early twenties; a number of couples and foursomes; one or two clusters of young men, an odd lone drinker older than this.

Kate voiced what each of the others had thought at some stage during the evening. 'This is a sodding awful place. I don't know why we come here.'

A male voice answered. 'For the talent, I expect.' Two young men, one in a sharp jacket, the other in a tight tee shirt to reveal his pectoral muscles, were standing by the table.

Kate answered. 'Not much chance of that, but if you'd care to move a yard to the left I could at least check it out, you're blocking my line of vision.'

The tee shirt, who had been the one to speak, did not look crestfallen. He smiled and revealed a broken incisor. 'You were in school with us, weren't you?'

'I don't remember you. Did you stay on past Year Nine?'

The boy beamed again. 'You're watchucallit's sister!' He turned to the sharp jacket. 'Member that piece with the big tits in our year? This is her sister!'

Kate mimed slow motion recognition and put down her drink. 'I know you now! You're the brother of that boy with the brain cell!' The remark was half-lost because the two men were still laughing at some mammary memory. Ronnie had started hiccoughing, but this time not from laughter. Alison patted her back absent-mindedly. 'Well,' Kate went on, 'It was super talking to you. Did we ever talk before?'

The sharp jacket ignored this. 'Where you working then?'

'We're putting together a motorcycle stunt team,' Kate said. 'Wanna come and watch us some time?'

'Where's that to then?'

'Byker Grove, where do you think?'

Alison rallied to her support. 'This is our manager, Ronnie. She's a man really, but she likes to dress up when she comes out with us, doesn't she, Zoe?'

Zoe turned away from her young man, who was staring into the middle distance now anyway, and smiled blankly. Ronnie, recovering from her hiccoughing and a subsequent coughing bout brought on by the back slapping, held out a long slim hand. 'Pleased to meet you boys. Any friend of Kate and Al's.'

Tee shirt twitched a smile. Jacket scowled. 'You're bananas, you are,' he said. He mumbled the word 'dykes' to his muscular friend as they moved off.

Ronnie laughed loudest, for she was newest to this type of badinage, but Zoe looked happy too. She had been told how beautiful she was, and that was always nice. She had had two vodkas and had been able to forget about the state of the kitty for a while. Kate and Alison, despite their verbal victory, looked glum by comparison.

'Why did you drive them away though?' Ronnie asked. 'They weren't all that bad looking.'

55

Kate groaned. 'You don't get it, do you? We're out to have a grin, not get caught up with some morons who'll talk about themselves all night and then complain when we don't let them paw us at the end of the night.'

Alison perked up. 'They can *paw* us drinks, if they like.'

Ronnie understood this well. She nodded in vigorous agreement.

Half an hour later they were in a small disco which was little more than a pub with an imaginary supper licence and a dance floor no larger than somebody's dining room. The place was hot, extremely crowded and noisier than a stock exchange. It took the girls several minutes to work their way into a corner where there was a pocket of air and a pillar to lean against. They decided to wait until they had drunk the cold ciders Ronnie had managed to squeeze over from the bar before trying to get to the dance floor.

They had just got used to the level of shouting that was necessary to communicate with each other when Kate shouted even louder.

'Good Lord! Look who it is! Mr Whatsit!'

Ronnie and Zoe had their backs to the newcomer and were astonished by Kate's delight. They manoeuvred their shoulders around to find themselves facing an oldish man. He was paunchy and balding but had the bright glittering blue eyes of a much younger man.

'Don't tell me ... don't tell me ...' he was starting to say. 'Begins with a letter of the alphabet ... and it's er ... don't tell me, I'll get it in a minute ... you used to sit together. See? I don't forget everything.'

Kate held up two fingers, the Churchillian way round.

'Two words. First name and last name. Am I right? Yes. Brilliant.'

Kate banged her finger against her arm, spilling her hard won drink in the process.

'First syllable. No, first word. Sounds like...'

She was pointing at herself.

'You! Sounds like you. Boo. Do. Sue! I don't remember that. Oh, you haven't done it yet. You ... your name is ...'

She told him. He seemed glad that the game had ended.

'But we can't remember your name. Alison and me - remember Alison now? - we were trying to recall your name earlier on. It's an amazing coincidence, isn't it?'

Alison had been busy shouting the information to Zoe and Ronnie that this was the teacher they had been referring to, who had come with them to the pub and on to the restaurant on their London trip. She greeted him now. He announced himself as Tom.

'We'd put you down as a Bill, but Tom is okay. How are you doing anyway? Where are you? Are you still up at the school?'

Tom steadied himself as a passer-by pushed him dangerously towards Alison. 'I'm everywhere and nowhere, baby, that's where I'm at ...'

Kate shrugged. 'Well, there was always a bit of truth in that.'

'But where are you guys at these days?' He gave a general sweep of his head to indicate that anybody could answer.

'We're down for the holidays. We're in London. We all share a flat.'

He was looking horrified at this news. 'London! Did I leave you there? I thought I counted you all back on the bus!'

Ronnie was stage whispering to Alison: 'Is this really the guy who used to teach you?'

Tom pushed himself nearer and shouted at her. 'I teached these girls everything they know!' At the same time he was making great efforts to extricate a cigarette from his packet with one hand. He finally succeeded, and to everyone's surprise he pushed it up one nostril. Then he repeated the one-handed routine and pushed a cigarette towards Ronnie's lips.

'Anyone else smoke?' he said, pulling out the cigarette from his nostril. 'I've only got one left, but you're welcome ...'

Kate pushed at his arm. 'How did you know Ronnie smoked?'

'Listen, shweet heart,' he purred. 'When you get to my age you kinda get the feel of these things.' He waved his lighter past Ronnie's cigarette a few times. 'Being an English teacher is like being a cop - you're always on the lookout for clues, see.'

Ronnie glanced at Kate and Alison. They were both smiling and still listening,

'It's not so much the tell-tale little signs, like the thirty or forty cigarette ends on the floor by your feet. That could be coincidence. And the packet of Silk Cut sticking out of your handbag, that could be just you carrying them for somebody. No, what I couldn't help noticing...' He paused to allow his grammar to catch up. ... 'Cos it's like forensic evidence to the trained eye, is that you have a broken nail on your right thumb.'

Ronnie instinctively pushed her thumb into its own fist.

'And that's almost certainly been caused by friction on a lighter wheel. Or perhaps by flicking a match alight, you know, like George Raft used to do?' The speech had exhausted him, for he suddenly stopped and looked a little glazed, but then he brightened again and took a gulp from his beer glass.

'Am I right or am I an utter heap of bullshit?'

Ronnie grinned, accepted the light at last and exhaled. 'Not bad bullshit,' she said.

'Ah,' he said, 'When I grow up I want to be like me.'

'Old, you mean?' This was Alison bursting back into the arena.

'What d'you mean, mean?'

'I said old, not mean.'

'You said mean. Well, if I'm so mean, you get the next round. Buy everyone a drink. Then you can call me mean. You old.'

'I'm not old! I'm in my prime.'

He laughed a smoker's laugh. 'As soon as anybody says that, you know really they're afraid they're past their prime.'

'How old are you anyway?' Alison demanded.

'Guess,' he replied.

'I don't think I can. I've never met anyone quite as old before.'

'I'm a hundred and sixty, but that's including both my parents.'

Ronnie hazarded forty-four, more to get involved in the talk than out of any real sense of how old he might be. Alison and Kate demurred simultaneously.

'He was at least that when we were in school,' Alison said. And that's a lifetime ago.'

'Small lives you people have,' Tom mumbled.

'Perhaps you're only about thirty-eight,' Kate suggested.

'I'm not so old as to love a woman for her singing, and not old enough...' He faltered in the quotation. 'I have years on my back...' He looked appealingly at Ronnie. 'Forty-four, did you say? You can't be much less than that yourself. Look at the state on you: your lips are bloodshot, your nails are shot to pieces...'

'He's definitely been married a couple of times, and he's got three or four kids, we know that,' Kate interrupted.

'I've had more kids than you've had hot dinners.' He grinned sheepish-drunkenly. 'As long as you've only had four hot dinners anyway. But I bet I've had more hot dinners than you have.'

Ronnie looked genuinely surprised. 'How many times have you been married then?'

'How many hot dinners first, since we're getting personal.' He sipped his drink. 'Well, in truth, I find I can't hang on to my wives.' He resisted a laugh. 'Suppose I shouldn't take them rock climbing really.'

After only a few more moments of shadow boxing he admitted to being forty-one. Said it was sadder than a runaway cat, but there it was. Then he proposed marriage to Ronnie, who choked on her cider.

'No, you're right,' he added quickly. 'We'd never understand each other. You, because I don't talk much sense. Me, because you don't talk much. How about you Kate? You look like a nice sort of girl. No, don't answer now, just give me leave to speak further.

59

Perhaps when I'm not quite so tired. Or drunk.'

'It's good to see you enjoying yourself, Tom. I always thought you were a little bit serious in school.' Alison said graciously.

Tom reacted as if somebody had burned him. 'Serious? You cannot be serious! And as to enjoying myself, I've never had less fun in my entire life. No one'll marry me; no one's bought me a drink for upwards of three minutes...'

'I'll get you a drink,' Kate said. 'Everybody ready for another one? Where's Zoe gone?'

They all looked round. Zoe was leaning against another pillar a few yards away, being surrounded by a man. She looked as if she were being tied to a stake, and enjoying it.

Tom resumed speaking. 'No, it's alright. You girls get on with your lives. I'd better get home anyway. Got a wife waiting for me. As far as I can remember. I usually have.'

He lumbered away without waiting for a response. Kate turned to Alison and spoke both their thoughts aloud: 'Teached us all we know!'

'Yeah, nothing.'

Ronnie said he was quite nice.

Zoe never returned. Ronnie departed quite early for a taxi. Alison and Kate danced together for a while but suddenly their hearts were no longer in it.

'I used to want to grow up so much when I was younger,' Kate said, as they made their way to the cloakroom. 'But I'm not so sure I want to grow up any more than this.'

Alison linked her arm. 'Were you thinking about Mr Whatsist? Tom, I mean?'

'And that bloke Gary with the Moet. I wonder what they were like when they were our age?'

'Probably just like us. Looking at someone else and thinking, I wonder what it's like to be that old?'

'And now they are that old,' Kate said. 'And they're probably

60

trying to think what it's like being twenty-three again.'

'Footloose and twenty-three.'

'Or screw loose and forty-one.'

'Perhaps we ought to get married after all. Alison said, then quickly, 'Don't ever tell anybody I said that!'

'You can get married, just as long as you still come out with the girls.'

They had reached the front door and a gust of cold air caused them to pull together. They strode rapidly to the taxi rank and huddled there against the wind like penguins.

'Mmm,' Alison said. 'I suppose we can still have the girls. You don't have to give up your life.'

'Of course,' Kate said. 'No one can stop us. We're the tide!'

'The tired anyway.'

There was no call for further discussion. They waited to be swept home by their taxis.

BIG JEFF AND LITTLE JEFF

I heard that Jeff was back living in the town where I live the other day. I was playing squash with someone who knew the girl he'd got married to. Of course, I didn't connect at first because he'd always been known as Dick in school. Even the teachers called him Dick, and his parents gave up calling him by his real name because he got so used to Dick that he forgot to answer to Jeffrey. Practically the first time I heard him use his real name was when he introduced himself to the workmen as Jeff that day when we started working on the building site.

I suppose he was what you might call my best friend, when we were sixteen, seventeen. We kind of hung round together all the time anyway, and we got our first job together that summer as labourers.

'Can you handle a pick and shovel?' the man said. That was the interview and we both said we could, so we passed. Dick ... it's no use, I can't get used to Jeff ... Dick looked like he could. He was six foot two with big bony shoulders and arms that were too long for him. He looked like he'd been nailed together from old bits of wood, I guess, but he must have looked like he could do a day's work. I'm a small person, wiry now, but perhaps a little frail-looking in those days, I don't know.

I know I felt out of place when we got to the building site. We arrived early that first morning but there were four men already there. They had started brewing tea and talking about how they'd got drunk and fought with their old women the night before. The first of them to address us only looked a couple of years older than me but he had just been talking about his wife and the baby like he was a veteran family man.

He said, 'Don't get married, you'll end up like me and Brian here.'

I laughed, but not much. He had tattoos and shiny slicked hair. I guessed he was nineteen.

'Welcome to Stalag 17,' he said.

Dick didn't say a word, so I thought I'd better make some reply because the others were looking at us and we were going to be work mates.

'What's it like then?' I said,

A stout old man that I hadn't really noticed, because he was in the corner of the shed making tea, laughed and then coughed sickeningly.

'You'll learn,' he said, and then he started spluttering and coughing again.

The man I took to be Brian unpeeled his donkey jacket and pulled on a red bobble cap that he'd taken off a hook by the shed window. He was ugly and very big. He had a wrestler's massive torso balanced on thin denim legs and he looked as if he was buckling under his own weight as he bent over the table at us.

'You work like piss when the boss is around, and when he slips off for his pint at ten to twelve you do piss all for an hour. Then you work like piss when he comes back.'

He said this with a leer which made me smile but also feel a little sick. My mother had made me eat a full fried breakfast at six o'clock in the morning, to set me up for the day, so I was feeling a bit queasy anyway.

We sat down for a few minutes and I had a good look round the shed, though it was dark in there and there was a lot of steam from an ancient boiler by the door. There was just the table and two benches that some carpenter had obviously banged together out of old shuttering boards. On one wall there were a few nails that served as hooks for kit bags and three darts were grouped on another wall just by my head, but I couldn't see any sign of a dartboard.

I wished that Dick would say something, but he never did say much. He pretty well used to agree with what I said. I was always the dominant one, deciding where to go, what to do, which girls we'd fruitlessly try to pick up. This going for a job in our summer holiday was my idea, he'd just acquiesced without a word, as usual. He was the same age as me, but he was like a kid brother, trailing around.

The door opened and a funny little man with a felt hat pulled low over his forehead stepped up onto the threshold. He had a stinking grey coat on like tramps wear and he had dirt in the lines in his face, but there was a sudden change of atmosphere in the shed when he appeared. Brian adjusted his bobble cap and the old man put down his tin mug of tea as if he'd just thought of something else.

I had a shock when I realised this was the foreman. I thought he must have been the watchman or something. I had another shock too when he spoke, because it was a croak that came from his diaphragm, something like a voice synthesiser. I was told later that he'd had cancer of the throat and that he'd never been a happy soul in the first place, but this had soured his temperament even further.

The foreman didn't say much, he just croaked or burped something, but everyone started shuffling out and across to another shed I'd noticed, where the tools were locked away. Dick and I followed but I was stopped by a leathery hand on the upper arm.

'You're the new boys,' he said, but it came out as four rasping grunts, like when you've been sick and you rack your throat for the last bits.

We nodded.

'What's your names?' This time I did manage to pick it up a bit quicker, but Dick must have had some relation or other who'd had the same operation because he understood straight away, and he spoke before I did.

'Jeff,' he said.

I was so surprised to hear this name that I must have mumbled when I said mine. Anyway, he misheard and said with another croak, which was probably his laugh, 'Two Jeffs, eh?' Then he went over to one of the other men, the one who hadn't said anything in the shed, and said something, pointing to Dick and me.

The man beckoned us over and handed us a pick and shovel each.

'Jeff, you go over by that big tank. You'll see a trench started there. Square off the sides and take it down to about three feet, okay?' He turned to me. 'Right, Jeff,' he said, 'Hang on to these, you'll need them later. Follow me now and give me a hand with these drainage pipes.'

I was thinking about telling him my name wasn't Jeff but something else, but it seemed a good sort of name for a building site. After all, I wasn't going to be here for long, and it didn't matter much what they called me.

The man didn't say more than four words together all morning, just shouted the odd instruction and swore at the big pipes he was laying, but I didn't need conversation much. I was learning the agility of jumping and clambering in and out of drainage trenches, and learning how to fumble for, and slowly light, a cigarette when my back was hurting a little too much or my arms ached from the work.

It was a long time till lunch break that first day. It seemed like this stranger and I had been working for days. I'd been measuring the passage of time not in hours but in lengths of pipe that had been laid, but I soon realised it didn't matter how much work got done, there was always more. So I started to invent things to do to take up the time.

'I think I'll just slip back to the canteen to get my jacket,' I'd say. Or, 'that spirit level looks like it's done for, I'll go and get the other one.'

The man didn't mind me disappearing for five or ten minutes at a time. He just carried on working while I strolled off to where I was supposed to be going and enjoyed a cigarette on the way. It was on one or other of these pretexts that I passed where Dick was working.

He had a big expanse of pallid back with shoulder blades leaning dangerously out as he bent over with his shovel. He looked different with his shirt off, though I must have seen him in the changing rooms at school. It had never struck me before: he was like a man now, not a boy.

Brian was leaning on his pick shouting at him: 'Come on, Big

Jeff, put some muscle into it.'

I guessed Dick was working as hard as he knew how, but if it had been me there, and I'd known right then that Brian had just got out of jail after three years for grievous bodily harm, I would have done just what he'd said and stretched every muscle till it screamed. He saw me standing there looking and he gave me an ugly grin.

'Alright, Little Jeff? Come to have a spell working with the men then?'

I almost blushed. I did a sort of half-shrug, which was meant to be both ingratiating and non-committal, and hurried off to fetch whatever I'd said I was going to fetch.

So by lunchtime Dick was Big Jeff and I was Little Jeff. I think he liked that. I thought I heard him laughing when I walked away from Brian, though I wasn't sure.

Whatever, we never saw much of each other after those four weeks on the building site. Guess we drifted apart. I hear he's back now though. Married too. The guy at the Squash Club didn't say if he had any real Little Jeffs of his own now though.

LAUGHING MATTER

Josie's gone now. I handle every cigarette like it was new to me, examining the name, thinking her name. Thinking her fingers.

Once, my ego arching like a stroked cat, I told her she was right - I was a genius. She told me - this was near the end - it wasn't that sort of genius she meant. A genius at wrecking, she wanted to say. But she was the real genius, in a different way. I mean, at making me happy. She never said much, she lived in her eyes, which were blue and deep enough for both of us. I kissed them and it made them sting. Old cigarette breath.

First time I saw her she had a dress on like she shopped at Woolworth's. 'Ago' must be the longest word in the English language. It was a while back, I can't say ago. I told her I spelled my name with a silent 3. I spelled it out: DAV(3)ID. She didn't laugh but I was still hooked. Great sea bass hanging on to a kid's string and bent nail, the pain through the lower lip. Fish have lips? Birds don't. No birds where we were though, unless they were overhead, just travelling through.

She said, 'What?'

I blurted out something: 'I just wanted to make you laugh, so I said something stupid. Just wanted to say something to you really. It's actually a silent 2 but I always have to exaggerate, try to impress, you know?'

She smiled then. It was like eating my first profiterole. I couldn't believe how sweet something could be. Like my first glass of white wine too.

I said, 'You're twenty-two, aren't you?'

She said, 'How do you know that?'

Cool. She was older. I could tell from the bra strap. Nobody taught me this trick, I just kind of picked it up. The nearer it is to the shoulders, the younger the girl. Some fifty-year-old women, the back of their bras could double as a belt.

I said, 'It's the hair. No one over twenty-two would wear a band.'

I guess she felt foolish. Either that or I was getting a little slick. I changed tack. 'You're a Pisces, your name's Anne-Marie, you've got a boyfriend called Doug who's in pharmacy and your old man's got silver hair. Probably late fifties. Doug, that is.'

She slowed down walking. Either time to cross the street and get rid of me or she's thinking that she's got half an hour. Anybody has half an hour in circumstances like this.

'My boyfriend's name is Jurgen.'

'Is he French?'

'And he's an optometrist.'

'Would he see his way clear to me buying you a coffee?'

She didn't cross the street.

'But my father does have grey hair, and I'm on the cusp between Pisces and Aries, that was pretty good ...'

Silver. That was flattery. Grey. All old guys have grey hair, even if they're bald, they imagine their hair would be grey. I impressed myself with the Pisces thing though, and pharmacy/optometry, that was genius.

'Since I know you so well already it seems pointless to carry on talking, but I've got time to waste, so let's go and get a coffee, okay?'

'Why should we waste time?' she said.

'It's the only thing to waste,' I said. 'Apart from money. Come on, there's a place near here.' I might have added 'life'. It seems like that now anyway.

'So was I right about the name? It was a one in two thousand shot you know.'

She told me. Josephine.

'Pas ce soir,' I said, sophisticated as a turd on the pavement.

She might not have heard. She said, 'I like to be called Josie though.'

'I'll try and remember that, Jo.'

You can't gag all the time. In the end they gag.

She said, a lifetime later, 'Your pathetic jokes make me sick, you know that?'

'You should have got health insurance,' I said. I didn't think it was very funny either. Odd I remember it really.

Living with someone is like climbing a brick wall. When you think you've made it there's a roll of barbed wire at the top. I can't remember the wall, just the barbs. Like: 'You smoke too much.'

'I do it to keep my mouth occupied. Otherwise I'd have to use it to laugh.'

'And what does that mean?'

I pondered sweeping this one to the boundary.

'I'm a joke, is it? You find me funny?'

I suppose I must have sniggered. Four leg byes.

Another time, she'd bought a dress. I said it looked like camouflage for a blind man. She burst into tears. 'You're not funny anymore!' she said. She said it with the force of her own realisation.

I said, 'I am!'

She'd started taking this dress off, unzipping at the back with her hand reaching over her shoulder, like they do.

'You don't understand jokes. When I said at that party you were so lacking in culture you thought Burnt Norton was a motorbike wreck I was NOT getting at you. I was just trying to help the atmosphere along.'

I hadn't even said this. It had just come to me at that moment, and I was puzzling over why I'd said 'wreck' not smash or crash. It might have been better if I had said it at the party. She stepped out of this dress of a hundred colours and walked out of the room.

She left a week later. My parting words were: 'And don't bother coming back for your books. I've coloured the rest of them in myself!' She wasn't a great reader, but this was just me being inadequate. She told me this, but she didn't speak, of course. Her eyes were enough.

And I suppose it was. Long time ago now. There, I managed to say it. Ago. It's over three weeks. I was right, there is only time to waste. So much of it. And it's no laughing matter.

BREAKDOWN

It started with a broken spring.

Ash heaved his sleep-heavy legs over the side of the bed and felt a sharp stab just behind the knee. He looked down uncomprehendingly at the red bead of blood inside his thigh. Gracie was still sleeping, her face blanker than a soft toy, her mouth open and ugly in the flabbiness of slumber. He pressed his finger against this wound that looked like a bite then unconsciously put the finger in his mouth. He recoiled from the taste. It took a few seconds investigation to find the sharp wicked curl of the broken bedspring, but he could not push it back into the mattress. It was too rigid to bend over and disarm, and he pinched his finger in the attempt. He got up. Bed, a useless place for years now, had become a dangerous place. But it was time for other things than emergency repairs.

In the office the new girl's bright red lipstick reminded him of the blood. It set him thinking. He told Sonya he would be out for lunch, and he drove home as quickly as the town traffic would allow. He entered like a thief, darting a glance backward as he slipped through the frosted front door. He never normally went home at this time of day and the house appeared stiller, deader than he knew it. There was a letter on the mat, but it did not interest him right now. He loped up the stairs like a teenager released from school. Gracie had not made the bed, which was good. He threw back the heap of covers and wrenched at the mattress. It slipped from his grasp and flopped back on the bed frame. He took a firmer grip on the braided edge and doubled it over. It was old but it was a firm, expensive mattress, bought for his back, and it resisted until with one more heave he managed to turn it. He ran round to the other side to inspect. His concept of geometry had failed him for a moment, and he had expected to find the protruding spike lower down the bed. It was, of

71

course, at the same crucial position. As she swung out of bed it would gash her thigh. She was even slower and more ponderous in the mornings than he was; it could rip an inch long tear in her flesh.

It did not start there. That was just the first in the acts of attrition that had brought him here. It started, of course, long before.

The plan did not work. She normally got up just as he was finishing in the bathroom, but for the next three days he hung around brushing his teeth till they tingled, combing his thinning hair again and again. He was waiting for the yelp of pain but all he heard was the sleep-thick voice complaining that he was supposed to be out of there, it was ten to eight. On the fourth day she caught her stocking on the spike as she draped it over the bed.

'Look at this!' she called. He came out bright eyed and groomed from the bathroom next door. 'There's a dirty great bit of metal sticking out of here!

He touched it gingerly with his finger. 'There's a spring broken,' he said, his voice quiet and sad.

'We'll have to turn the mattress round,' she said.

'But I'll get stabbed then,' he complained.

'Upside down, I mean.'

They turned it together and inspected where it stuck out.

'I could still catch my leg on that,' he mumbled.

'Buy a new one then,' was all she said.

He thought for a mad moment of repeating the exercise on her car seat. When he examined the thick coils of steel, however, he realised he lacked the technical expertise to cut through the metal and cause a sharpened end to gouge out through the vinyl. He was glad after the mad moment passed. Too much of a coincidence. So the next act was non-violent, just a distraction for the sake of amusement.

Though the new telephone had been installed long since, Gracie had only just discovered the last number repeat function. She was delighted, since she rarely rang anyone except her mother in Keynsham and it saved the effort of all that button pushing. Ash took to dialling random numbers at first, but it did not produce much effect. She would look a trifle baffled and then simply dial the number she wanted. Once, he dialled the Samaritans but again there was less impact than he might have hoped for when she pressed the number repeat button.

'Some wrong number telling me not to hang up,' she said. 'Cheek.'

Another time he wasn't in the room. She approached him with a wry but accusing smile.

'Who have you been ringing?'

He could not remember this time if he had planted the Samaritans' number or whether it was an 0898 number, or possibly even a harmless call that he had had to make.

'No one,' he said.

She looked at him like his mother used to.

'I reckon the cat walks over it,' he said.

'Oh yes, and I suppose she takes the receiver off first?'

He shrugged. 'Bloody clever creatures, you know.'

'Well, I'm glad the cat is so clever.' She stressed the word 'cat'.

He was only discomforted for a short while. He began to practise his retributions, as he had come to call them, on a daily basis. He took a twenty-pound note from her purse. She did not notice, or if she did she didn't say anything. He switched off the freezer late one night and switched it back on early the next morning, his blood trembling. His prime target was the container of strawberry ice cream that she loved so much. He hoped it would melt, then solidify in some new shape, like molten volcanic lava. It would probably taste the same, but it was designed to confuse, to suggest a hostile environment tweaking at her securities.

He replaced the fuse in the iron with a dead one. She ironed in a spare bedroom, always her own things and invariably last minute before going to work. She would iron his shirts without enthusiasm but in bulk once a month and he had a fortnight's stockpile. He hoped this retribution might run for a few days. The first day he drank his coffee in the room below, imagining her spitting uselessly at the cold metal triangle, fretting at the impossible world of electricity and gadgetry. Nothing happened. The next day there was a degree of success. She strode into the dining room and switched on the lights.

'I thought we must have a power cut. The iron's broken down.'

'This is a different circuit,' he said. 'But the radio is on upstairs. It can't be a power failure.'

'Can you sort it out then? I need to iron a blouse for work.'

'It must be a fuse,' he said, looking serious and full of male knowledge.

'Just sort it out for me, could you, love?'

He was not her love. He rummaged slowly in a box of plugs, screws and drill bits for the thirteen-amp fuse that he had in his pocket.

'I'll never find it now,' he said.

She looked at him with eyes narrowed. He replaced the fuse when he got home that night.

But he soon grew tired of these sniper's shots. He wanted to launch a scud missile against her bright life and air of self-containment. Her car was always on his mind. Brakes? Far too criminal. Disconnect a battery lead? She would make him fix it. He would get oil on his shirtsleeve, and he would be late for work. Or she would simply call out the breakdown recovery service. He had once borrowed her car and scraped it on a pillar in a multi-storey car park, but she had not noticed for months. This gloomy memory prevented him running his screwdriver along the side of her driver's door.

What was dissatisfying him, more than the work he was causing himself, was Gracie's lack of response. She was too engrossed in whatever it was that engrossed her - her work, her clothes, her hair appointments, to betray more than the mildest annoyance. His own mechanical environment under attack like this would have driven him mad. It needed something major, but he wanted it to be a

74

machine breaking down in order to be sure that he could be abjured from all blame. He had considered exchanging the smoke detector battery for one that was nearly run down. He knew from past experience that this caused the detector to utter a painful bleep every two minutes. Surely that would get to her? She would have to turn to him for an explanation of what was wrong in this house. Only he could decode such signals. He even took the battery out and tried to think of another appliance he could put it in to speed up its loss of power, but it was a stubby PP9 and nothing else he could think of used this type of battery. Disconsolately he replaced it. Then he had the brain wave.

The cooker was quite new, but it had a timer which had become faulty within the first year. Gracie had never bothered to find out how it was supposed to function as a timing switch for the oven. She just seemed to know when things were done. But she did use the minute timer to time vegetables boiling. When the mechanism malfunctioned, it took a tedious half hour of him fiddling with it till he finally silenced its high, shrill noise. He commanded that it never be touched again.

'The ratchet is worn. I'll never get it to go off again. Please don't ever try to use it,' he said.

Under the pretence of waiting for the mail he hung round one morning till after she had gone to work. He turned the electricity off at the mains then prised off the plate that housed the timer dial. Behind it was a nasty serpent's coil of wires. He pulled off a spade connector then switched the mains back on. With his screwdriver he delicately touched the loose connector that was poking out like an entrail from the cooker's white body. There was a joyous bright spark and he leapt clear. He went to work happy. He even smiled at the girl in the lipstick, much to her gaudy surprise.

There only remained two doubts in his mind. Firstly, how to persuade her to go near anything as mechanical, or electrical, as the dismantled timer. Secondly, the question of the electric shock killing her. He was not possessed of enough knowledge in these matters. Without doubt it would be dangerous, but in all probability she would only burn the tip of her finger. That would be appropriate retribution for his own pinched finger and the spike wound in the back of his leg. Other things he could punish in future tamperings. Stains could appear on her work clothes, he had already decided. Bills could go missing. It would be a simple matter to report that her credit card had been stolen and thus have it cancelled just when she might need to use it.

He timed his return to perfection. She had got home a few minutes before him, gone straight into the kitchen to boil the kettle for tea, then seen the dangling timer mechanism. He sighed as he came in, as he always did, to indicate the gruelling nature of his day's work, and caught her just reaching out to touch what could be her nemesis.

'Hang on,' he cried. 'I had to dismantle it to stop the damn thing tinging. I accidentally touched it this morning and it started making that intolerable noise. See that bit of copper?'

She touched it.

'This?'

Nothing happened. He realised he must have left the mains switched off. 'Yes,' he snapped. 'That connector. I'll go and make sure the electricity is off. When I give a shout, push it on to the prong thing at the back of the clock.'

She exhaled noisily. She wanted the electricity on. She wanted a cup of tea.

'Alright. Hurry up.'

He went to the fuse box. He pulled the lever down. 'Now!' he shouted.

There was no sound from the kitchen. He went quickly back. She was still standing by the oven.

'Push it on. Hard!' His voice was brittle and too high pitched.

'Oh do it yourself,' she said. 'Don't scream at me like that. You're supposed to be the man round here.'

She moved over to stand by the kettle, which had started to make its gurgling noise. There was a pause of a few seconds. It took them

76

both that long to realise. She knocked off the switch at the back of the kettle.

'This isn't on a different circuit,' she said icily.

Ash did not move. He dared not speak.

She switched the kettle back on. It began to bubble again. She knocked it off.

'Polly put the kettle on. Suki take it off again.' Her voice was calmer than he had ever heard it. 'You turned the electricity on, not off!'

'I ...'

Her eyes were not narrow now. They were ablaze with all the years' contempt. The smile on her face echoed down the centuries.

'You despicable...'

She was calm enough to take a step towards him and take a glass from the cupboard above her head. She even returned to the kettle. Then she spun and threw it at him. It caught him a glancing blow on the side of the head and smashed on the door behind him.

'You don't think that ...' he started.

'The Samaritans,' she said. 'Pathetic. But not really. You need the Samaritans!'

'Don't you dare accuse me,' he began. He felt the warmth of a drop of blood as he touched his ear lobe. 'And don't you dare throw crockery at me!'

'What?'

Her face burst into vicious life. She was awake with rage and quick with the sense of her abuse. She picked up the next missile, a heavy whisky tumbler that stood on the draining board next to her and hurled it at his eyes. He ducked, trod on the cat's dish and slipped backwards in the same pantomimic motion. He cracked his head against the handle of the door behind him as he stumbled. This time the blood flowed freely.

HOW TO MEASURE THE VALLEY

His name was Nick something. Strange, I can't remember what now. I saw him the first day I arrived in the chemicals firm where I worked as a porter, but he didn't speak to me until near the end. I suppose if I'm honest, that's why I was happy enough to leave. I'd been there for about four months, and they said they'd have to let me go. Cutbacks. I said I was leaving anyway. I was only eighteen and it was a boring job. More than that though that night with the flashlight had put me right off.

But it was me who started it, not him. I was carting some gear through his lab one day and I saw that he'd laid out some kind of experiment on the bench. There was a pencil torch on a wire frame he'd rigged up at one end and a mirror about ten feet away at the other end. I said, 'What's that in aid of then?'

He looked at me and went stock still, as if I was a noise he'd heard that he couldn't place. Then he relaxed a bit. 'Oh,' he said, 'It's a measuring device.'

'You could measure it from the floor tiles,' I said. 'They're a foot square. That bench is about ten foot long - count the tiles.'

'I'm trying this out late tonight,' he said. There was a sort of excitement in his eyes. He wore these thick glasses, like paperweights they were, and it may have been them magnifying his eyes, but I still sensed the pupils getting bigger, like a cat's, and I wasn't even standing particularly close to him.

'Oh tonight, eh? That's why the torch then, is it?' I said. I was trying to be jokey. You'd never see anything with a tiny little torch like that, obviously. He didn't smile, so I went to move off with my tray of bottles, but his voice sounded strange, cracked almost, when he spoke. 'Would you like to come and see?' he said.

I put the tray down. 'See what?'

'How to measure the valley.'

My face must have been a picture. He obviously realised I didn't have a clue what he was on about because he explained: 'Do you know High Point? There's a car park there.'

I knew the place he was talking about but I was getting a bit worried now. It was a courting couples sort of place, though I hadn't heard it was a gay car park or anything. Nevertheless, I must have stiffened slightly.

'It's just that I've worked out that it's a straight line from there across to the Dunsfield Estate across the valley. That's where I live, you see. I was going to set a timer for a lamp to go on in my bedroom at ten tonight, but I've got a better idea now. If you could be in the car park at High Point you could switch the lamp on there at a set time and I could operate this from my bedroom. It's refraction system.' He was pointing at this mirror he had. 'It's bound to be more accurate that way. We'd just need to synchronise watches.'

'Why do you need to do that?' I said. 'If you know roughly what time the light's coming on you can measure it when you see it, can't you? If you can't see it, it's not going to work anyway.' Though this was logical enough I couldn't help myself being intrigued at this Aldis lamp business. He could tell he had me hooked too.

'Well, there's no strict need to synchronise watches, but I've got to be sure it's the signal light, not just a car headlight, haven't I?'

I wondered why it made a difference, if it was distance he was measuring, and the headlight was coming from High Point anyway. I started to say something, then changed it to a question about how this measuring thing worked. He started explaining, but I have to admit, I'm a bit of a dickhead. I haven't even got a GCSE in Science, and I couldn't follow what he was saying about refraction and light waves and so on. I nodded a couple of times, not wanting to let on that he'd lost me.

'So, would you like to help?' he said.

'I wouldn't mind,' I said. 'But I haven't got any transport.' I was still saving up for my first Honda 250 at the time.

'No problems,' he said, 'I'll drop you off at the car park. Where can I pick you up?'

It was all a bit strange still, so I didn't tell him my address. I said he could pick me up by the bus station at nine. I sometimes went to a pub near there, I told him. 'Tell you what, make it 9.30,' I said. I wasn't sure whether I wanted to hang around with him too long.

'9.30 then,' he said. His eyes were huge.

'As long as I remember,' I said with a laugh. It unnerved me that he was so into this daft experiment. I mean, he could have found out the distance from a map if it was that important, I would have thought.

I went down to The No Sign Bar early, but there was no one I knew in that night. As a result, I had three pints on my own, which is murder, and I was pretty glad to get outside and see him driving up bang on time in this crummy old cream Vauxhall he had. He didn't say anything on the way up to High Point, but when we got there he took out a tripod thing, like they use for video cameras, and something which did actually look like an Aldis lamp. He had a car battery too and he connected the lamp to it with these jump lead things.

'If you could switch on for five seconds at a time at exactly ten, and at one minute past, and again at two minutes past,' he said. This was simple enough, but I hoped no courting couples would turn up. Maybe somebody'd even take me for a Peeping Tom or something. Then he looked at me kind of seriously and insisted on us synchronising our watches. I was embarrassed, though I didn't quite know why.

'I can't stay out too late,' I said. 'Got a couple of things to do when I get back.'

'I'll pick you up again straight after,' he said. 'Shouldn't take me more than twenty minutes to get back over here. That okay?'

I had a thick coat on because it was November. I was doing someone a favour. I said it was okay.

But it was bloody cold on top of that hill; the wind hit me in sharp bursts like gunfire, but at least no one came along to see me hanging around there. The last few minutes to ten o'clock lasted an age because I kept looking at my watch. It was funny, I was afraid I'd mess up this stupid business by being a few seconds late. I kept picturing this poor bloke Nick tensed up in his bedroom, as if he was Galileo or something, sitting there in the dark behind those pebble-thick specs, waiting for someone he hardly knew to reach out to him across the silent valley. Then at exactly ten I did what I was supposed to. I felt stupid, like I'd said something in a pub that I thought was really funny, but no one was laughing. Then, when I'd flashed the light like he'd said, I just stood there. I wanted to do something, but I didn't know whether I should dismantle the tripod; he might drive across and say it hadn't worked and ask me to go through the whole rigmarole again. I just stood there with my arms wrapped round myself. I felt like Captain Oates.

Twenty-five minutes passed. I had a sudden thought that it was all a practical joke, like when they ask you to hold the end of a piece of string and they disappear round the corner. I started to walk off, but the lamp and the tripod looked like they might be worth a bit. I thought I couldn't just leave them there.

I decided to give it five more minutes, and then I was definitely off. With a bit of luck I might find a pub before it got to closing time and I could have a whisky to warm myself up, I thought. Then, just before half past, I heard a car grinding up the hill and I saw his headlights through the trees at the side of the road. I don't know what came over me; I was like a girl deciding not to turn up for a date. I ran and hid behind some bushes at the back of the car park.

I heard him crunching over the gravel, but I had my head down low. There was a silence for a few seconds, then I heard a sort of groaning. There was a bit more crunching and then the bang of the car door. I stayed crouched down with my head tucked into my duffel coat until I heard the car start. When he'd gone, I looked up. I was blushing. Imagine, me squatting behind these bushes in the freezing cold like I'd been taken short, my face blood red in the bitter November night.

I soon decided what I was going to say the next day. Thought your car must have broken down, but I couldn't carry your gear because I was on foot, I'd say. Sorry, but I just had to leave it up there. But the following morning he wasn't in work. It was a Friday and that meant I wouldn't see him for the next three days. I wasn't sorry. By the time I bumped into him again I'd be able to pass it off as some misunderstanding, or just a stupid thing that didn't really matter anymore.

But I didn't see him on the Monday either. His boss told me he was off sick and wouldn't be back for a while. I imagined him catching a chill, like I nearly had, and sweating in bed. Then something his boss said made me think it wasn't that at all.

'Not that we'll miss him, mind,' he said.

I wondered about that. It seemed like he was iller than I thought, which was how it turned out, in point of fact.

That was a couple of weeks before I left and got another job as a caretaker. I didn't actually get to see him till the following February, when I was walking through town one day. He was coming towards me, his arm linked through an old woman's, and he looked like he'd aged forty years in those few months. I found out later it was his mother he was with, but it looked more like she was supporting him than the other way round, despite the fact that she was a spindly little old woman. He said hello and I stopped, knowing I'd have to speak, but I couldn't think of what to say, apart from 'Hello,' back. I was thinking about the time I'd hidden from him in the bushes, but it didn't seem like the time or place to go into explanations of things I hadn't really understood myself. I just said 'Hi,' and tried to look as if I was pleased at running into him.

A couple of days later he telephoned. He must have got back in touch with work to get my number. I didn't recognise his voice at first.

'Would you like to come round for a cup of tea some time?' he said. 'In fact, my mother says you could come for a light meal.'

It was such a strangely worded invitation I didn't know how to get out of it. Partly, I wanted to know quite what a light meal was when it was at home, perhaps. Anyway, I said I'd be happy to, and I went round the following week.

He was sitting in an armchair, and he must have had a blanket round him before I knocked, because it was sticking out behind him, where he'd obviously stuffed it in a hurry. I said he had a nice home, largely because it was a good deal warmer than my bedsit, but it was an old person's house, full of patterns, brass and cheap pictures and stuff. I took this in at a glance, or rather all this jumped out and took me in.

'I left the old place, I said, as if the lab had meant something to me.

'I haven't gone back yet,' he said. He was tapping his fingers on the arm of his chair, like he was counting at the same time as he was talking. 'When I'm better I'll go back perhaps though. Got to get things back in order there.' He smiled. 'As soon as I sort everything else out, I mean.'

I nodded, though I didn't understand what he was on about, of course. His mother came in then with a cup of tea. 'Would you like an omelette?' she said. 'Nick likes an omelette round about this time of day.' She looked more sprightly than when I'd seen her in the street, but I still couldn't quite imagine her whizzing round the kitchen. She was about sixty and pretty frail. I said I'd pass on that because I was going out for a meal later, which wasn't true because I had no money, and I didn't have a girl friend or anything. I was planning on having yesterday's pasta when I got back to my room. I took a sip of the tea, which was lukewarm and in a fancy cup.

'So, you haven't been well then?' I said.

'A bit up and down,' he said.

I nodded slowly and took another sip of my tepid tea.

'You see, I tried too hard to see into things,' he went on. 'And it ends up getting all confused.'

I said I knew all about that.

'I thought you looked like a person who could appreciate things

83

like that,' he said. He started rummaging down the side of his chair, as if he had something important there. I half expected him to pull out a piece of paper with a set of equations on it, proving he wasn't barmy by the aid of diagrams or something. Then he stopped rummaging. There was nothing there, or he'd thought better of it.

Neither of us said anything for a minute. It was too long. 'Did you ever switch on?' he said suddenly. His voice was harsher than I'd heard it before. He was always a soft spoken sort of bloke.

'I did, I did!' I said.

He was looking away, as if I wasn't there or he didn't want to hear an answer now anyway.

'Didn't you see the signal?' I said.

He shook his head. Then the shaking started to take over his whole body. I was glad I was holding a cup and saucer; otherwise I would have had to reach out and touch him, grab him by the shoulders, or perhaps stroke his hair. I gripped that cup like it was a handrail, or like it was a torch and I was a thousand feet underground in utter blackness.

Eventually he pulled himself together enough to speak. 'No,' he said. 'It must have been too far.'

'I suppose so,' I said. 'And the valley's deep enough, isn't it?'

He smiled the thin smile of someone who knew all about measuring distances and depths. 'Deeper than you'd ever imagine,' he said.

SITTER

Catherine needed trees, and so did the baby. Though she had been brought up in Harlow, a desolate new town in many respects, she had lived her early years on an estate where the roads were lined with, admittedly sparse, trees, Even in the dull, functional late sixties planners had realised that people couldn't face each other across the no man's land of a grey street, and young elms had been planted every hundred feet. Catherine's house had been one of the lucky ones, with the mystery and murmur of branches a few feet outside her front bedroom window. Now, after seven years with Gary in a neat but soulless city centre apartment, she had found herself a first floor flat in a different town, but though it was a suburban house it had a strong elm whose branches shaded the bay window of her lounge. Catherine never drew the curtains. She liked to stand by the plant table in the bay window, cradling the baby and telling it long rambling tales of the old woman who lived inside the tree trunk, or of the squirrels who came up from the park nearby to climb Catherine's tree, for it was safer there than in the municipal sycamores and beeches of Singleton Park. The baby would sometimes open its huge violet eyes and stare at its mother's murmuring lips in wonder. When the baby was tired enough Catherine would put it down in its crib and continue to stand by the window. She would open the top part and smoke through it, feeling a little guilty, but aware that her new habit of cigarettes was a small vice.

And it was on account of her smoking that she began talking to Felicio, the new neighbour who moved into the flat downstairs. Felicio asked her for a light one day as she was struggling through the front door of the house, Alice slung over her back and two Spar carrier bags biting into her palms. She put the bags down and took out a lighter from a side pocket of her denim jacket, her one extravagant expenditure on herself.

'Thank you,' he said, holding on too long with his cupped hands round hers. 'I am Felicio. You are ...?'

'Cath, she said, surprising herself that she had shortened her own name.

'You have a beautiful baby,' Felicio said. The baby's head had appeared over her left shoulder, slightly bobbing, but evidently interested in this dark-complexioned stranger. Unusually, the man's heavy beard and thick black moustache did not cause any alarm in the infant.

'Thank you,' Catherine said. 'She is lovely, isn't she?'

'And I am most grateful to you, Caterina.' The man's lengthening and foreignising of her name unnerved her more than her own abbreviation of it.

'It's only a light,' she said, and she hurried upstairs.

The next day Felicio knocked at her door and asked if she knew where he could get a bus timetable. He was new to the city, he told her, and wanted to find out how to get around. Catherine told him quite curtly that any bus from the fare stage on the nearby main road would take him into the city centre. She presumed they'd have timetables at the bus station. When she closed the door she was sorry that she had been so abrupt, but he had seemed a little nosy. He had peered round her and remarked once again that Alice was a pretty baby, seeing her sitting on a bean bag in the middle of the floor.

'What the big nasty man want with mummy den?' she asked the unblinking infant. Catherine felt she'd known precisely what he'd wanted the previous afternoon as he had put his hands round hers to cup the flame from her lighter. Now she thought perhaps he just wanted someone to talk to. She glanced out of the window and saw, through the swaying branches of her elm tree, her neighbour striding down the pavement towards the main road. Maybe he had actually wanted to know about public transport.

She bumped into Felicio several times over the next few days as she was coming in from or going out to work. Once or twice he just smiled; other times he made harmless conversation. He had located the bus station. The local Spar was very convenient, wasn't it? The house was rather damp. Was it as bad in the upstairs flat? Catherine responded genially enough but didn't initiate topics of her own. Then one night at about nine o' clock he knocked on her door again.

'Would you like to share a bottle of wine with me?' he said. His voice was not as confident as it normally was, and Catherine didn't feel this time that her space was being encroached upon. 'It is from Chile, my native land,' he added, in a tone that was almost plaintive.

'Why, that's very kind of you,' Catherine said, 'I ... I'm afraid the baby is still awake...'

'Bring her down,' Felicio said. 'But she is a little young for this good wine, I think.'

On an impulse, Catherine decided to go down with him to his flat. She would not have left Alice anyway, so it was just as well the baby was still awake. Though she didn't mistrust Felicio, she preferred to have a drink with him on his territory. That way she could decide when it was time to leave. Felicio insisted on carrying the seat that detached from the highchair and that Alice was still occupying. 'She's not as light as she looks,' he said. Catherine peered over the man's shoulder as she followed him down the stairs to check that the baby was happy about being held by someone else.

They talked about the difficulties of settling in a new town. They talked about their hopes, and Felicio talked nostalgically about his homeland. He didn't try to sit near her, or suggest that he had any physical intentions. In a way Catherine was disappointed. He was a big man with strong, very manly features but amazingly small, delicate hands that reminded Catherine of the nuns in her Catholic secondary school. At eleven she said she had to go, she had work early the following morning.

'Oh, and I suppose you have to drop this delightful baby off with a sitter. Your mother, I suppose?' Felicio said.

Catherine picked up the sleeping baby. 'No, Alice comes to work with me. We don't need anybody else, do we Alice?'

Felicio nodded and held open the door for her to squeeze past with the baby and the chair.

'I'll see you tomorrow perhaps,' he said.

'Maybe,' Catherine said.

But she decided to avoid him the next day, though she was uncertain about her own motives. It was partly perhaps that he was so solicitous, so gracious. They were qualities in a man which she was not used to. Gary had been great at first, but that was while they were still free to go out to pubs and chat to mates. Since Alice was born he'd lost interest completely and that had been the beginning of the end. He'd never shown the slightest affection to the baby. When he'd got a job working away they both recognised that the marriage was over. Perhaps Felicio was different because he came from a different culture. Then again perhaps he was simply one of those insinuating types whose goal was the same as other bold young men. They told you that you were gorgeous out of the blue, but maybe Felicio was going about the chase more deviously.

Over the next two weeks Catherine twice accepted invitations to watch television in his flat, for she had no set of her own as yet, and at the end of that fortnight she invited him to supper in her flat. He accepted with his customary grace, and he brought two bottles of good wine. 'Just in case,' he said. I'm not trying to get you drunk, you know.'

'I wouldn't mind getting tipsy,' Catherine said. 'For once.'

The evening flew. Catherine apologised for her leathery, inedible lasagne and Felicio apologised for neglecting to mention that he was vegetarian anyway. They ate the green salad she had prepared. The Chilean wine was strong and warming, however, and she found herself topping up her glass repeatedly. He drank little however. She poured herself a large tumbler of water, because she was starting to giggle too loudly at everything that was said. Then as she was returning from the kitchen, stepping with exaggerated care round the furniture, she saw him standing by the bookcase. He had picked up a gilt framed photograph of Alice and was studying it.

'She is very beautiful,' he murmured.

Catherine decided instantly that she would not drink any more wine. She took a deep breath and sat down on a low upholstered stool away from the table, where her guest had sat back down.

'Were you ever married, Felicio?' she said.

'Alas, no,' he said softly. There was plainly more to be said, but Catherine could not find the words to frame the questions she wanted to ask.

'Tell me about your home. Back in Chile,' she said at last.

'It is a beautiful country,' he said, putting down the photograph. 'But I lived in Santiago, you know. In two rooms in the suburbs. Not so very different from any city, when you are sitting in a room with just a bed and a TV set.'

'At least you had a TV,' Catherine said brightly.

He smiled. 'Sometimes though I used to go out to the country and walk in the woods, just to breathe the same air as the trees.'

Catherine understood and started to tell him about her own tree outside the house when she was a child. She said she was thrilled that she had a fine elm outside her window now. He nodded, but unenthusiastically.

'Alice needs trees too,' she said. 'As much as me, though she can't express it yet, of course.' She fell quiet. The evening's buoyancy had been pricked, though she didn't know how. Then Alice started to cry. Catherine looked nervously at the clock on the mantelpiece. 'I ...'

'It's alright, it's getting late,' Felicio said. They both stood up. Catherine was unsure whether to respond if he offered to kiss her, then was surprised as he took her hand and shook it.

'If you need to get out, take a break, I'd be happy to look after the child' he said. 'As long as you show me what to do.'

Catherine went to speak, then stopped. 'That's very kind,' she started again, 'but I'm fine. You'll have to excuse me...'

'I know,' he said. 'I'll go now. See you tomorrow, or when I see you.'

Catherine stood for a few moments after he'd gone, listening to her daughter's sniffling from the bedroom. In a few minutes the sounds ceased and the baby was asleep again. Catherine poured herself a full glass of wine and drank it down in one long gulp.

Over the next couple of weeks Catherine came to accept that Felicio wanted only a platonic relationship. They sometimes chatted about innocuous things like the changing weather - winter was giving way to spring - but there was always something sad about him. Evidently, he didn't want to talk about the past though. She formed a theory that he had had a lover back in Chile who had miscarried, and he was gazing at what might have been, when he glanced down at Alice's bright face and tiny mittened hands. He asked again if she ever needed a sitter for Alice. She repeated that she was happy enough to stay in at night and that she was fortunate enough to be able to take the baby with her to her morning job as a cleaner. Then the day after he had repeated his offer she was forced to accept. There was nothing else she could do. Gary's brother was standing, crash helmet in hand, on her front doorstep when she returned from her morning's cleaning.

'He's in hospital. In Cardiff. It's not bad, it's a couple of broken ribs, I think. He asked me if I'd fetch you.' Gary's brother was only eighteen, and he looked helpless, like a child delivering a message to a stern headmistress.

'I can't come now,' Catherine said. 'I've got Alice. What does he expect me to do, catch the train? How am I going to get from the station to the hospital? Is he in The Heath? Oh God, how did it happen?'

'He'd been drinking.' Gary's brother looked down again in discomfort and rubbed one boot with the toecap of the other.

Catherine saw a curtain move in the downstairs flat. 'Wait here,' she said. Then she turned back. 'Are you safe on that thing?' She motioned towards his Yamaha 250.

'As houses. I don't drink and drive, Cath.'

'My name's Catherine,' she said quickly. Then she swept up Alice from the pushchair and struggled to insert her key into the lock.

Felicio agreed that it was best for her to go straight away. She assured him she would only be a couple of hours. 'I must be mad, but I'd better see what state he's in,' she said.

She made up a bottle of formula and brought down a jar of savoury and a jar of sweet and two nappies. 'If she cries, she's either hungry or she'll need changing. She's very placid. I'm sorry about this. Three hours. I'll be back by two at the latest.'

Felicio touched her arm. 'Two thirty is fine. Any later and I may run out of Chilean folk songs,' He smiled.

Catherine sighed and kissed Alice on the forehead and touched her tiny fingers. 'Mummy'll be back in a minute,' she said, then to Felicio: 'I can't thank you enough for this.'

Gary's brother drove fast but safely, and they were in Cardiff and approaching the hospital in less than an hour, but as they slowed down in the traffic Catherine made her voice heard at last. 'Stop now,' she screamed.

Gary's brother pulled in and turned his head slowly. 'What?'

'Take me back now. Or to the station. Now!'

He did not understand.

'I insist!'

Gary's brother's shoulders collapsed.

'Or I'll walk to the station. I've got to get back!' She could not explain any further and Gary realised that there was nothing to do but take her to the station,

'What am I going to tell Gary?' he said.

'Tell him not to drink and drive!' she said.

The train took an hour, and no amount of coffee from the buffet could calm her racing blood. With her last five pounds she took a taxi from the station rank.

There was no answer when she beat at Felicio's door. She rapped

91

with her knuckles, then banged with her fists, and finally beat with the flat of her hands till they were stinging, and she could beat no more. She hurled her slight body at the dull wood, but it didn't move, and she was left rubbing at her sore shoulder. She slumped down by the door sobbing and broken by grief.

Meanwhile, in the park, Felicio was holding Alice high above his head so that she could she grasp at an oak branch. The smooth bark of the new branch and its bounciness as she tugged at it felt good. A middle-aged couple strolling past in thick winter coats smiled at the man and the child. They could not have imagined the atavistic howl that was coming from the slumped figure of the child's mother in a dark passageway a few streets away.

WHAT'S THE SMELL OF AMERICA?

'It smells like America!'

Lucy has picked up an old handbag of mine from the bottom of the fitted wardrobe and is holding it strangely, like it's evidence or something. I look at her amused, though a moment before I caught her looking at me in the mirror. Her expression seemed to suggest that she thinks I'm letting myself go. I'm in my slip and I suppose a certain Christmas excess has dramatised my cleavage and, well, thickened my waist a little too perhaps.

'Don't be silly,' I say. 'Countries don't have smells. Not America anyway. If it was India now ...'

'Don't be so racist,' Lucy says.

'What does America smell of then?' I say, pulling on my old purple jumper. It used to be really huge on me.

Lucy shrugs and drops the handbag on the floor. Doesn't even put it back in the wardrobe.

She was ten when we took her to Florida. Six years ago. America smells of diesel, or hamburgers, or laburnum, depending on where your self-catering apartment is, I suppose. I don't keep any of these in any of *my* old handbags.

Strangely, I can't get it out of my mind.

'She says weird stuff,' Jim says when I relate this tiny anecdote to him later on in the evening. 'Remember when she was little, and she said about the acrobat inside her head?'

'Acrobat?' I don't know what he's talking about now. 'It's you that's weird, not Lucy.'

'I never did find out what she meant,' Jim muses. He's got a droplet of Bolognese sauce at the side of his mouth, and I can't take him seriously.

'You're such a messy eater,' I say. 'D'you want some more?' It's him that made the sauce, a huge pot of the stuff that he made in the pressure cooker that we lost the whistling thing off, so much that it's lasted us yesterday and today, but I still act as if I'm the provider and do the offering. He holds up a declining hand.

'It must have been her imagination she meant,' he says, still worrying over a three year old's malapropism thirteen years later. 'I suppose.' He likes to annotate our personal history, the three of us. Or the two and a half of us, as he sometimes says in his gloomier moods. Lucy's undeniably her mother's daughter and I can't say but I'm glad it's that way.

Lucy has eaten already, made herself some exotic salad of healthy raw vegetables and unhealthy chocolate biscuits. She comes in but Jim doesn't want to embarrass her with reminiscences of her childish utterances.

'I think I'll be a dancer,' she says. She pirouettes past the kitchen counter and only manages to bang herself on the hip. 'Ouch!'

'I'd practise where there's no furniture,' Jim says lugubriously.

Lucy sticks her tongue out at him, but he's not facing her. She hasn't hurt herself.

'Can I have some of your old clothes, mum?'

'I haven't got anything that'd fit you, love,' I say mechanically. On reflection I realise this may not be true.

'Your mother hasn't got any *old* clothes,' Jim says, sliding in the last slimy strand of spaghetti.

'Mmmbly mmmble grmm,' Lucy mimics.

Jim speaks clearly this time. 'She only has new clothes. And what would you want with suits and blouses? You've got a uniform for the daytime. And your jeans and sweatshirt uniform for evenings and weekends.'

She's wearing Levi's and a Heaven sweatshirt right now.

'These are for easy movement,' Lucy says languidly. 'I told you,

I'm going to be a dancer,'

'What happened to the acrobat inside?' Jim says, suddenly sounding sharper. Lucy screws her finger into her temple. They don't get on too badly though. Jim is stressed out at work. I decide to remind my daughter of this unassailable fact, despite myself.

Apropos of nothing Lucy speaks: 'You guys don't get it, you're not taking 'A' levels,' She obviously can't imagine anything more stressful than her examinations.

'And you don't do a job of work,' Jim says. 'I, on the other hand do, and I have also in my time sat one or two exams, you know.'

'City and Guilds probably,' Lucy flounces. I lower my eyebrows at her, but Jim catches me doing it.

'And I sometimes wonder why I bothered,' he adds. This is one of his parting shots. Lucy knows it as well as me and we stay silent as he gets up and goes off to sit in the living room to catch the news on TV.

Lucy doesn't say anything, and she just stands there for a while. After a bit she starts nosing through a cupboard, though she's already eaten. There's only jams, marmalades and a few old dried foods in there anyway and I'm getting annoyed by the clink of jars as she rummages.

'What are you looking for, for heaven's sake?'

She bangs the cupboard door shut and glares at me. I still can't get used to her scornful looks; when she stares at me as if I've dribbled on myself, or put my makeup on wrong.

There's nothing on television, just programmes, so I read for a bit then decide to go to bed early. It's only half past nine when I announce that I'm going up. Jim looks at me and I wonder if I've said it too loudly and he thinks I mean for him to come up now. The thought makes me wonder if I want sex myself. Perhaps.

Next morning I wake early and can't quite remember if I've dreamed about it or whether Jim did actually try and initiate something last night. He's fast asleep with his mouth hanging open. His lips are cracked and he looks ugly, or as if he's in pain. He doesn't even stir when I push his shoulder. I decide not to ask what time it was he came to bed. I'm not moist and I don't remember any details from a sexy dream. I sit up in the bed and look in the mirrored door of the fitted wardrobes. I'm thirty-seven, or is it thirty-eight? I'm puffed up by sleep of course and my breasts are heavy, but they always get like that before my period. I might go on that three day diet though. Next Monday. Today is Friday and I need to unwind over the weekend. Dieting makes me hyper.

Jim's body suddenly gives a mighty jerk, then he rolls over as if he's been kicked. He splays out a bony arm and it nearly catches me across the side of the head. I fold it back away from me and he throws himself back round in the bed and digs his coccyx into me. The radio comes on just at this moment and he hits the button, still foundering in his oceanic sleep.

'Put it on,' I mutter, unsure if he can hear me. 'I want to hear the news.' An arm creeps out of the bunched quilt and switches the soothing voices back on. 'Are you awake?' I ask, but Jim hasn't opened his eyes, and I guess he's still operating in some subconscious mode.

The news tells me that things are getting worse, then a politician comes on and tells me that things are getting better. My mind drifts off and I feel a flush of warmth and sudden tiredness again, so I nestle back down into the bed.

'What's the time?' Jim mumbles. He's facing the digital display again, but he doesn't even want to open one eye.

'Seven.'

'Five more minutes,' he gurgles. He always says this, then gets up few seconds later.

I listen to him urinating long, then in shorter bursts - his private morse code for something - then I hear the familiar sounds of his energetic toothbrushing and the softer sound of the shower. The bathroom is next door, almost an ensuite but not quite. I've closed my eyes again and my hand goes down for a lazy stroke or two. When I open my eyes again it must be a few minutes later because

Jim's back in the room rattling wire hangers in his half of the wardrobe. He's taken up running again recently and I look at the tighter skin round his waist. His hair needs cutting at the back, but he's taken to combing it over the thinning bits and he won't listen to me about this.

When he's finally out of the bedroom I roll out of bed and pause by the window to see what's happened in the world while I've been away from it overnight. Nothing much. Grass might have sneaked a millimetre higher, I suppose.

I take a bath and luxuriate in the heat and flux of it for longer than usual. I have an important meeting at nine thirty and I usually like to get into work in plenty of time to get my mind really active before I have to talk to a client. Today I can't get motivated somehow. When I'm clean and nice smelling - gardenia, I think, this morning - I flick through the suits and dresses in the wardrobe. But today they all say the wrong thing to me. Where are all the delicate patterns? I only seem to have red, grey and black. I sit back down on the bed with a thump and take off the towel round my head. A cold wet snake of hair flops against my shoulder and I don't feel so good anymore. But I have to rouse myself. I put on a skirt and blouse and go downstairs. Lucy and Jim are in the kitchen. She's looking through her school bag and Jim is staring past the steam of his coffee at nothing in particular. They've breakfasted themselves, as they do these days without word. I get out the coffee percolator, though there's a jar of instant on the counter and the kettle's only just boiled. Jim notices this slight deviation from normal routine.

'I don't have to be in till ten,' I say. He shrugs and starts to put on the jacket that he's draped round the back of his chair.

'Well, I'm off,' he says.

'Have a nice day, dad,' Lucy chirrups.

'You too, Darcy Bussell,' he smiles.

They're both gone by half past eight and I'm still sitting here. I've no intention of wearing this tight skirt and this silly silk blouse today, but I've no alternative plans either.

After a bit I put on the radio, but I don't like the man's accent and I switch him off again. I take my coffee into the living room and try the television instead. There's a woman in a leotard and she's got music pumping away that she's stretching and jumping about to. She looks older than me; when the camera gets in closer you can see the tight lines under her eyes, but she's obviously super fit. I look at her shape more closely and I see that her thighs are firm and sinewy, but the vee of her leotard reveals how bony her ribcage is. Her chest is far too flat as well and her hips are unnaturally narrow. She's not a proper full woman, I decide, she's what that novelist called a social x-ray.

I switch off the TV. If I'm going to get to work, I've got to get my mind clear and dress for this meeting. I go back upstairs and stare at the suits again. My eyes are drawn to the floor, where I've thrown in that old handbag amongst the shoes. I pick it up and sniff deeply into it. It doesn't smell of anything but leather. I start to fiddle with the zip inside to see if there are any old tickets or credit card slips but it's seized up. All of a sudden it seems terribly important to get the thing open and I wrestle with this damned zip until I can get two fingers inside the little compartment and feel round for anything. There's a piece of paper. I try and tell myself it could be a £20 note maybe. I know really it's bound to be a receipt or something. But now I can't go to work until I find out what it is. In the end I take the bag downstairs and get a kitchen knife and slash at the lining. Of course it's a receipt. I look at the amount and I wonder what on earth it was that I bought that cost this much. I'm going to have to do something. Phone somebody, or something.

When Jim and Lucy come back, they both comment on me sitting in the living room with the TV on mute. I don't say anything to Jim, but I admit to Lucy that I haven't been in to work.

'What's wrong?' she says. 'Are you ill?'

'No,' I say. 'There's nothing wrong with me. I just felt I had to have a break.'

She looks like she'd like to say something nice to me, but she obviously can't think of anything. Eventually she says, 'Shall we have a takeaway tonight?'

Jim comes in and hears this. 'I was going to make a chicken dish,' he says.

'I don't know if I can eat anything,' I say. And it's true. Everything's gone wrong and I can't taste or smell any more, it feels like.

Suddenly I say it out loud. 'I'm fat,' I say. 'I'm hugely, obscenely, grossly fat. Why didn't you ever tell me?'

They both look at me with hope and despair swirling like oil and water in their eyes.

'I can't dance, I can't cook, my clothes are all awful and now I can't even smell things anymore! How could you let me get like this?'

Jim smiles wanly. 'What do you want to smell that you can't smell?' he says. I think he's trying to be funny to cheer me up.

'America,' I say.

Jim sighs a smiley sort of sigh, but Lucy shows no sign that she recognises what I'm talking about. All of a sudden I see what she will look like in twenty odd years. There's a little hard line round her mouth and her forehead's showing the first wrinkles, but of course they disappear as she stops frowning. Her skin goes pale, translucent again. She doesn't know anything about what twenty years will do. I'd like to start telling her, but I'm glad I don't. You can't anyway. Backwards is the only way you can look at what anything means.

CONTACTS

It's funny, it's the sort of thing that everybody knows about, the sort of thing some bright young features writer might write an article about in *The Sunday Times*, making everyday observations an art form. Or a journalism form anyway. But I've never come across any article about this, and I've never heard about it happening to anyone else quite in the way it happens to me. It's these overpowering visions I get of people I used to know, and they occur just as I start some mundane task, like peeling a clove of garlic, or shaving, or adjusting a wing mirror on my car. And it's not as if the people I recall are particularly special, despite the way they come to me so vividly.

One's a girl I went out with, but I never even kissed. She wasn't very pretty. She had mousy hair that was short and in tight curls and she was a funny shape. Her body was longer than her legs, sort of thing, but she was fun, and intelligent. Maybe that's why she finished with me so readily. She comes into my mind when I'm applying shaving foam to the bit between my lower lip and the cleft in my chin, which is to say every day, except if I'm on holiday, or ill in bed. Then she's gone again as soon as I start smoothing the stuff into my cheeks and throat. I mean, it's not as if she ever touched that nameless bit of skin in our brief relationship or anything.

When I'm slicing an onion there's an old guy who I worked with once. I quite liked him, though he was a bit boring, to tell the truth. He wasn't funny, or particularly intelligent though. We were working in a hospital, and he was one of the other porters, and he mainly just gave me a nod or a smile. Actually, I always found an excuse to rush off when he'd start telling me about the corner shop he used to run, before he came down in the world.

I said garlic and I said onion, but I don't think it's anything to do with smell. Sometimes I use a lemon scented shaving cream, but most often I buy the cheapest, and that smells of nothing. Anyway, there's no particular smell to my wing mirror, and that's for definite.

Today I saw my brother Lou. In my head, I mean. He died eight years ago. Obviously, I've thought about him plenty of times, but I mean he came to me, like the girl and the old man, and the woman who used to serve in The Duke (she's my garlic visitor). I was just taking my glasses out of their case, which I keep in my top pocket since I started wearing them a couple of months ago. I slid them out of the case, leaving the case in my pocket. I suddenly knew that this was going to be a habitual action which was going to bring Lou into my head every time I do it from now on.

It was unnerving. Lou killed himself after Theresa left with the kids. Every time I think about him normally, I try to shuffle the pictures round and catch him in one of his laughing moods. But the trouble with this association thing is that the people come to me in a set pose. I can't do anything about it. I slice the first sliver of garlic clove and here's this barmaid handing me a pint, like she's in a photograph or an old postcard. I touch that wing mirror and there's that old German teacher, whose name I don't even remember, just frozen as he's passing out the marked exercise books.

Lou is holding his hands out to me as if I'd just asked to inspect them. I don't even recall the time I must have snapped this mental slide. He's sort of smiling, but with a look of regret too.

Every time I see Graham (he's the hospital porter) I think I should get in touch with him. He's still working at the hospital, so it'd be easy. But what could I say? 'I think of you constantly.?' I mean, he'd get the wrong idea, wouldn't he? And you can't go writing to people out of the blue, telling them what's happened to you over the past six or seven years. It would be a lot longer if I managed to get in touch with Amy, the girl with the frizzy hair that I never kissed. I'd have to say, 'Dear Amy, I grew up and had all sorts of jobs, all sorts of relationships. My brother killed himself. A whole lot of stuff has happened, I guess. More than you'd care to read about ...'

Or: 'Dear Mr German Teacher ('Dear Sir' would be okay in this instance actually), I never did German after the Third Form, but I still picture you, handing out the exercise books in that inimitable way of yours ...'

He used to throw them at us. Or rather, skim them through the air like Frisbees. Sometimes one would threaten to land short, and some bright spark would backhead it on to the right desk. 'That's the way,' the guy would say. Other times he'd say things like, 'Don't interfere with the flight of the book, boy. I have developed my outswinger over a number of years, and I know what I'm doing. Let the book spin in flight, it'll find its owner.'

I don't remember a word of German, but I can still quote the things like this he used to say. Funny.

The woman who served in The Duke has probably moved on. Got married. Remarried even, by now. The Duke isn't called that anymore, it's The Goose and Granite, and you aren't allowed to go in there if you're over 21. Or that's what it feels like. I think her name was Babs. Might have been 'Babes' we called her though, I can't remember now. She looked a bit foreign, but not so that you could tell where she was from. Like she was Maltese, or Swiss, or something. Some nation that hasn't got a look, but you're not surprised when you hear that a person's from there. Well, not Maltese, because you'd think Italian probably, and not Swiss, because you'd probably think German in that case, but you know what I mean. Something of a different complexion, perhaps it was. She was lovely, actually. She called me Barry because she always confused me with a boke called Barry that we used to hang around with. But who stopped going to The Duke. I never liked to tell her it wasn't my name, because she was so attractive. She had a huge smile and lovely big black eyes. When she said, 'Pint of cider for you, Barry?' I think what I mainly did was blush.

I'd like to see her again. I mean the real her, not this frozen image I have. I'd like to see what she looks like now. Even if she's changed those eyes would still be there. But it's that same mental photo I see when I make the first incision into a smooth creamy clove of garlic. It's Freudian, I think. Whatever that's all about.

Sometimes I wonder why I don't think about more significant

people. Until today, when I saw Lou with his large white hands out in front of me, I mean. My grandfather died when I was about eight and I can picture him too, but he doesn't come unbidden like the rest of these ghosts. It's only when it's on the news that someone has died, and there's a picture of an old man with grey hair and a hard looking lined face, that I remember my grandad. He had soft eyes in that craggy face of his though. You kind of accept death, even when it's through illness, when it happens to people from a different world, or a different generation. Obviously, Lou was another matter, but even then, there was a reason, of sorts. It didn't make any proper sense, but in the end you force yourself to accept that there was too much pain, or he felt there was, to go on. I thought I'd accepted it anyway.

Then I started to wonder, was I seeing all people who'd died? I don't know for definite if Graham's still working at the hospital, do I? Any more than Babs and Amy and Herr Whatsisname are alive and thriving. Maybe death's a cool blade that's sliced them in half somewhere some dark night in a head-on, or in a corner bed in an intensive care ward.

I don't really believe in any of that stuff about telepathy or the supernatural. But these figures from the past do all look dead in a way too, or rather, they're two dimensional, like they're one of those famous people who've died and are frozen on the TV screen for a few seconds. It's got me thinking, I have to say. And one of the things I think is, do people get images of me? When they pick up a letter from the front door mat, or turn over the corner of a bedspread, or hear the first coin drop in a vending machine? Life's always thought of as a swirling mass of movement, but it might be like a movie after all – made up of a million still frames. I could be a momentary déja vu in a hundred people's lives; a smiling spectre as they half turn their head at the whistle of a kettle or the sound of a fridge turning on. It's a spooky thought. I'd want to say something if I turned up for someone else, like Babs and Amy do for me. I'd want to say, 'I'm alive, I'm moving, I'm real, this is only one frame from a thousand reels of beating existence.'

103

If Lou could say anything, he'd say, 'Do it, son,' I'm sure that's what he'd say. But of course he just stands there. The German teacher is caught for all eternity mid exercise book fling. Babs is handing me the same pint that I'll never drink. Amy is throwing her hand up in the air as if she's just got the joke and Lou is showing me these clean, unstained hands.

I'm going to put my glasses away. I'm afraid of seeing so clearly with them. A few months ago I realised that words and pictures in the newspaper were getting grey and blurred, so I bought these specs. Readers. Now everything's stark black and white, the pictures clear, the words sharply defined. I can see clearly now, as that old song goes. It was quite a shock at first, I can tell you, when I realised I'd not been seeing things properly. Everything must have gone grey without me noticing it, but you kind of blame it on the light. You say to yourself. 'I'll have to put a stronger bulb in this lamp,' and so on. Nobody wants to admit they're not as whole, not as unblemished, as they used to be, do they?

If I didn't live alone perhaps I'd have had someone to tell me that I was squinting and peering to see the small print in the paper or on the backs of food wrapping. Anyway, I bought these glasses. I did consider trying contacts, probably out of vanity, but I also thought I wouldn't like it having something that close to me, right on my eyes. Now with these half-glasses I've got, I feel more in touch, despite the slightly swotty look. I mean, I don't have to wear them all the time, it's just for close scrutiny of things. I've decided to keep them on the table next to my chair, not in my top pocket, because of how powerful that feeling was when I took them out today. It's not that I don't want to think about Lou, of course, it's just that I know I'm going to feel so helpless when the same image of him comes back to me. In fact, I may give up using garlic and onions when I cook my chilli con carne. I always make enough to last for the next three days, but there's nothing wrong with cooking myself something different every night really.

I could even give up shaving, I suppose. I might look even swottier with a beard, I think. That might get rid of Graham and Amy and Babs at least. But I can't do anything about the business of having to adjust my wing mirror occasionally. I think it's wonky; it keeps going out of line. It'd be dangerous if I couldn't see what's coming up behind me properly. Especially since, as it says on the glass, things are closer than they seem. But imagine if all my 'visitors' congregated there instead. A group photo of the dead and the lost, all speeding up the outside lane to catch me. It's not funny after all, it's a tragedy. And that's probably why no bright young features writer has done anything on this association phenomenon in *The Sunday Times*. People like that can send words flying through the air even more effectively than my old German teacher, but who wants a message like the one I'm seeing so black and white all of a sudden landing on their desk? Making contact with your own past is making contact with yourself, I'm realising, and I'm not sure I like it.

LIFE GOES ON

I've been here all day. Not doing much but thinking. Of course, nobody just *thinks* all the time. You can't. Well, perhaps Socrates did. Or maybe some of those other Greeks with names ending in -ites or -ates. *At ease?* And weirdos like Nietzsche and Newton and Einstein perhaps. But most people can't just dwell on ideas for more than a few minutes. Unless you're working out a money problem or doing a sudoku you can't focus on one thing for long. You spot someone walking past your window, or a fly lands near you, or you're dreaming of Maggie and an image of a meal you once had with her in Rome. And you cartwheel off into other images of food you like. Or restaurants you discovered in the middle of nowhere in France. I've watched my cat thinking about whatever cats think about and then seen her just giving up and staring away at nothing for minutes. I've been a bit catlike all day. But I have been thinking about Maggie a lot.

Of course there was no guarantee we'd make it. There never is. How can two people, made up of different genes, atoms, experiences, hopes and dreams even, randomly come together and mesh? Like jigsaw pieces you can't separate again for fear of tearing off a corner? She wasn't as precisely formed as a jigsaw piece, mind. She was more like a blob of mercury suspended in water. Not shapeless of course, but capable of becoming anything, I suppose. Well, that's true anyway.

We were in our twenties. My twenties started when I was about fourteen though. Even the teachers thought I should be less uptight, less focused on my future. I was a mini-adult far too early. You're only young once. Hah! Actually, you do get a second chance when you get to your seventies. They don't tell you that of course.

Maggie was twenty-two and I was twenty-five, going on forty. That first time she looked at me like she wanted to sort me out. Take a comb to me. Whisk me off to a boutique on The King's Road and make me buy orange and purple shirts. Of course, we weren't in London so that wasn't going to happen. She did encourage me to grow a moustache though. A weak, bedraggled affair that I soon got rid of. Not like this sophisticated facial hair I have now. But she was definitely interested in me. I don't know why. Perhaps she thought I was a corner piece in the puzzle of life she'd just sat down to solve. You start with them, don't you?

So we started dating. Courting, my parents would have called it. I called it 'going out', though we mainly stayed in of course. She was 'into her music'. I'd had a record player as a teenager. Everyone did. Even the really poor kids. But I'd already moved on from Radio One to Radio Four by that time. She'd insist I put Radio One on though. I don't recall all the names of the bands – groups, I think they still were then – but we never went to any gigs (are they all concerts now?) so it was just something we heard, or she'd speak about now and again, not any cable tie around our relationship.

Earlier on I was trying to picture what she looked like when we met, but I'd need a photo for it to be accurate. And of course I haven't got any anymore. That was rash of me, I know. Still, I could describe her in terms of her hair and face and shape if someone asked me. Like if the police found her wandering around after an accident. Back then, I mean of course, when she was twenty-two. Not now. I'd want to say she had a bit of a kink in the bridge of her nose, and maybe I'd suggest her eyes were neither grey nor blue but a sort of dirty pavementy colour. That wouldn't help though. Some stubborn sergeant would say, 'Is she short or tall, blonde or brunette, slim or well built?' And I'd tell them nothing of any use at all. 'She's average height, mousey hair, average build,' I'd say. Then I'd add, 'But you'll know her from her sense of humour. Unless she lost it in the accident.'

I wouldn't have the first idea what she looks like now. But I'd guess she would have let her hair grow grey and kept it long, like a feminist critic on TV. She's bound to have put on weight. Everyone does. Thickened, rather than got fat, I'd say. Started off a taper, turned into a candle. But not a yankee candle.

Would she be bitter now? Who knows? Am I bitter? A bit. I never saw it coming, but you never do, do you? After, she said, 'He turned out to be just like you.' As if that was a criticism. I would have wanted that to be a compliment. But I never found out what our supposed similarities were. I'm sure he wouldn't have been a United supporter, he was from somewhere else. He certainly didn't look like me or talk like me. Of course, I don't really know what I sound like to other people. Perhaps I sound posh to some folk. Or affected. Or dim. Who knows? He did have a sense of humour, but why would she think that was something that meant she could stay with him? He was actually quite a nice guy. A good friend etc. Not in my case obviously, but nevertheless.

It was all my fault of course. I was too constrained. Fully formed too early, stuffed into my sense of myself like a model ship in a bottle. I don't think I was very good at sex either. Nobody wants to think that about themselves, but you get so you don't mind admitting things about yourself when you get to my age. Well, it becomes possible anyway. Especially if you're on your own. Like, people will admit to being not very good cooks, or not very good musicians or runners or swimmers, but they don't often say, 'I can't satisfy a woman, or I'm an inadequate kisser.'

I used to like kissing. Strange thing, putting your lips against another person's and wriggling them about. I found it strange. She used to wipe the top of the coke bottle if I offered her a share. With her cardigan! Not very ladylike. Then five minutes later she's rummaging around in my mouth, our tongues exchanging oral liquids. Usually as a prelude to an even more intimate exchange of fluids. And all the time it transpired I was doing it unsatisfactorily.

She burnt bright. Brighter than a candle, so I should have used a better phrase just now. She *felt* things. I think things, know things. Quite a few things actually. But she experienced the world directly through her flesh almost. Lots of stuff bypassed her brain and went straight for the viscera. It meant she was suffused with life rather than jogging alongside it, as I almost certainly was. One time she came round to my place in tears because she'd seen a mother in the street shouting at a little kid for some unknown misdemeanour. She felt the poor child's pain. 'He was cringing from her, from his own mother,' she said, drying her eyes with a tissue I'd left on the table, and which I'd probably used already. I didn't say anything of course.

She loved food. I mean, approached it like a lover. I like it too, but it's not an affair for me, it's a work colleague. She'd throw things together in the kitchen, as if preparing a meal was just another chore, like doing the laundry or tidying the living room. But then she'd drool over every mouthful as if it had been put together by a Michelin chef. Not in the sense that she was proud of her culinary achievement, but as if her true being had been recognised and congratulated by her pasta sauce, and she was honoured by it. She didn't look for my approval particularly either. It was a type of communion with another type of being, her affair with her dinner.

I saw the binmen this morning. I don't wear a watch these days, but I can tell the time by the passing of bin lorries and the click of next door's front gate as their kids set off for school. I like sounds. I don't mean indoor ones like the fridge or the boiler, but the sounds of other people's lives. The postman, the Amazon van door opening. The birds too. They seem to give up after a bit though. Saving energy for the racket they make when it's time to go to roost, I suspect. Time is slow, of course. Just as well, the old guy in the local shop says, we haven't got so much of it left. I resent the 'we' but I don't respond. You tend to start measuring in bigger chunks as you grow older. Seasons even, rather than days and hours. I was with Maggie for four seasons. That's all. But it was 383 days. Countless hours. Some of them spent watching her sleep, which sounds creepy but wasn't. I loved her so much. I couldn't get enough of her and resented being away from her, even in the sense of being mentally away from her because I was asleep. She was next to me, but it wasn't quite enough. I wanted to be fused with her. Two electric wires soldered together. I guess she had more current going through her though. No, that's just fanciful. She was red and I was black. Black is negative.

She'd recently started working for a printing firm. She said it was boring and the people at the printer's were dull. One of them wasn't, it turned out. I said she should look out for something else. She had a lot going for her, with her personality, her wit, her quick mind. I should have said 'with your looks too' but I didn't. I didn't want to be shallow. She said she'd stick it out for a bit until something turned up.

Then after about a year she started coming home at different times. Rush job on. Tudor wanted us all to stay on. That sort of thing. I'd either cook something we could heat up when she came in or say, 'Let's have a takeaway.' They'd opened a McDonald's not long before and there was a KFC too. They called it Kentucky Fried Chicken then, of course, because at that time nobody was afraid of the word 'fried'. Then, early in the new year, she said she had to go away at the weekend. 'It's an annual thing,' she said. 'Nothing grand, but the parent company treats all its workers to a bonding event in Birmingham. I have to go. No partners, naturally, or we wouldn't bond.' She laughed. I shrugged.

That was probably the weekend she decided to leave me. I mean, she didn't up sticks the moment she got back from Birmingham or anything. If it was Birmingham even. But she'd clearly changed course, like she'd been warned she'd entered a shipping lane that had been heavily mined. We still had sex, but she wasn't *feeling* it like she used to. She didn't use those words. She didn't actually say anything. But the light seemed to have gone out. The candle had burnt out, you might say.

I once tried telling Sally about this emptying out I'd gone through with a past girlfriend, but she didn't want to know. And I don't think it would have been a good idea now. How do you tell your wife of thirty years that you had a yearning, a love that still consumes you when you think about it, and it wasn't her? Sally died five years ago but I don't talk to her ghost. I do talk to Maggie. But she looks at me like the cat does. Then slinks off somewhere where I can no longer see her. Also like the cat.

It's probably about eleven o'clock. Time for a coffee, methinks.

Charles, his name was. Is, I suppose. She said, 'He loves me. I know you probably think you do too, but I really think he loves me. He can't do without me, so I have to be with him.' He managed to be without her a few months later though. After he'd got her pregnant.

I saw her just the once after all of that. She was dragging her son along - he must have been four or so – and the poor kid was having a tantrum about something. She stopped dead in the street and smiled. She looked me up and down. 'Theo, you look great. Have you been working out?'

'Just working,' I said. Working in, as ever.'

Neither of us knew what to say next. She was still as beautiful as ever. In my eyes anyway. But she had a slightly faded air about her perhaps. She was still shy of thirty, but a spark seemed to have gone out somehow. Like she'd fallen into water and come out flatter, more bedraggled even than my youthful moustache attempt. She told me things hadn't worked out with Charles after all. But little Tim was a blessing of course. I must have nodded wisely.

'You were and always will be the only one,' I said. 'If you'd had young Tim here with me, I don't think I could have shared you. No offence, young man.' Naturally. I never reported saying this to Sally.

Next door's kids will be home for lunch soon. I'll hear them arguing through our parti-wall. Life going on, whether I like it or not.

LOOKING FOR THE PATTERN

I was born at an early age to a woman who eventually turned out to be my mother. I didn't speak to her for about a year, then later on not for several years. Mainly I cried, which was something she was rather partial to as well. She did influence me in my clothing and diet though, at least until I could buy stuff for myself.

The best thing about being alive was breathing. I did it all the time, and sometimes quite heavily. Occasionally when I forgot to do it I would faint, so I've now made it part of my daily regime. It's about the only exercise I do actually, because I can't afford gym membership or an exercise bike. Or shoes.

I had to go to school, because apparently IT WAS THE LAW, but I didn't learn very much. Neither did anyone else, which was encouraging because it made me feel part of a community of utter ignorance. Men in black gowns moved about unheroically eating sticks of chalk and wiping off strands of tobacco. They had mysterious powers which they didn't use.

Still later I discovered females (they had been hidden from me since I was eight) and also the universal truth that a single woman is a strong and independent creature, but as soon as she gets married she NEEDS SUPPORT. A corollary of this is that men are rarely strong, almost never independent and never ask for any support because that would be too girly.

I had to get a job because IT'S THE LAW, so I went to the council Highways Department. I was asked if I could handle a pick and shovel. I didn't know what a pick was, but I said yes in case it was a trick. So I stood at the side of a road for six weeks and listened to dirty jokes from men who could actually handle picks and shovels. They paid me too.

I wanted to write a great work of fiction, perhaps a big long saga about all the members of a dysfunctional family, but every time I

112

tried I found I couldn't think of any relatives to put in. There was mum, but she never said very much and didn't have any particular characteristics. And I never knew my dad, but I'm told that was a good thing.

When I switched my literary ambitions to poetry I was made up! There was a thing called a quatrain, which was a bunch of words written in shortish lines, sometimes with rhymes at the end. Since I always try to keep my paragraphs to four lines this promised to be just the thing for me. And I could cut down the actual number of words I'd have to write!

So I tried this quatrain business. It was alright, as long as you could get the bumpety bumpety bumpety BANG thing right, but it was difficult. Some words just aren't bumpety enough, it seems. Pity. Well, bum pity, in fact. You try and get 'I'm a hexagon with just two sides to me' or 'If only I could climb a hawthorn hedge' into a bumpety quatrain!

So I gave up on the verse malarkey and tried DIY. Not a great success. I thought I'd start by making my own tools, but I got stuck after my rudimentary mallet. So I grew flowers. Well, I say I grew them, actually they did all the hard work themselves. I mainly watched. I was very successful at growing bright yellow ones in the middle of the lawn.

People used to knock on my door and ask if I'd heard the good news. I'd reply that good news wasn't really my scene, but I soon realised they didn't actually want to know, they just wanted to smile beatifically and drink my tea. Eventually I'd ask anyone who knocked to come right on in, I was just finishing making their coffin. I still had my mallet, you see.

When a strong independent woman came into my life needing support I said okay, though I was unsure what help I could possibly be. We stood in front of somebody in the council offices (back again, but no pick this time) and they said 'Here's a piece of paper. Good luck. Off you go.' So off we went, though it took a few years, if I'm honest.

But we had some kids. Two, as I recall. Interesting creatures.

Smaller than real people but a lot louder. You soon find out that they're a lot heavier than you'd think too. Sometimes I would read stories out loud in front of them. Not very successful, this. They invariably fell asleep and I'd never find out what happened in the end.

After a few decades I got a better job than standing by the side of the road listening to dirty jokes. It was indoors. It was a bit like school – people moving around aimlessly wiping stuff off their clothes, but mainly food now. No one knew what anybody was supposed to do but everybody was afraid of someone finding out that this was the case. I fitted in very well.

Now I was earning a bit of money I thought I'd give this shopping business a go. So I went to Marks & Spencer, Primark, Tesco, everywhere I could think of. It didn't turn out well. I've got a suit, but it doesn't fit, and I've got some ties, but no one wears them anymore. I only buy black socks though, so I'll always be in fashion, and I'll always have a pair.

I bought some cookery books. You know, colourful, very expensive hardback books with picture of delicious meals with ingredients you've never heard of. 'Take a pinch of sacremento and grind it to a pulp with the juice of an organtilla.' And 'Let your spinozas stew for eight hours.' That sort of thing. I put the books on the kitchen windowsill to go damp.

I bought a car. A saloon. I always thought that was a place you went to drink, but you're not allowed to in this type. It's like people saying 'I own an estate' when in fact they just live on one. The car I bought is a Ford. That's actually where you cross a river. Better than Qashcai though. That sounds like you've run over your nephew.

I don't really have friends. They're too expensive. 'Shall we go to Romero's for dinner?' 'What would you like for Christmas?' Meaning they want something bought back. I had one friend, but he got boring. Or maybe it was me who got boring. In all probability we both bored the daylights out of each other, so we called it a day. (Or a night, I suppose).

Then one day I stumbled on politics. This is the business of

114

pretending that you care for people you actually despise and where people ask you to go out into the cold and rain every five years to guess who'd be the least damaging to your precarious existence. I thought, 'I could do this!' But it turns out you have to have a deposit, so I never bothered.

I got ill and had to go and see the doctor. He said he suffered from what I had too. That was encouraging. At least I was part of a community. Another time I got ill again and he sent me for tests. This is what GPs do when they don't have a Scooby what's wrong with you. They say they'll tell you when they've got the results. They never do though.

Nature. Ah, nature! What can you say? I used to think it was a bit overrated. Some water moving about aimlessly, like a teacher, or an office worker. Some trees blowing in the wind. Some flowers of different hues. But when I got a bit ill in the head I spent more time having a proper look at it. They said,' Take your time.' So I did. In front of nature. It was good.

Now I'm on my own. Kids grown and gone. Women getting supported elsewhere. I watch TV but it's not much cop, is it? Presenters smiling beatifically and talking about stuff that's nothing to do with me. At least they're not drinking my tea though. They have shows set in the East End or Manchester, where everyone's on about their community, as if that's a real thing.

I've taken to looking at things. I don't mean the mantelpiece or the picture rail. I mean stuff like clouds, because they're always on the move. I also like neighbours' pets because they're funny and they look back at me. Passers-by too. I took down the net curtains so we could accidentally catch each other's eye. They look embarrassed but I don't care. It's a community of strangers, isn't it?

And lately I've been going on the internet. This is a device created by teenagers in California to make you think that life is all people saving animals from tricky situations and appeals for £5 donations to someone who's going to run somewhere for no real reason. I skip past the videos and the appeals straight to the 'epic fails'. I can identify, you see. I'm not so sure about epic though.

I've got a grandchild who's allowed to visit sometimes. I like it when he comes. He loves stories more than anything. Even food! The trouble is, he's got more stamina than me and it's me who drops off as I'm reading them. He prods me awake though. And we stare at each other. Obviously there wouldn't be a net curtain anyway, but it feels like one's been removed when he looks at me.

I'm going to sleep now, as a matter of fact. Perchance to dream! Not likely. I've never dreamed. Seems like a waste of effort to me. Creating stories that no one will ever hear? What's the point? I can look at some things before I drop off. Stars and stuff. Maybe patterns in the wallpaper, though that's not really my scene.

I'll see you in the morning. I'll be the one wiping off the night's detritus. I might even be smiling beatifically, whatever that's supposed to mean. Lots to do tomorrow. A bit of normal breathing, nothing too heavy. A bit of cloud watching. Then I think I'll look up a definition of the word 'community' on the internet. There should be one.

If by some chance I don't wake, that's alright. I've already put the bins out and the goldfish should be good for a few days. It's been a hell of a ride. It hasn't, of course, that's just something people say, isn't it? When they know it's all been something of a drab affair in fact. I might give the wallpaper a go tonight though. See if there is any discernible pattern.

NEW YORK AND MERTHYR TYDFIL

Her name was Petra and she had been away from South Wales all her life – all her real life, she said – until the last two years. She was a sad-eyed, sensual woman who changed the subject charmingly when I tried flirting with her, but obviously remembered times when she wouldn't have done.

I didn't really flirt. I said, 'How does Wales seem now then?' That surely didn't count. But it was the way I said it, the way I hung onto her answer, the way I was apparently so fascinated by everything she said. When she mentioned having lived in New York for a number of years I said, 'Well, I've been there, but I can't say I know the city really. I spent nearly the whole time I was there in The Museum of Modern Art. There was a Munch exhibition on, and I stood there for ages with my mouth open, a bit like *The Scream* actually.' This was, I realised later, calculated stuff. She'd been an art student. Now she was back in Merthyr after living abroad all those years and, after the sophistication of the Big Apple, an art literate reference might well have been welcome in these more provincial parts. Even if the reference was pretty lame.

There's a whole thing about art galleries and sexual attraction that is well documented. There may be a less documented but equally self-evident thing about Edvard Munch. Any man in the 1990s who talks about that other nineties' scream has to be well apprised about female angst. Quod erat demonstrandum. 'Shall we go back to your coffee or mine for out further exploration of post-Chagallian sexual liberation?'

I didn't tell her anything about myself. Cunning. I found out she was that rare thing in Merthyr Tydfil, and that common thing in so many other places, a yearning, imaginative, artistic beautiful creature with dreams of Miller's Paris, Brecht's Berlin and Fellini's Rome. She got a job as a dancer, spent two years in Greece and then discovered America. She'd worked as some sort of assistant to a costume designer in Hollywood and then ended up in a brownstone in Manhattan as an editor. Now, three loves and a few more lovers later, she was in a nondescript town in South Wales, the place where she'd started and tried to avoid for twenty odd years. I put her at 41, but that's just me – I like exactness. She could have been 40.

She'd been ill, she said. I couldn't help noticing traces of alopecia, but I didn't like to interrogate her that far. Very ill, she stressed. I suspected the C-word and leapt nimbly away to the neutral ground of postmodern literature. I'm no expert, understand, but if you read the Sunday newspapers you can do a reasonable job on any conversation, except quantum physics perhaps. I have tried that actually, but the jukebox was on loud, and I may have got away with it.

I said a few provocative things about Umberto Eco. Not a great response, so I switched back to David Hockney. I could relax again for a while, watch her lower lip and the sweet shape of her breasts against her thin coffee cream blouse. I'd started off just for a bit of practice, as unreconstructed men like me do, but I was beginning to fall for her vulnerability. Now that's a strange thing. You should admire strength not weakness, but I suppose this was her strength though. A quivering, delicate, totally feminine strength, and that's what gets me.

Eventually, despite numerous evasions, it came to finding out who I was. I toyed with extravagant lies. You know, film producer, novelist, graphic artist, reviewer and so on down the cultural line. I was somewhat reluctant, congenitally, to be candid, but her almond eyes and all this quivering of breasts and lips betrayed me into a near-truth. I told her I was a poet. I know, I know, anyone can say that. 'But what do you do for a living?' they riposte.

After a while I told her I wasn't a poet at all. She looked abashed. She wanted me to be a poet.

I said, 'Actually, I wanted to be one, but I couldn't afford the uniform.' Surprisingly this didn't even get a smile. She gave me a serious dressing down instead.

'You're afraid to admit it but you shouldn't be, you *are* a poet.'

I was in, but I didn't want to be – not quite this easily anyway.

'You're a Sagittarius, aren't you?' she insisted.

Here we go. I had been one of those for a few weeks with a girl from Biarritz, but I've also come on as a Scorpio, because of the reputed sexiness, and my favourite, Gemini.

'I don't know anything about all that stuff,' I risked. My first refusal. Four-point penalty, but we weren't in the jump-off yet.

She looked abashed again. 'I was born in February,' I said. It was close to home at least.

'Ah, Pisces.'

'I think so, yes,' I lied.

It shouldn't be true. It defies all mathematics, but Pisces is a woman's sign. I was back in. I was a sentimental, emotional, torn soul, admittedly with a touch of Capricorny bluntness, but this at least made it a challenge for her.

We talked about Peter Greenaway for a bit. Safest thing in the world. Everybody's seen at least one of his films, everybody's got a theory and everybody's partly right. Even Greenaway perhaps. I said I deplored the supposedly anti-right wing message in *The Cook, The Thief, His Wife and Her Lover*. She wasn't so much abashed as astonished this time.

I don't mean I deplore anti-Thatcherism,' I said. 'What I deplore was the passing off of an aesthetic and essentially visual artistic work as some sort of squib against the Docklands mentality. I mean, as a director he's totally apolitical, but he's keen enough to cash in on the liberal vote. He's a box office poacher dressed up as an auteur.'

She hmmmed. I had to tone it right down. 'The colours were very interesting though,' I added.

She looked at me with those chocolate box eyes and used them to ask me to stop patronising her. If my object had been purely polemic,

119

I would have slapped this down as a woman's trick, but let's face it, I had a different agenda. Anyway, I'm a sucker for all that stuff. I glanced down at my feet to give my brain time to shut up; it was spoiling things for my heart. Not my heart, but something about my emotional system, I suppose.

Her turn to look down. 'Listen,' she said, 'it's very flattering of you to be paying me all this attention, talking to me like this.'

'I'm not talking *like* anything,' I interrupted, 'Nobody talks *like* this – this is it. This is me, a complete stranger who quite likes talking to people, such as they are, but who's having a whale of a time talking to you. And I'm frightened, excited, miserable, laughing, elated, drunk on it …' I had to stop because it was almost right. This didn't feel like a lie. I was unused to talking in words, rather than lines. 'I'm sorry,' I said, 'Sometimes, and it's rare actually, but now and again in your whole life you start talking and you never want to stop. Except when you know it's time to kiss instead.'

It seemed I'd formed a sentimental attachment to her upper torso and her pale, forty-one-year-old face, somehow before I knew it.

She didn't reply for a moment. Then she decided she couldn't. I reached out and touched her hand where it lay on the table. It was bony and veiny. On its own there it looked like it was a hundred years old. I touched it with a surprising gentleness. Then, just as I withdrew my hand, the guy who was meeting her came hurrying up, apologised for being late and asked her solicitously if she wanted to eat, or whether she wanted another drink. I was introduced. She nearly said I was a poet. She bit her beautiful lower lip on the word and said, 'We were talking about Peter Greenaway.'

My blood ran cold as a tap. The man shook me by the hand, and I tried to make my mouth give some sort of smile. He went away to get their drinks.

'Listen,' she said. 'I'm awfully sorry. I'm just too faithful.'

I wondered whose screenplay this was. Not a Greenaway for certain. Not enough encodings. This was blunt, simple, banal. A guy in a pub. I looked over at the girl collecting the glasses. She was tall and beautiful, in a horsey way. I mugged up in my mind on Vivienne Westwood, Billy Bragg and D H Lawrence. She had to be a student, with delicate un-bar-like hands like those. I finished my drink. I hadn't quite fallen out of love with my older woman yet; it would take another few drinks, perhaps another pub. I cursed my life for its learned lines and incredible speed.

Petra had decided to move to another table and now she was talking animatedly to the straightforward and rather drab man who had brought her drink. It was no good wishing. If I'd met her fifteen years ago, I'd have had to talk about Billy Bragg and D H Lawrence anyway. As it was, I had almost reached out. Nearly told the truth. Got within a month of my birth sign. Something in her Merthyr blood had pulled her back. That didn't make Merthyr a bad place, I suppose.

'Have you finished with that, sir?' The horsey girl was standing by my table.

I smiled. 'Where are you from?' I said.

SAY PORTHCAWL

I should have phoned this Ivy woman. I could easily have made some excuse, like enquiring whether we could rearrange the date for my talk, and then found out how she'd got gold of my name and how she'd come to invite me to address her little writing circle. I didn't call. I wrote back, almost as soon as I had deciphered the thin handwriting, and said I'd be delighted to talk about fiction in general, or a particular genre or author, if that were more appropriate. The next letter I received was a couple of days before I was due to give the talk. It merely reiterated the terms of my fees and the rather all-embracing topic: 'The Art of Fiction.'

Luckily, I didn't just copy out a few pages from the David Lodge book of the same name that I have on my shelf above the desk. I have, of course, written stories. What academic in my field hasn't? What English graduate hasn't? *Everybody* writes stories. From the age of seven to the age of sixteen you have to anyway. It's like acne, or masturbation, only legitimised in the curriculum. But what made me take along a dozen crumpled word processed sheets that were all that was left of the stories I have ever written? Both Ivy's initial letter and her almost identical and equally illegible second letter mentioned a *small* writers' circle. Small, but fascinated with the art of fiction. I suppose I thought I could pep up a rather dry, academic account of the Rise of the Novel – another title I have on my shelf incidentally – with an illustrative example or two from a couple of unpublished stories I happened to have about my person.

The truth is, I get paid to bore people on a salaried basis. But this writers' circle payment – tiny though it was – was an unbidden gesture of faith. It said we *want* to listen to you. Our small but fascinated band of amateur writers wants to know what it is all really about. Reader response theory, postmodernism, intertextuality; we could read it all up in books, but by the sound of your name you're

122

the type of man who could bring it to life for us. You might be able to direct us into the path of writerness.

I think I must have reasoned that if I read some of my own work and got a titter or two, or any minuscule sign of appreciation, I might be nudged into thinking about working on those twelve pages of deathless, but twenty years old, prose and fashioning them into marketable fiction. Twelve pages isn't bad. Another 238 and I'd have a book. I have written a book, of course. It's in the library here at college, though I note no one has taken it out for the last three years. *And* I put it on the required reading list of my Fictions and Factions semester 2 course. But I mean a real book. A book that someone buys when they don't have to. A book that someone passes on to someone else to read, rather than tries to sell, unopened and unread, at the end of their degree course.

My talk was to take place in the District Council Offices in Porthcawl. In winter. In summer Porthcawl is quite a pleasant, though somewhat windy little resort on the Bristol Channel. From October to March – but sometimes it's September to June – it's a bitterly windswept one-horse dorp with nothing equine and very little that even rises to the level of dorpishness to recommend it. It's just nothing but grey house and closed hotels. The council offices are in fact the upstairs of a terraced house. I had no difficulty finding the venue, however. Mrs Ivy Double-Barrel – I wasn't able to decipher either Barrel from her letters and I was too embarrassed to ask when I got there - Ivy anyway, provided me with a map in her second missive. It was, in contrast to the handwriting, very neat and tremendously detailed, but really there was no need. The street was one of the two interconnected streets that lead off the Promenade, or Esplanade, as they probably call it in the summer months.

When I pushed open the door that said, rather grandly, 'Council Chamber' I began to realise the gravity of my mistake in coming. Six people were sitting at the long conference table. The three who faced me were all ladies in their late eighties. Just in front of me, with his back to me, was a man with the silver hair of someone in his early sixties but the quivering voice of that man's grandfather.

There were two other ladies, the youngsters of the group, on his side of the table. They could barely have been more than fifty five or so. The quivering voice was trembling on towards the end of a long sentence that he might have started several minutes before my entrance, but the expression on the faces of the others warned him its owner that a stranger had entered the room.

'I … er … I wonder if I'm in the right place …' I began, knowing full well that I was, in the strictest sense of the word, but that I wasn't, in any normal person's apprehension of things. 'My name is …'

Everything was in order. A few things had to be dealt with as preliminary business, but I was very welcome to the Porthcawl Writers' Circle. I put down my briefcase and looked longingly for a sign that might read WC, or Staff Toilets.

'Would you mind if I just … er …'

'Down the hallway, last door on the left,' one of the youngsters said, in alarmingly accurate anticipation of my micturational needs.

I would have just run away if I hadn't left my briefcase in the room with them. I even paused to consider if there was anything in the briefcase that I would ever miss that badly, but of course there were the two unfinished stories. I hung around in the toilet and pushed my hands through my hair a few times; repositioned my tie; flicked a speck of dandruff off my jacket. I was gone for about three minutes. This was time enough, however, for them to deal with the minutes of the previous meeting, or whatever it was they felt they had to do. When I re-entered the room the old man motioned me towards a chair at the head of the table, as if I was an interviewee. I looked longingly at the circle of armchairs and settees at the far end of the chamber.

'Do people feel comfortable round the table like this?' I began. 'Would it be better perhaps if we sat round in a circle over there?'

One of the late-eighties women, whom I could now see was closer to a hundred, shook her head gravely. I felt like I was Sydney Carton asking if the executioner's blade was quite sharp enough.

'Perhaps I should say at the outset,' I remarked, 'that you've allowed me a pretty open brief, so I hope it's okay that I've responded to it in the particular way I have.' This meant absolutely nothing, and the open mouths of my audience let me know that was a truth that had not eluded them either. What it did do though was alert them to the fact that I was a practised public speaker, not to be thrown by the aggregate of their ages, unthinkably huge though that number was.

'I feel perhaps that, because we are such a small number, it might be best for us to maintain our discussions as in informal level, rather than me undertaking a full-scale lecture, so to speak.' My own choice of words doubtless belied my call for informality, but I was aware as I spoke that two of the old ladies seemed to have dozed off, and at their age there was no guarantee that they would ever reawaken, If I could at least get them to participate, to say anything from time to time, then I night feel confident that I hadn't reduced anyone to irredeemable catatonia. No one said anything. All that happened was that a half-smile on one of the fifty-five year old's faces coagulated into a deep frown. I pressed on: 'The Art of Fiction is, perhaps, an infelicitous phrase …'

An octogenarian whispered to her older friend and the words went echoing round the cold air of the chamber. 'What's he saying?'

'… because fiction might rightly be construed as a science as much as an art …'

The silver haired man began a paroxysm of coughing. He gasped and choked my next few words into meaninglessness, but on one paid him any attention, or looked as if they cared to hear me repeat what had just been drowned out. Indeed, the only words I heard myself were 'postmodern … alarming … playful interchange … therefore.'

About twenty minutes passed (with the length of long winters, if I were to quote Wordsworth) and the expressions on my auditors' faces did not alter one whit from the alarming air that they had assumed at the beginning of my awful talk. They resembled nothing so much as a group of snakes looking at a small animal and

125

pondering whether it was a rabbit or a mongoose. But I am no Rikki Tikki Tavi, nor was meant to be. I dived into my briefcase for the pathetic crumpled sheets that lurked within. I produced them in a fair impression of Neville Chamberlain, my face now as red as the old man's had been during his coughing bout.

'So, I thought I would just read you a part of this unpublished story, to give you an illustration of what I mean.'

I began reading, and the fact of having a script in front of my face calmed me down, at least for a few seconds. Then I saw the expletives coming up in a paragraph of dialogue halfway down the first page. There were three fucks, a bollocks and a clitoris in quick succession. I slowed down my reading, to give myself time to come up with acceptable synonyms. But there is, of course, no synonym for clitoris, except the even more unacceptable 'love button'.

'Drat, drat, drat ...' I attempted. It didn't quite have the same ring for my hero in the hour of his greatest existential angst. Then straight up I was forced into paraphrase ... and there's a section where the protagonist reflects on his relationship with his former ... er ... colleague ...'

Silver Hair had moved a heavy crystal ashtray a few centimetres towards himself, perhaps preparatory to hurling it at me. I looked at him expectantly.

'I was just going to intrude for a moment to ask something,' he said.

'Please,' I whined, 'yes, by all means, please do.'

'Maybe I'm a little old fashioned, but I do like a story which has a beginning, a middle and an end. Do you subscribe to that feeling, or do you think that a writer should ignore his obligations to his readers and follow his own course?'

I could have embarked promptly on a critical discourse on Primo Levi and Italo Calvino. I could have rapiered this objection aside with a quick reference to *The Crying of Lot 49* or *A History of the World in 10½ Chapters*. I could have said that Aristotle had been dead for quite a whole now. I didn't want to mention people dying right now though. I said, 'You're right of course, but beginnings, like endings, can happen anywhere.'

An octogenarian tightened her claw-like grip on the handbag she had on her lap. It occurred to me that she had misheard, that my words must have sounded strangely like, 'Give me your cash and your pension book, dude!' It was hard to understand why.

'Should I carry on for a bit?' I said. No one nodded, but neither did they indicate any wish for anything else to happen. It was like addressing a group of Inuit in demotic Spanish.

'Well anyway, this guy goes on for a bit wondering what's happened to Saffron, that's his former colleague, and then he's looking at the hamster cage he's got. There are two hamsters in it, but they're both stuck to the bars of the cage. They've been frozen to death overnight, you see ...'

Of the six of them I guess now that five must have kept hamsters and at least two been on the Rodent of Great Britain Executive Committee. I riffed through the remaining sheets in my hand, looking for anything uncontroversial. A nice description of a country garden perhaps. But this was incontrovertibly an urban tale. Not a hollyhock or a parsonage in sight. Not much you could call 'in sight' at all, as a matter of fact. Just this dismal character's puerile thoughts about some dubious sex he's had once and some tedious speculation of the nastiness of living on your own in a bedsitter with two dead hamsters. I found the opening page of the other story.

'Reader, I didn't marry her,' it began. The curse of intertextuality reared some of its gruesome heads at me and I wondered how it was that I must have begun this story immediately after putting down *Jane Eyre*. I ploughed on regardless. 'I raped, in due order of things, her mind, her handbag, her bedroom and, though I'd always deny this, her body. That cool internecine body ...' I shuddered to a stop. Internecine? What the fuck? Or what the drat, I suppose, was that supposed to mean? I looked up. One of the fifty-five year olds was apparently reading her library card. An eighty something was staring at me as if I'd just claimed I was a gasman and was trying to gain entry into her house. Mr Silver Hair was studying the grain of the wooden council chamber table as if searching for something. He wasn't actually Mr, I was to find out when I eventually collapsed into silence and the coffee and cakes were brought out; he was Reverend Oats. He gave me a story he'd written, passing it to me discreetly in an envelope that conveyed this prenominal information.

'Well anyway, what I'm trying to suggest,' I said weakly, 'is that the art of fiction is an art that involves self-interrogation. The fictive world is less a window, more a half-glazed interior door into reality.' I couldn't believe I was saying this. I was going to get paid for uttering preposterous nonsense about going down someone's corridor. I couldn't stop my metaphor careering on, however. 'But forgive me if the door has to swing closed again for tonight. I should really stop at this point and allow time for some questions.'

No one spoke. Eventually, the most sprightly of the octogenarians dragged herself to her feet and headed slowly towards a tea table at the other end of the room, walking as if she were aboard a very unstable ship into the teeth of a gale. Reverend Silver Hair managed a brief thank you speech and then suddenly the chamber was a flurry of activity as tea and coffee were poured, spoons clinked against the sides of bone china cups and macaroons and home-made ginger cake made their appearance, to remind people that life was not such a sorry affair after all.

I ate a glutinous piece of ginger cake and sipped at my weak coffee. I accepted the coy offer of the Reverend's story, which I should read 'at my leisure'. I blithely promised a full critical analysis, though I don't feel this was quite what he wanted. I shuffled my twelve pages of self-indulgent, expletive-ridden and pathetic prose together and replaced them in my briefcase, as if I didn't know I was going to dispose of them in the bin as soon as I got home. Finally, I thanked my hosts for a stimulating evening. 'We must do this again some time,' I said gaily and without any warrant whatsoever.

'It was very …' The woman who must have been Ivy started to say, but she struggled for so long to find an adjective that I had to offer her one.

'Different?'

'Yes,' she sighed.

She looked like Queen Victoria coming out of Stranglers concert, but I guess by this time I looked like one of The Stranglers coming out of an audience with Queen Victoria too, only less self-assured.

I haven't tried to write any more stories, though the twelve pages stubbornly found their way back into a desk drawer. Reader Response Theory is great as far as theories go, but it's all a bit too real in the flesh.

I took my book out of the library the other day though, partly just to have it date stamped of course, but partly to have another look at what I'd written. It's called *Fiction – Theory and Practice*. It's crap, to tell the truth. It's all middle. No beginning and end.

WEST OF EDEN

When Derek and Francine decided to splash out and go to America for a fortnight, they had just one child, Poinsettia, their outwardly delightful three-year-old daughter of the dark curly hair and Pear's Soap smile. This was in the relatively unencumbered days before Mandrake, before Bernard, and before the need for a large estate car to accommodate the writhing boredom of family touring holidays.

'Let's have a touring holiday,' Francine said.

'I'm not going to North Wales again, Derek said, looking up from the pools coupon he was checking.

'I mean abroad.'

'The car isn't reliable enough,' Derek responded on automatic, for these were also the days when he sanguinely relied upon Ford technology.

'We can hire a car,' Francine said.

'We've already got one.'

'But, as you say, we can't rely on it for long journeys.'

'How long is long?' Derek crumpled his losing pools coupon and inwardly cursed Stranraer.

'I was thinking about touring the States.'

Derek dropped his biro and choked on his last mouthful of tea. 'We can't afford America!'

'I've been doing some sums, or my mum has anyway, and we could just about afford the flights, though we should have taken advantage of Poinsettia going free and done it two years ago.'

'How could we have flown two years ago? How would we have transported the pushchair, five dozen nappies and enough spare dummies? Anyway, what's your mother got to do with it?'

Francine clenched her teeth. 'She's good at finding bargains, you know that, Derek. She's always wanted to go there herself. Actually, she suggested that we go with her and dad. It'd make it cheaper in the long run.'

'I don't think it's a sensible idea to go on holiday with your parents, you know that, least of all to somewhere like America. Please don't go promising ...'

'I didn't promise anything. But what do you mean, it's not a sensible idea?

'Well, America's dangerous. And it's got lots of K-Marts that we'd probably never see the outside of.'

'What's that supposed to mean? Are you saying my mother's a cheapskate? She regards herself as a bargain hunter, you know that.'

'And there's precious little warm British beer to be had, as far as I know.'

'Are you saying dad would moan all the time?'

Derek did not need to reply, for Francine's pause indicated that she was running through a likely scenario in a Florida bar, with her father drumming his fingers on a beermat and staring off into the middle distance, then insisting that he could not possibly drink this cold American rubbish so would have to drink orange juice for the fortnight then. 'They can't afford to go at the moment anyway,' she said. 'But I think we could, if we stopped at motels and did things economically.'

The absence of the in-laws was one blessing but the word 'economically' and the phrase 'Francine's idea of doing things' could never appear in the same sentence, or in the same hemisphere of the brain, Derek knew. He took a more prudent sip of his tea and demanded to hear the preliminary costings Francine had done. The figures were nightmarish, but the image of a big Buick speeding down Route 66 with Derek at the yard-wide wheel was an infinitely more palatable notion. 'If we start saving ...' he began.

'You know you couldn't save if you were a worldwide religion! No, we're not having any of that shilly shallying saving nonsense. We'll borrow.'

131

'Are there any banks or credit companies left that we haven't already tapped?' Derek asked, quite reasonably.

'This is 1987!' Francine shouted. 'Things are looking up. You should borrow as much as you can lay your hands on. Mum was reading the *Daily Mail* about it.'

'Oh well, it's got to be true then,' Derek sighed. 'How much?'

'I think three thousand would do it.'

By the summer of 1988 the appeal of borrowing large sums of money had dwindled for some people, though of course this would not last very long, but Francine had set her heart, and a new bank loan, on going to America. She was less keen on the economising idea, however, as the time to depart drew nearer.

'Let's stay just one night in a hotel near Heathrow,' she said. 'If we go up by bus, it'll save the car parking fee at the airport.'

'Don't be ridiculous,' Derek snorted. 'I can't go catching buses at my age. No one over thirty should be seen catching a bus, unless they're also over sixty five anyway.'

Francine found an offer in a magazine. It involved an exorbitant night at a hotel outside Heathrow, but it also involved free parking at the hotel for the duration of the holiday, and a free shuttle to the airport. Honour was thus saved. The hotel was a drab building in the middle of a wasteland just off the M4, but Francine fought back her architectural disappointment with great strength. 'We'll have a really nice evening meal and an early night, be fresh for the plane tomorrow,' she said.

Derek knew it was pointless being fresh for an eleven hour flight. However fresh you started, you still got off at the other end like a car mechanic's rag. But he rarely baulked at the idea of a leisurely evening meal in a hushed restaurant. He had still not fully learned that such a thing was impossible with a young child at, or more often running around, the table. Poinsettia's Pear's Soap smile was a good deal more angelic than her behaviour. A few seconds into the meal she spilled Francine's soup and received a harsh rebuke; so harsh in fact that she careered away into Derek's side, causing him to spill his wine. Derek offered the little girl another rebuke, which caused her to collapse underneath the table. There she consoled herself on the corner of the tablecloth, dragging it to her tear stained eye and upsetting Francine's wine in the act. The adults hurried on to the next course, but Poinsettia reappeared and put her finger in Derek's gravy, burning herself quite badly. She promptly remonstrated with the gods, restaurants in general and her abusive parents in particular. A waitress asked if there was anything wrong.

'Just take her to the room, Derek," Francine snarled. "I'll come and take over when I've finished my meal.'

Derek felt there was something wrong with this arrangement. Francine ate at normal speed, whereas he could have demolished his huge plate of roast beef and six vegetables in under three minutes, if left untrammelled for that short time. Nevertheless, he grasped Poinsettia's hand and led her away firmly. The child fell asleep in twenty minutes. Derek knew it was risky, but he crept out of the room and hastened back to the restaurant.

'Where's my dinner?' he gasped.

'It went cold,' Francine said, shocked by his reappearance.

'So?'

'You don't like food that's gone cold,' she said. 'That's why you eat so fast, you always tell me.'

'But I'm starving,' Derek said.

'Well, I'm sorry, but the waitress took it away. Do you want to order another meal?'

Derek groaned. There was a single boiled potato left on Francine's plate. He picked it up and swallowed it. It was freezing. 'Never mind. I've lost my appetite. Give me a glass of wine.'

Francine looked guiltily at the empty bottle of Sancerre. 'I drank it,' she said.

'All of it?'

'You know what I'm like about flying,' Francine mumbled. 'I always have to have a couple of glasses of something.'

'We're not flying till tomorrow! And there's six glasses in a bottle.'

'Poinsettia spilled two.'

Derek threw a credit card on the table. 'I'll be in the bar,' he said. 'Your daughter is alone in the room. She's quite safe. I know this because I personally chained her to the oil heater.'

He did not go back to the room for over an hour, by which time Francine was tucked up with Poinsettia in the double bed. Derek threw himself like a heavier credit card on the single bed.

Francine had chosen California as their destination because she hated flying so much, she said, that you might as well go as far as you can once you were on the plane. It was not faultless logic, but Derek had not argued. He favoured the far side of America because he rather imagined that the East coast was a long strip of Disneyland with New York and Boston just above it. But then on the plane Francine had some sickening news for him: they were going to be more or less perfectly situated at their first stopping point for a trip to the Disney Park at Anaheim.

'I thought Disney was in Florida, Derek said aghast.

'They've got two.'

'Can't we go to Montana or somewhere then?' Derek asked. 'They can't have one there as well - it's desert. I think.'

'Don't worry,' Francine said. 'We'll be going to the desert, but the one in Nevada. I don't know anything about Montana.'

'Why are we going there?'

'It's a treat for you,' Francine said smiling. 'Las Vegas. Casinos, brash noisy bars, lots of tastelessness. You'll love it. Anaheim is for Poinsettia and me.'

Derek wondered what his daughter, now nearly four, would get out of huge rollercoaster rides and hour long queues, but any challenge had been forestalled by Francine's generosity in thinking of him, and how he would appreciate the loud shiny joys of Las

Vegas.

Poinsettia was not well behaved on the plane, but no one, not even the air stewardesses, thought to comment on it. Derek's idea of hell was a leg constraining plane trip that lasted forever, so he fully understood that his daughter was bored to distraction, even if her short legs were less inconvenienced by the seats in front than his own. Eleven hours in the air was close to forever, even in adult terms; it probably seemed as long as her entire life to poor Poinsettia. But even forever ends.

When it did, Derek remembered that there was a worse hell than flying six thousand miles tourist class. It was the hell of queuing. They queued to get off the plane, then they queued to get through customs. After that they queued for their luggage. It was still not over. They had to deposit their reclaimed suitcases on a conveyor belt that took them off somewhere else, so that they would have to queue once more to re-reclaim them. Then, finally released from the airport, they were faced by a queue the length of the Nile at the car rental outlet. Derek's eyes had become so unfocused by the end of all this that he had difficulty signing the forms. Then he realised that the whole queuing process was a form of torture to soften up those who were intending to hire compact vehicles, and to render them incapable of rejecting arguments to upgrade. Derek nodded like a drunk at everything the counter clerk suggested.

'This is a nice car,' Francine said, as soon as they were outside.

'I'm just glad they didn't have a Rolls Royce,' Derek sighed. 'I would have upgraded us out of house and home, just to get out of that place.'

Derek drove the huge Chrysler slowly but competently to their hotel, a dubious building in a slum area of Santa Monica.

'This is a slum,' Francine said forcefully.

'I booked it by phone,' Derek said lamely.

'I'm surprised they've got one,' Francine said, bitterness rising like a yellower sap.

'We'll move on tomorrow,' Derek said. 'That's the beauty of a touring holiday.'

For the second night in a row they had to eat at an hotel, rather than a nice restaurant. There were no restaurants where you could take a child anywhere near the Santa Monica Majestic, not even a child like Poinsettia.

'If she misbehaves tonight, you take her to the room,' Derek said. 'Tonight I eat.'

'Gladly,' Francine said, picking out a piece of gristle from her teeth.

Derek ate, but though Poinsettia was becalmed, there was still insult and physical discomfort ahead, this time from an unexpected source. Francine asked for some ice for her cabinet sauvignon, which she claimed was as warm as a beach sandwich. The waitress, a Mexican girl, obliged promptly, but spilled the ice bucket down the back of Derek's shirt as she reached over him to drop a cube into Francine's glass. Derek did an impromptu St Vitus dance and glared at the girl furiously.

'Hey, sorr - ee!' she said. Then she laughed. Francine laughed too. Poinsettia woke up and gave a sleepy giggle. Derek was left to wonder where he could find an ombudsman on this run down part of the Californian coast.

'I thought American waitresses - or servers, whatever they call themselves - were supposed to be the politest form of life known to man,' Derek complained, when they were back in their room.

'I think it might be because you hit on a Mexican rather than a native American,' Francine smiled.

'I'm glad it wasn't a Native American," Derek grumbled, "I probably would have had a tomahawk on the back of my neck, not just ice.' He was peeved because he had determined not to tip the girl, but she had added fifteen per cent to the bill anyway.

*

The next day Derek tried to drive to Universal Studios via Sunset Boulevard. He imagined this to be a leafy little avenue with a handful of exotic houses belonging to people like Sylvester Stallone, or

136

perhaps Gloria Swanson. It turned out to be nearly twenty miles long, though for one stretch of it they did pass some electrified fences round long sloping front gardens, indicating a substantial degree of wealth, if not movie fame.

'L.A. is big, isn't it?' Francine purred.

'You could drive through it all day and still never get out,' Derek groaned. It seemed at that moment that such might be his fate. 'And I can't get this bloody automatic transmission to go any faster.'

'There's a pedal next to the brake,' Francine said absent-mindedly, as she looked out at a huge sign on the mock Gothic gates of a long driveway. It was a warning to visitors that they were likely to be mauled savagely by half a dozen Dobermans if they had the temerity to ring the bell. She turned back to see Derek looking at her in a very old fashioned way. They both fell quiet until they reached Universal Studios. It was now eleven o' clock.

'We've only got six hours to do the place,' Francine said.

'Six?' Derek echoed.

That evening, exhausted, they removed to a motel near Anaheim, their destination for the following day. Francine was entranced at the free ice machines at the corner of each block of rooms. Derek was entranced by the people in the bar where they took an early evening drink. The clientele comprised, as far as he could tell, two hookers, a derelict of dubious ethnic origin and a dozen or so operatives from a local branch of Rentokil on their works outing.

'It's a land of such contrasts,' Francine sighed, as they lay in bed that night, Poinsettia between them.

'Yes,' Derek said. 'The poor people and the people who live behind electrified fences and rows of rottweiler kennels.'

'I was thinking of the palm trees and the deserts, the mountains and the valleys,' Francine said happily.

'All we've seen is streets the length of a medium size English county,' Derek said.

'There was the beach at Santa Monica.'

'Yes, but we didn't *see* that, did we? You were too afraid to go out walking.'

'And you were.'

Derek shrugged. It was true. He had seen Santa Monica on a trashy American TV import, but it didn't have tramps, people screaming in the distance and prowling patrol cars running its length then. He had been glad he had hired a car with a lid, not the Pontiac Convertible of his idle fancy.

'Can we clear out of Los Angeles as soon as you've seen Disney World?' Derek asked plaintively.

'Uh huh,' Francine said.

America was getting to Francine badly, Derek decided.

Disney World was a cacophony of colour, lights, noise and fat people. Derek sheltered from them all for a while by a burger stand as Francine looked for a ride that was suitable for Poinsettia. Luckily, she was not tall enough for the more thrilling rides, so Derek was saved from some of the more extensive queues. Unluckily Disney had thought of this, and there was a huge area packed with docile rides for short children. It was another long day, but the longest day, like the shortest ride, soon comes to an end. Back in the motel, Derek and Francine got out a map and set about the serious business of planning the rest of the holiday, for only these first two days had been absolutely fixed in Francine's itinerary.

'We could go straight to Las Vegas,' Derek volunteered.

'Mmm, but I think I'd like to see San Diego first,' Francine said. 'We could go up to Vegas from there. It's probably quicker.'

'But speed, my little chickadee, is not of the absolute essence, is it?' Derek quickly countered. 'Besides, if it is, this way looks much more direct.'

'We don't have to go to Vegas at all,' Francine said mistily.

'And I don't have to trek round bloody San Diego!' Derek said firmly.

They eventually agreed to follow Francine's plan. This was pretty much par for the course, since it had long ago been settled that if Derek needed to make decisions, he should get his decision making done in work, where it didn't interfere with Francine's life. Derek hadn't really been serious about giving San Diego a miss anyway, although if he had known that the city contained the world's largest zoo he might have made a stronger case.

They visited the zoo, which was tremendous if you liked that sort of thing, but very large if you didn't. The next day they went to a place called Sea World, where huge sea mammals did a lot of leaping. Derek watched in awe, less at the gymnastics of the seals and whales, than at the thought of the money that must have gone into building what was plainly the most tedious tourist attraction in the western hemisphere. Even Poinsettia was bored after a short time.

'Can we go back and see the giraffes, mummy?' she said.

Francine smiled gently. 'No, my darling, that would cost another eighty dollars, and I don't think your father wants another eight-mile walk today.' Derek had his shoe off and was rubbing at a blister as she said this.

The next day was less fraught. They visited a charming tourist trap called Old Town, which had once perhaps been an old town, but was now a collection of Mexican restaurants and stalls selling silverware and leather goods.

'It's very Spanish here, isn't it?' Francine said.

Derek put his shoe back on before answering, for he had been worrying at his blister again. 'Yes, dear. Indistinguishable from the real thing. Rather like the food here, in point of fact.'

'I rather enjoyed my tostada,' Francine said. 'Whatever was in it. But I expect it's because we're so near Mexico.'

'Yes dear.' There did seem to be a lot of Mexicans in California as a whole. Luckily, the ones he had come across since they had left Santa Monica had not attacked him with ice buckets.

'We could go across to Mexico,' Francine said.

Derek realised she hadn't simply been making conversation; she had been busy working in an extra stop on the go-as-you-please itinerary. He looked doubtful.

'It's not far,' Francine said.

'Alright,' Derek replied. He surprised himself by his sudden acquiescence. Francine must have been surprised by it too. She looked at him darkly, as if her husband knew something he wasn't telling her.

So they drove down to the border, parked the car and caught the local bus into Tijuana. They were mobbed as soon as they got off the rickety coach.

'One dollar!' a small child cried, gripping tightly on to Derek's trousers.

'Quick, quick!' an older Mexican said. 'This way!'

Derek wondered if there was an earthquake due, but the man merely dragged him over to the edge of the pavement to inspect a stall of silver jewellery. He seemed most reluctant to let go of Derek's sleeve. Derek said that the rings, bracelets and brooches were indeed very attractive. The man intimated he already knew this but was anxious to know how many items Derek's beautiful wife and beautiful daughter required. Derek got away with a pair of earrings and a butterfly brooch for Poinsettia, which she misplaced on the bus going back across the border a couple of hours later. They only managed to get ten feet further down the pavement before they were accosted by another street trader.

'Beautiful jewels for the jewels in your life, sir.'

Derek led Francine and Poinsettia out into the middle of the street, for it was plainly impossible to proceed down the pavement unmolested. It seemed safer to negotiate the oncoming traffic. Despite this manoeuvre, the family was forced to stand next to a donkey in a hat for a photograph, and Francine twice more felt the compulsion to invest in further silver jewellery.

'Mexico is just a car boot sale,' Derek said despairingly.

'But everything's such a bargain,' Francine sighed happily.

They stopped for lunch and ate genuine Mexican food in an empty restaurant. Later that night, back in San Diego, they had genuine Mexican stomach upsets. When they woke up next morning Francine's ear lobes had turned green. She threw her new earrings in the bin and they packed for the next leg of the tour, the drive to Las Vegas.

'It says here we ought to make sure we've got plenty of water in the car if we intend to cross the Mojave Desert,' Francine said, as they set off.

'I checked the level yesterday,' Derek said blandly.

'Not for the car, for us!' Francine said. 'We're crossing the world's hottest desert, Derek!'

Derek decided to take the driving more seriously. He switched off the radio and stared fixedly out of the windscreen, but his efforts at concentrating were not needed. The Mojave was perhaps a desert, but it was bisected by a four lane motorway amply served by filling stations and rest areas. Derek felt confident of driving all day. By four o' clock he was bored sick with the arrow straight road, however, and he insisted they stop at a place called Barstow.

Barstow was not exactly a ghost town, but it had definitely attended seances, they quickly realised. There was a hotel, but it seemed to be from the future, for it was totally unmanned. Derek had to insert his credit card in a machine to gain entry, and the machine flashed him a diagram to show him the location of a free room and a code for its automatic door.

'It's very quiet, isn't it?' Francine said.

Derek had already noticed that there was only one other vehicle in the car park, a badly dented old Ford pickup that looked like it belonged to a farmer still suffering from the Depression. He very much doubted that it belonged to another touring family, unless *The Beverley Hillbillies* was based on true life.

'What are we going to do tonight?' Francine asked. This was quite a question.

'There must be a bar or a restaurant somewhere,' Derek said.

141

'There wasn't even a receptionist,' Francine said.

'I mean in the town. This hotel, I realise, is completely deserted. I wonder if this is where they filmed *Invasion of the Body Snatchers*?'

'*Invasion of the Brain Snatchers*, more like,' Francine said half an hour later, as they were sitting in a bar in downtown Barstow. They had waited twenty minutes to be served, despite the fact that the bar was empty. The youth who had eventually served them looked like a banjo-playing Appalachian, without his banjo. Derek agreed to Francine's suggestion of an early night.

By daylight the clump of hotels that was Las Vegas on the skyline appeared out of the desert like a spiky concrete cactus. The neon lights were not yet shining but there was a brashness already in the air. Derek sniffed the money in anticipation. Francine was silent and appeared depressed. Poinsettia was equally silent, sulking because Derek had refused to stop to look for poisonous snakes in the desert.

'It'll be cheaper than dirt staying here,' Derek said. 'After the weekend everyone goes home and the motels are prepared to practically give the rooms away.'

'Doesn't Sunday still count as the weekend?' Francine said.

'Nah. People have got to get back to LA for work tomorrow.'

'What about all the tourists? And what do you mean 'motel'? I want to stay in a proper hotel!'

Derek shrugged. 'We'll probably get in at The Sands or The Luxor. They make all their money at the tables, they're not worried about how much they charge for accommodation, or food even. That's practically free too.'

'Where did you find all this out?'

Derek smiled. 'I read it, my dear.'

'When? You never read up on where we're going on holiday! You say it spoils the surprise.'

"This is different,' Derek said smugly. 'This isn't some resort with a monastery or a castle a couple of miles away.'

'Oh no, this is somewhere steeped in history,' Francine scoffed. 'Vegas probably goes back as far as the forties!'

They were entering the main thoroughfare, which Derek insisted they call The Strip. There were instant marriages, instant mortgages and instant fortunes on offer outside every building they passed.

'A man could be happy in a place like this, if he had aspirations to be a family man,' Derek said.

'What do you mean?'

'Look, you can get married for $49.50, get an instant mortgage, no hanging round for legal searches ...'

'The most instant thing a man is likely to get here is a divorce,' Francine said darkly. Then, after a pause for thought: 'You're not seriously entertaining doing any gambling, here are you?'

Derek's shoulders sagged over the steering wheel. 'I don't think there is much else to do, my love. I mean, we're already married; we've already got a mortgage big enough to sink an ocean going liner. I just thought I might try a couple of spins on the wheel, you know. Perhaps even enough for us to pay for one of the meals we've had, maybe enough to buy a decent pair of sunglasses. Ray-Bans or something.'

'Oh,' Francine said, 'That's very nice of you. I do need new sunglasses.'

'I meant ...' Derek gave up. It was his own corner he had painted himself into, he knew.

It took a surprisingly long time to get a room for the night. Every one of the major hotels was completely booked. Derek was offered a room in a medium size hotel at the far end of The Strip, but the adenoidal clerk coolly demanded $120. This was about three times the rate Derek had been paying in San Diego and Los Angeles, and he came out of the hotel with an ashen face.

'So, Sundays the place is empty and practically free, eh?' Francine said.

They were finally offered a room in a hotel some way off The Strip, for only twice the usual nightly rate. Derek seized it, because

143

the hotel had a casino, which actually took up the entire ground floor of the building, with the result that they had some difficulty finding an elevator to the bedrooms. For some minutes they prowled around in a gloom that was only relieved by the eerie glow of the slot machines and the downlighters above the craps and roulette tables.

'I think I'll just pop down and try my luck on the machines, see if I can win enough for dinner tonight,' Derek said, as soon as they contrived to find an elevator and were at last installed in their room.

'I thought you said the food was practically free,' Francine demurred.

'Well yes, but I'll have to tip, won't I? You're supposed to leave something in chips, not dollars. It's the cool thing to do in this town.'

Poinsettia looked up at the mention of chips.

'We'll take you to get something to eat soon, my darling,' Francine said. 'Daddy's just going to lose some of our money first.'

'Why are you always so negative, Francine?' Derek said. Francine looked at him as if he had suggested oral sex in front of her parents.

Twenty minutes later he returned less bouncily to the bedroom, where Francine was dressing in her gaudiest garb for a night in the world's most decadent city. 'I only lost five dollars,' he said.

Poinsettia began to cry. She was perhaps thinking of the number of My Little Ponies she could have acquired for that princessly sum.

They ate in a dark corner of the ground floor that was supposed to be a restaurant, but was really an area fenced off from the tables for patrons to pause over a steakwich and reflect on life's unfairness, and the certainty that it would be black 17 next spin. Francine had Surf 'n' Turf and complained that it did actually taste of turf. Derek had Kickin' Chicken, a dish designed to send you screaming from your table and out to the real tables for any sort of relief.

Francine refused to watch Derek frittering away any more of her life's savings, or life's credit card more accurately, and she went back up to the room. Derek looked hard and long at a craps game but failed to understand a single element of it. He collected his wife and daughter and they drove down The Strip, which was now transformed in the dusk of early evening into a glittering fairy cake of greedy fantasy.

'We should see a show,' Francine said, as they made another pass down the brightly lit street.

'I haven't quite won enough for that yet.'

'It doesn't matter. I'm not fussed about Lena Horne anyway.'

'I didn't know she was still alive.'

'Neither did I.'

They got back in time for Derek to try his luck once more in the casino, though of course the very notion of time was one completely alien to Las Vegas. Derek noticed that there were no clocks anywhere, and that daylight was banned from the gaming rooms. He noticed too that some of the gamblers he saw at ten o' clock at night were still there when he got up the next morning. They were still dripping quarters from the buckets in their laps into the voracious mouths of the poker and keno machines. This was doubtless why the town had not emptied after Saturday night, as he had expected. These people didn't know what day it was.

Before risking any money himself Derek stood and watched the faces of these more acclimatised gamblers. They showed no despair, despite the regularity of their losing rows of fruit and king high poker hands. Instead, their faces looked emptied out, as if they had just been released from hospital but had not yet regained any memory of what accident it was that brought them here. Almost worse was the strange conjunction of mechanical noise and human silence in this bandit hell hall. Derek had noticed a sign advertising LIVE POKER outside one of the casinos they had passed earlier that night. He had always thought card games were the least lively of human pursuits, but he saw the attraction now of having actual people in front of you, even if they had expressionless poker faces, compared to the screaming blankness of a twelve inch screen. He turned away and nearly collided with a Malaysian waitress who looked as if she'd been inflated.

'Could I get a soda?' he asked in his best American.

'If you're not playing at the tables, sir, you'll have to go to the counter,' she replied impassively.

He went to the counter, which was not that but a row of Keno screens, this time laid out horizontally. He tried a few quarters as he waited for a barman, but whatever numbers he picked, the machine picked different numbers.

'I can't see the percentage in this,' Derek said aloud.

'About a hundred per cent to the house, friend,' a grizzled voice beside him said.

Derek was embarrassed that he had been overheard, and even more embarrassed that he had spoken in his normal English accent. The owner of the grizzled voice pulled himself off the stool he had slid onto, slapped Derek on the back and veered off towards another phalanx of slot machines.

'This isn't really very much fun,' Derek said, again out loud. This time there was no one around to hear.

He repeated the sentiment to Francine the next morning.

'Let's go to Yosemite then,' she said. She fully expected him to have lost all his money, but he had recovered all his losses in the one spin he had permitted himself on the roulette wheel, having placed a chip on zero, because it seemed appropriate.

'Actually, I think I may have come out winning,' he said, and he fished in his pocket, to find a single chip profit, which he placed proudly on the dressing table. Strangely, it wasn't there when they finished packing and quit Las Vegas.

'I talked to a bell boy, and he said we'd be best off going round to the other side of Yosemite,' Francine said. 'Apparently the roads are closed this side till the height of summer. He said we haven't got much chance of getting through.'

'Nonsense,' Derek said. He was studying a map that had come with the hired Chrysler. 'It's April, how can they close the roads?'

'It is way up in the mountains.'

'So is Switzerland. They don't close that at Easter.'

Francine shrugged and settled back in her seat. 'Whatever. Let's drive.'

Derek drove. He drove as far as the road from the East into Yosemite National Park. There was a 'Road Closed' sign.

'I can't believe it,' Derek said. He studied the map. 'This means we'll have to drive about another three hundred miles. This country is ridiculous!'

They had driven from the frying pan of the desert into the cool bag of the snow lined hills, through some of America's most beautiful scenery. Francine felt duty bound to point out that it was a very big country, and exceedingly picturesque, and therefore perhaps not entirely ridiculous.

Another half a day's drive brought them to a town called Bishop, where they stayed, despite the fact that it looked like a colder version of Barstow. A further fourteen hours on the road the next day brought them to San Francisco.

'I'm glad we gave Yosemite a miss,' Derek said. 'It's only scenery after all.'

Francine looked baleful, but she was glad they had reached San Francisco. She had seen *Bullitt* and lots of episodes of a television series with a young Michael Douglas and a somewhat older Karl Malden; it was almost like coming home, she said.

And then all too soon they were actually going home. The five days in San Francisco were busy and enjoyable, except for the time on Alcatraz when Poinsettia took Derek's taped tour guide off him and played with the controls on the cassette. Derek couldn't find where he was again on the tape and he kept turning right when the other tourists were turning left. He felt like a new prisoner, unused to the regime.

'I'd like to come back to the States,' Francine said, as they returned their hired car and were left with an array of suitcases and no transport. 'Do you think we ought to come back one day when Poinsettia's older? It might be nice to come with my parents.'

147

Derek wasn't listening properly. He had been looking in some awe at a newspaper on a bench nearby. It reported that there were forty-seven feet snow drifts on the Eastern route into Yosemite. 'What?' he said.

'I was just thinking about where we ought to go next year.'

'I'm not going anywhere with your parents, or anybody else, come to that. Don't you think that the three of us is enough?'

He had little idea.

GAMESMASTER

I'd just pulled up my pants when I heard the door banging in the next cubicle.

'Shitting, arsing, buggering, wank-wiping bastards!'

I think I remember this impressive list of participles correctly. They were the first words I heard Charles utter, and he hadn't finished, he'd just paused for that first flow of relief. He wasn't swearing at his fly buttons though. Still mid-stream he picked up his diatribe: 'pus-filled, bloated, pig-featured, dribble-mouthed pox doctors' runts ...'

I didn't want to open my door or press the flush, because I thought it might embarrass him that someone had overheard his tirade. This was, I see now, unnecessarily sensitive of me. But of course, I shouldn't have been listening anyway.

'... bollocks to their coughing language!'

I couldn't stay in there all day. I cleared my throat, although quietly, preparatory to saying something. I must have cleared my throat just as he was drawing breath. There was an intense silence for a few seconds.

'That's what some people would say anyway.'

There was an unmistakable zipping sound. A zip, not buttons then, I remember thinking. I slipped open the bolt and popped my head out. He did the same thing at the same moment.

I suppose we both raced back inside to flush, but I can't remember now. The vivid impression I have is of his florid face with its powerful grey beard and his steel wool hair looking like he'd just brushed it up, or more likely, pulled it up by the roots in his rage.

Apparently even before noticing I was female he said, 'You're not Welsh, are you?'

I shook my head. 'Just here on business, like you,' I said.

It was a Careers event we were attending in a small corner of West Wales. And this is part of the United Kingdom, believe me, where there are a lot of corners. Someone had once built a school in a particularly inaccessible cranny in one of these corners, and now someone had invited representatives from all sorts of unlikely professions to talk to school leavers about potential life choices. Perhaps the plan was to dissuade them all from becoming feed salesmen and farmers like their parents and accelerate the depopulation of the area. I had come all the way from Bristol to talk about the tourism industry. Charles, I was to hear soon enough, was a former barrister who had given up the bar to try and make his fortune inventing board games. He had agreed to come and give a talk about the legal profession as a favour to a friend. The one stipulation he had made was that he would in no way encourage any benighted sixteen or seventeen-year old to pursue that siren, a law degree. The friend must have been desperate, is all I can conclude. Or all the local solicitors were already booked up for a Rotary Club night.

'Couldn't find The Ladies, eh?' he smiled. We were standing close together at the two hand basins they had in there.

'I don't think there is a Ladies,' I said. Perhaps they like it this way. They can have good reason for not appointing female teachers.'

He chuckled. It sounded like Muttley, from the old children's TV programme.

'Are you going back to the hall? Or hell, should I say?' he said, allowing me first go on the damp linen towel roller. 'Buggered if I am. If anyone else asks me how I am in Welsh, I'll throttle them.'

I shrugged. 'I've done my talk. I was toying with the idea of the finger buffet, such as it is.'

He grimaced. 'I had a bit of it. Tasted like somebody's fingers actually. I wouldn't recommend it. Want to come for a drink instead?'

This was blunt. I'd decided not to drive back to Bristol that night, but I was still planning to drive back as far as Swansea. I should have politely declined, I suppose. Instead, I looked at my watch. He touched my elbow very gently.

'There's a pub two miles back down the road. The Dynefor Arms, it's probably called, they all are in this neck of the woods. It's the one lit up with fairy lights. Fancy a glass of wine with me?'

I started to explain that I was staying with an old friend and ought to be getting back before it got too dark, but he knew I was interested enough. Only one drink, I'd told myself.

'What do you mean, before it gets dark? It's blacker than an MP's tongue already. Let's get out of here. You can follow me, I'm in the Sherman tank.'

We were standing outside now by an emergency exit, and he pointed to an old white Volvo Estate that was straddled across two parking spaces in the visitors' car park.

'I'll just get my stuff from the main hall,' I said. 'I might stop for a quick drink. It depends how tempting I find the fairy lights at this pub of yours. You go ahead anyway.'

He rubbed a big hand through his wire wool. 'I just brought me,' he said. 'Have you got posters or advertising boards or something. Anything you need a hand with?'

I wasn't looking for an adventure. I was forty-one years old and had more than my share of adventures in California before I came to Britain, and a couple more in London before I settled down with Neil. Things conspire though. I could have driven past the fairy lit pub – it wasn't called The Dynefor Arms as it happens – but I'd smoked my last cigarette before going into the Careers Convention and I thought I'd like another one now. That's the way I smoke these days: if I want one, I have one. Days go past when I don't need a cigarette. No, that's wrong. I never need one anymore; I simply choose to have one or not, as the mood takes me. I could, of course, have driven past the pub and stopped at the services, but that seemed too deliberate, too needful. I know from past experience it's the craven act of an addict to stop for petrol when you don't really need it, but you do need a pack of cigarettes. Stopping at a pub is a caprice which speaks of spontaneity, not weakness. When you get past forty you can think like this about your own actions and it makes sense.

When I walked into the lounge bar it was empty. I'd seen the Volvo parked outside, but instead of turning on my heel and heading for the other bar, where Charles must be, I strolled up to the counter and ordered what I felt my taste buds wanted me to order.

'Do you have a Californian red wine?' I said.

The barman was not some youth who would need to make enquiries about such an outlandish order. He was old enough and miserable enough to have to have been the landlord. He glanced over his shoulder at the optics and the shelves. 'Not as such.' He said, as if he had just that minute run out. 'But we've got a very nice vin de table. He pronounced the first part of this as 'vindy' but 'table' as some hybrid of French and English. I smiled but declined, stumped for a moment.

Charles came in from the direction of the Gents. He looked surprised to see me.

'I'd like to claim prostate trouble, but I think it must be nerves,' he said. He nodded his head towards the toilet by way of explanation. 'Let me get these,' he added.

I thought I might have a Cinzano, but he pooh-poohed the idea.'

'Scotch, on a night like this. Or Canadian Club perhaps?'

I assented to scotch. What do my taste buds know?

'And a pint of the guest ale for me.'

The barman was not having a good night. A flash of incisors revealed this. 'Afraid the guest ale's all gone,' he said.

'Become the ghost ale, eh? Well, anything bitter. Preferable creamy, with a head on it like an Irish coffee. I don't know these Welsh beers.'

I frowned at him to warn him off another anti-Celtic outburst, but he smiled wryly. When we sat down he admitted he liked playing

152

the game of being a stranger. I pointed out that it wasn't exactly a game if he was new to these parts. He explained that he was half-Welsh and that these parts weren't exactly all that new to him.

'Well, what was all that I heard you shouting in the toilets then?'

'That was me railing against the full-Welsh. Nothing contradictory in that. If people were more honest they'd all admit they were half-something and not go round pretending they were ethnically pure and can't possibly make themselves understood unless they're communicating in a half-dead ancient British dialect.'

I took it that he was not a Welsh speaker himself.

I know half the vocabulary,' he said. 'So do you. So does anybody who speaks English. The other half of the word stock, as far as I can make out, is made up of the dying grunts of a stuck pig.' He sighed. 'It wouldn't be so bad if they went in for the odd vowel. It all sounds like consonants to me though, and calculated to soak you to the skin if you get too close to somebody speaking it.'

If you're half-Welsh what's the other half?' I asked.

'I'm not pure half and half,' he laughed. 'I'm more like half-Welsh and four eighths English, South African, German and Italian. Mind, my grandmother won't admit to the Italian bit. What about you?'

'English through and through.' I nearly said English rose, but I managed to stop myself. 'No hybrids here,' I was boasting, and he pulled me up on it.

'Which is to say, one eighth Viking, one eighth Saxon, and a few more eighths Norman French, Irish … Portuguese, in all probability. The English are the least pure race in the world.'

'Ah,' I said. 'So you don't save your spleen solely for the Welsh. That's interesting. And somewhat contradictory, if you don't mind me saying so.'

He didn't mind in the least. He admitted he was happy to vent his spleen on any group, and that included various trades and professions as well as a range of nationalities. His special target group was barristers, he said.

'How about travel agents and people in the leisure industry?' I said.

He smiled and would not be drawn. Instead, with a politeness which was a little surprising after his earlier hostility, he enquired about my work. I kept my answers short because I sensed that what I had to say was not of great interest to him, or indeed to most people, come to that. Tourism is like teaching: everybody knows something about it from personal experience, but it isn't a topic for a riveting conversation. I have to say I was more interested when he told how he had given up the bar for the business venture he was embarking on.

'Board games, eh?' I said. 'There are an awful lot of them already, aren't there? Don't firms like Waddingtons and Spears just employ their own research staff? That's what I would have imagined. Not that I've ever thought about it, that is.'

He seemed surprised that I'd been able to name two toy manufacturers that glibly. Indeed, I had surprised myself.

'I'm sure they do,' he said, 'but that's why there aren't any good new games. Trivial Pursuit is the only genuinely new game for years, and it was a couple of enthusiastic amateurs who came up with that, not some white-coated boffins at Waddingtons. No, the parameters are too fixed for the professionals; anything they invent has to fit into their pre-moulded plastic trays anyway. And retail at exactly £15.99, or whatever their current market price is. It was Trivial Pursuit that made me see there were new possibilities. Did you ever play it?'

I had, I admitted. I was no good at half the categories though. I admitted that too.

'Oh yes, it's a fearfully tedious game. But what got me excited was they thought to package it in a different shaped box and charge a fortune for it.'

I asked him if he was prepared to tell me about the new game he had invented. I said I'd promise not to steal his idea.

'Well, I've got a few different ideas,' he said. 'One is for a game called "Duck It". Or I might call it "I'm Donald".'

I raised an eyebrow significantly.

'But I might have to call it "Role Up" or something equally obvious like that. It's a role play thing anyway. The object is to be found out and end up bankrupted.'

'Sounds a bit like "What's My Line",' I said.

'Yes, except you have to say everything in rhyming couplets.'

'Phew. Isn't that a tad difficult?' I was thinking of the 8-14 age group that I imagined were the most obvious players of board games. Perhaps I was also unkindly thinking that anyone who still played Trivial Pursuit somehow reduced his mental age to about that level too.

'Well, that's at one stage anyway,' he continued. 'At another stage you have to speak in Cockney rhyming slang.'

'Is this all aimed at experts or something?' I asked. 'Like the spotty boys who used to play Dungeons and Dragons? Or the gaming addicts?'

He scraped his big hand down his chin. 'Yes, you'd think so, but it's all a question of thinking laterally though. Who plays with computers?'

'Teenage boys, I think. Oh, and men who are still teenagers. And … let me see, financiers, hackers, pornography addicts?'

He nodded. 'Exactly. So where's the big market?' This time he didn't give me time to think of an answer. 'Women! Girls!' He said this triumphantly. 'All you've got to do is turn things upside down, you see. Think of a game, or an activity, it doesn't have to be a game actually, that would grab the female population, and you've got a huge untapped market.' He looked at his drink circumspectly. 'Maybe it doesn't apply to "Donald" though.'

I sighed. 'I'm not sure girls are too keen on computers generally. Maybe I'm being unfair to female financiers though. But I would have thought girls are an untapped market for board games precisely because they refuse to be tapped.'

'Don't women like role playing though?'

This was a sudden change of tack. He was talking to me once more, rather than rehearsing a well-practised speech. I looked at him over the rim of my glass. I decided to go along with it.

'Is that a pregnant remark?'

'Did it look like it had a bump?'

I smiled. 'And what role are you playing at the moment?' I said.

'I'm just an ordinary Joe. I was hoping not to end up as a John Doe,'

Well, that rhymes,' I said, 'but I thought you said that the object was to end up bankrupted?'

'Do you want another drink?'

'Would another scotch ruin you?'

'Not exactly. What about you?'

I didn't get it at first. Then I realised what he must have meant by 'ruin'. This was too corny, and I let my expression tell him so. 'You're really old fashioned,' I said suddenly.

He gave me a little boy smile. 'I'd rather hoped that we could avoid correctness issues. Do you want to get the drinks? There's no power thing operating then. Listen, I'll get the drinks, and you can decide who you're going to be, and if you're willing to buy me a meal later on.'

I could not prevent myself laughing out loud at this. 'One drink, I agreed. One more drink doesn't mean we dine together, still less that I agree to pay!'

We did of course go for a meal. The pub we were in had nothing much on offer but, graciously enough, the hitherto morose landlord perked up and suggested an hotel a few miles away where we could get a decent meal. We drank up quickly, though trying not to appear in haste, and set off in our separate cars for the King's Arms.

Though the journey only took about ten minutes, this was enough of a hiatus in our conversation for us both to feel that we needed to begin a new topic when we sat down at our table. Menus arrived after a few fumbling minutes and we were both engrossed in our reading for a while before speaking again.

'I take it you won't be going for the cockles and lava bread to start,' I said.

'On the contrary. They are genuine enough. It's the learntness of this new breed of professional Welshmen that drives me crazy. Don't you hate how false it all is? Look at this menu.'

I said the menu looked fine to me.

'I don't mean what's on offer, though venison is an apricot sauce is something of an oddity, I'd suggest. I mean the curly handwriting, the *printed* curly handwriting. I might suffer it if it was in blue or black, but sepia! I refuse to believe that there is some medieval monk out there in the stainless-steel kitchen scribing these menus. On the other hand, I can imagine the owners of this place paying a fortune after drooling over a printer's catalogue of authentic scripts for their precious menus.'

'Do you rant at everything?' I said. 'Do you rant at greasy spoon menus because they misspell "potatoe's" perhaps? Or chalk things up in block capitals rather than genuine handwriting?'

He sensed my playfulness and grinned sheepishly. 'Okay, for once I will allow the red napkins curled lovingly into the wine glasses to go unnoticed. I will not wince when the waiter asks me to taste what is patently a perfectly acceptable bottle of Burgundy before flourishing the bottle round to pour you a glass fist, when it is me who is paying.'

'I thought I was paying.'

'Exactly, when he assumes it's bound to be the man who pays.'

'And what about your massive assumption that I will go along with your choice of wine? What if I find, say, burgundy somewhat acidic with my apricot sauce?'

He laughed. 'Aha! Caught you! Burgundy is the least acidic wine this side of the Barossa Valley. What is more, I defy you to opt for the apricot stew with the lump of thawed and microwaved venison.'

'I'm not even all that hungry,' I confessed. 'And do I look like the sort of girl who'd want to gorge herself on the flesh of some poor deer?'

He hoped with a heavy sadness that I was not a vegetarian, and if I was, that it wasn't out of some misplaced affection for the dumb ruminants of the Scottish Highlands, but at least that it might be because I just didn't like the taste of red meat. I told him that I usually ate fish when I dined out, and usually because it was likely to have more flavour and be better cooked than lumps of meat I'd encountered in so-called good restaurants.

This satisfied him and we both decided to choose the salmon. He mumbled that he felt it was most unlikely, however, that the salmon was Welsh, as it claimed to be. 'I shall interrogate it about its spawning round when it arrives,' he said darkly.

'You're making me feel like one of those 'companions' who have to escort journalists who write pompously about food,' I said. I didn't mean it to sound irritable, but I realised it might have sounded a bit acerbic as soon as I said it. He looked hurt.

'Can I be honest?' he said, 'I'm playing all these roles because I'm afraid you won't like me if I'm just myself. I believe lots of people do this, you know.'

'Why is it important for me to like you?' I said. 'We're just having a drink, and a meal now admittedly, but we didn't arrange this. We're not on a date after all.'

He sighed. 'I'm Donald,' he said.

'You're Charles. You told me.

'Donald Ducked. Cockney rhyming slang, remember?'

'It doesn't all have to be a game, 'I said. I was forced to look down because he was searching my eyes.

'You're right,' he said. 'I haven't actually given up the bar, by the way. I'd just like to. I lied about that.'

'And I guess you're married with two teenage sons?'

'Two teenagers, yes. Son and daughter. And you?'

'Married. Two daughters, one eleven, one fourteen, both incredibly beautiful …'

'I can believe that.' He said it with sudden feeling, and it almost made me blush. I hadn't been looking for a compliment.

'Happy?'

I shrugged. 'You?'

He gave an identical shrug.

'I'm also Welsh. Full-Welsh, not half-Welsh, as I tried to make out earlier.'

I told him I'd suspected this much from his irrational fury at the language of the land of his fathers. 'What about the board games?' I said. 'Have you ever thought of inventing one really, or was that something that came out on the spur of the moment?'

'Not exactly spur; I do think about odd things when I'm driving about. Sometimes in court even. But I have toyed with the idea before tonight.'

'So,' I said, 'You claim that you despise everything false, and then you present a totally spurious image of yourself to me in the hope that I will prefer this false picture to your real self?'

He nodded, a small boy caught in the act again. 'That's about the size of it,' he said.

He was lying though. We booked into the hotel for the night. Reader, I slept with him, but he did lie to me. I saw the board game in a toy shop window the other day. It was called Role Up, of course, It was in a triangular box and cost a small fortune. I bought it to play with my youngest daughter, who's twelve now. She's very good at it too, but I have to admit I don't mind losing occasionally. It's not a bad game, but Charles, or whatever his name was, did have an enormous cheek. He's managed to produce a version in Welsh, someone told me recently.

TEA FOR ONE

Gary threw down his rucksack on the battered sofa. He went to the little table by the window and pushed the potted plant that stood there to one side in order to look through the faded net curtain. There was no sign of his mother. She was usually back by now; it was gone half past four. He looked at the old-fashioned clock which she had picked up in some jumble sale or other and which she always kept running ten minutes fast. It gave her more time, she said. Ridiculous. He looked out through the window once more, this time pressing his face to the glass to see as far as possible up the quiet suburban street. It was 1968 but not many people owned cars in this rundown part of the town.

The corner of the table was sticking into his midriff when he leaned forward so he turned to face the musty room. There was not much sun, but a shaft of light penetrated the room and made the particles of dust look like they were suspended in a straight line across to the opposite wall. When he looked at them for a few seconds though, as his eyes tried to focus to the dimmer light inside the room, they seemed to be falling and rising and circling in some crazy motion. It was the dance of protons and neutrons in a molecule, only slower.

He slumped into the fireside armchair and wondered whether he could face his homework before tea. His friend Tom had said he could take over a new album he'd bought so that they could play on his expensive hi-fi, which he insisted would make it sound better than Gary's old second-hand Dansette. Gary decided he would like to get his work out of the way first and go over to Tom's by about seven o' clock. He wished his mother would hurry up home and get his tea.

She was strange lately. Only just got in a few minutes before him the previous day. Been to the shops. Started going up the

160

supermarket lately, though she never got it all in one go like everyone else's mum. She could never remember it all, he supposed. She'd forget to take a list, even if she had the sense to make one. She'd always said they couldn't afford a weekly shop but they both knew it was more expensive getting things from the corner shop all the time. She would pop out for this, pop out for that. And that bloke probably robbed her blind every time with the change. Even if he didn't, his mum said herself that it was much dearer than the supermarket, but here she was now, spending the money she could have saved, catching a bus into town to go to the supermarket.

He wouldn't mind, he told himself, if she'd just get his tea ready on time. She knew he'd be wanting to go out. All he wanted was some faggots and peas, or sausage and chips, or something. She'd gone mad since she'd been going to the supermarket though. He thought about what she'd given him the day before, prawn curry. It was foul. All this flashy stuff out of posh packets. Tuesday he'd had fish at school; a horrible, soggy bit of boiled fish and a couple of scoops of mashed potatoes with little hard lumps in. Then when he got home, she served up a weird looking lobster thing and something called Spanish rice. She was fussing about too, asking him if he liked it and saying what a nice change it made. He hadn't really had the heart to tell her he found it nauseating. And that other time; those asparagus tips, or whatever they were! She'd served them with paste, or pâté, as she called it. He'd have to put his foot down soon; a growing boy couldn't survive on all this rubbish. He'd have to be a little bit careful telling her though; he knew how easily hurt she could be. She seemed to be trying so hard to do something special. He would say something really nice when she gave him something proper, like liver and onions, or cheese and potato pie. Besides, she surely couldn't afford all this pre-cooked stuff on her paltry earnings as a cleaner, could she?

He felt sorry for her in a way. She'd struggled to bring him up on her own and she'd taken all sorts of jobs, doing as many as three different part-time jobs at a time, just to keep going. But he couldn't really sympathise either because she was so stupid about the money.

She bought things whenever she had the cash, like the record player, the tape recorder and the new television set. He was glad to have these things, of course, but he wished she would just put some money away now and again instead of splashing it out straight away. They'd have cream cakes on her pay day and when he was younger, she would take him to the cinema two or three times a week during the school holidays. Then a bill would arrive, and they'd have to manage on watery stews for a couple of weeks, and he'd even have to take a cut in pocket money.

He got up from his chair and went to the shelf where he stored his records, He had almost as many as Douglas Stanton now. He looked through the titles, feeling proud but at the same time a little guilty about the way he'd asked for all the money he'd spent on them over the past few months. But that was the trouble. He'd only have to ask her, and she'd find some money from somewhere and let him have what he wanted. He supposed he might be able to get a job this summer holiday, but he couldn't think about that yet, not with his exams a couple of months away. And he wasn't mad keen on the idea anyway. You had to spend your life working, so it didn't seem right to have to work in his holidays.

*

Gary's mother was aware of her son's attitude towards getting a summer job. She knew she'd almost certainly coloured his view of work very strongly from the accounts she had given of her own jobs, since she'd nearly always regarded her employers as exploiters and her employment as an irksome necessity, rather than any duty to oneself or to society. She was secretly hoping, actually, that something would turn up which might prevent Gary's needing to work this summer. He would need a good long break after his examinations, she felt. She'd been thinking about it, in fact, that very afternoon, and wondering if there were any way she might get some extra money, so that the boy would not feel it necessary to pay his way during the holidays, as he had intimated he might.

When she got back from work she had put the kettle on for a cup of tea and sat thinking for a while. She was considering the question of what to give Gary for his tea when he returned from school. There was some bacon in the larder, but that wasn't enough for a growing boy. She had decided to slip up to the supermarket to see if she could get something special. She'd noticed he was off his food lately. Perhaps it was because he was worrying about his schoolwork, what with the examinations coming along so soon. He'd be entering the unknown territories of 'A' levels in September; he had already done so well getting into the grammar school. She felt that a nice treat would buck him up no end.

She drank her tea quickly and put on her hat and coat. As she passed the mirror in the little passageway, she glanced briefly at herself and hesitated, but then she hurried out into the street, her head lowered and he coat pulled round her, though it was a fairly mild day and the sun was bleakly peering through the clouds. She did not have to wait long at the bus stop, and she saw no one she knew as she was waiting. There were just three people on the bus, each of them gazing mistily through the windows at the posters advertising the local repertory theatre and a three-day trip to Dartmoor by coach. The bus conductor ignored her for a while too. She pushed the fare into his hand as she got up to alight from the bus and hurry to the supermarket.

Once there, she paused in the doorway and surveyed the rows of merchandise before picking up a basket. The shop was not crowded and there seemed to be quite a few girls in blue overalls and young boys in grey dust jackets busying themselves in the main body of the store. She moved up the first aisle and gazed at the shelves without seeming to see them. She looked over her shoulder occasionally at the boy who was working a little further down the aisle on the opposite side. He was stamping tins as he took them out of a cardboard box and rattling them on to the shelves. After perhaps half a minute she focused her eyes properly on the food before her: there were jellies and cake mixes and currants and sultanas in cellophane bags. She saw vanilla essence and glacé cherries and, a little further on, the different brands of baking powder and flour. She picked up a jelly after a few seconds and placed it in her basket.

It was at this moment that Mrs Carlton, the Supervisor, took an interest in the little old lady in the shabby overcoat and imitation fur hat. As she had appeared from the packing room at the rear of the hall, the first thing that had caught Mrs Carlton's attention was this woman standing before the home bake section, obviously not very interested in what she was looking at and apparently uneasy at the proximity of Roy, the shelf stacker. It was probably nothing, but you just got a hunch sometimes, and it was always worth keeping your eyes open. She couldn't make it too obvious, however, so she decided to go up to the office and have a squint down through the observation panel. She took a good look at the woman's face and noticed also the green and brown leatherette shopping bag that hung from her wrist. It was flat and apparently light. Nothing so far then, at least. But as she made her way up the stairs to the office she met Swinburne, the store detective. He gave her a wry smile as he went to pass her. She hesitated for a second, but decided to say something.

'There's a character down there I think you ought to keep an eye on.'

'Oh, there's always plenty of dodgy looking characters,' he said with a grin, but seeing her frown he stopped and added, 'Who is it then, somebody with an overcoat four sizes too large for them?'

'No, no, it's nothing terribly suspicious, just a funny feeling I had.'

'Yeah, I'm always getting them myself,' Swinburne said.

Mrs Carlton ignored this. 'She's wearing a brown overcoat, and she's got one of those plastic leather shopping bags, you know? About fifty, I'd say.'

He nodded and she carried on up the stairs. She did not in fact go to the observation panel because someone had deposited a pile of invoices on her desk, and she promptly forgot about the woman downstairs. Swinburne was watching her now though, making mental notes about her behaviour at the tinned meat section.

She had by this time put three or four small items in her basket. There was a faint flush on her face as she moved down the rows of tinned foods. She glanced about her as she turned into the next aisle and shifted the mock leather shopping bag on to her other arm. As she did so, Swinburne, seemingly browsing by the pies and pasties at the top of the aisle, noticed a little bulge appear at the bottom of the bag. He was surprised, for he had not seen her taking anything from the shelves while he had actually been watching her, though she certainly bore the nervous air of many of her type of shoplifter. He watched her for a few moments more, but she added nothing to the small stock of supplies in her basket, and presently she went to one of the checkouts and fumbled in her shopping bag for her purse. Swinburne was rather at a loss as to know what to do, since he realised it might well have been the purse that the woman had dropped into the bag, and not something she had taken. He could not see from the limp shape of the bag if there were anything further in it. As the woman paid for the goods he decided to have a good look at her face, to see if he could see any sign of guilt or fear there, before she disappeared into the High Street. He stepped quickly through an empty checkout passage and pushed open the glass door. He held it open as she hurried out and, as she turned to thank him for the courtesy, he stepped in front of her, forcing her to look straight up into his face.

She stopped and jerked her head up quickly to see the square shouldered frame and blunt expressionless face before her. Her body went limp as she saw his steady features and she turned back to go into the store.

'I suppose I'll have to see the manager,' she said, in a thin high voice which did not sound like her own. Her mind was racing with excuses, denials, appeals, and yet she felt surprisingly calm about it at the same time. She half heard the man saying that he had reason to believe, and that he would be grateful if she would accompany him, and she let herself be guided, gliding as if in a dream, to the back of the food hall. They went up a flight of stairs and along a narrow corridor to a veneered door which was embossed in gilt lettering with the name 'P.H.Roope. Manager.'

During the next five minutes or so she was unaware of almost everything that was said. She co-operated mechanically as the manager asked her to empty her shopping bag on the desk, and she made no attempt to deny or argue or redeem herself in any way. It was all a dream and all the time she could not stop thinking about Gary. What would he think? What would he say? She looked blankly at the manager and tried to listen to him. He had the tin of salmon in his hand. He was looking rather helplessly at her.

'Is this the only item you took, madam?' He said it as if he were repeating the question for the third or fourth time.

'I'm sorry,' she mumbled. 'I didn't quite catch …'

'Is this tin of salmon …'

'Yes. Oh yes. Just a bit of salmon before he goes out.'

The manager continued to question her. Was it the first time she had taken anything? Did she realise the seriousness? She admitted to the other times, though without really deciding to do so, and waited nervously for a verdict. She wanted to get back. It was getting late. But the manager was picking up the phone. He was asking for a constable to be sent round. She had no way of getting a message to Gary. She looked up at the clock on the wall behind the manager's desk and automatically deducted ten minutes, not remembering that other clocks kept regular time. Gary would be home already. He would be wondering where she had got to.

But Gary had given up wondering. He had discovered the bacon and was now devouring a good fry-up of bacon, eggs and fried bread. It was the best meal he had had for ages.

LANDED

Near a curving aberration of the River Cleddau in Pembrokeshire, a hundred or so yards from the quaintly named Landshipping Quay, a new sign was being hung over the door of the village inn. On a deep blue background was painted a white anchor and the words Hope and Anchor. Free House. Hope was not so easy to portray graphically, but the young woman watching thought it was a good name for her home. The boy fixing the board leaned back to admire his work and the woman smiled up at him. The sign shifted slightly in a gust of wind from off the river.

She went back indoors and rearranged the cloths over the pumps. Her husband Ray came through from the cellar, a stonewalled room on the same floor as the tiny bar and newly refurbished lounge.

'With this weather they'll be coming from all over,' he said.

They had taken over the pub six months before, at the start of the year, and trade had so far been very poor: nothing more than a few regulars who drank the cheapest bitter and never ate more than a packet of nuts. Now, with the summer holidays started and the weather glorious, they had reason to expect the camping families and day trippers. These would drink wine, minerals, coke, all with a good mark up, and they would eat their landlord and his wife to enormous wealth.

She had wondered what she was doing here over the past year. Ten years previously she had moved to London from her native Brighton to attend art college. She was going to be a designer then. At twenty-one she had thought to teach English as a foreign language in Dubai or Nigeria. In fact, she had stayed on London temping for a year, then lived in Birmingham with Mike for a while, before Ray rescued her from that and transported her back to the city. The move to Pembrokeshire was a brainwave brought on by the mortgage hikes; their semi in Forest Hill had become too expensive but its sale financed the purchase of this tiny pub in a backwater in West Wales and left them with what promised to be a manageable mortgage.

But the days and nights were long. They never went out of course; they socialised as they worked, as Ray put it. The company invariably consisted of a bloody-minded and bloody-complexioned old farmer, drunk apparently before he ever came in; a couple of labourers, including the lad who had painted the sign from her design; and sometimes an oldish primary school headteacher and his thin, rat-faced wife. These regulars did not even pay for the fuel bills, and Ray had had to delay completing the improvements he intended till after the summer season. The labourers spoke Welsh when left alone but made polite enough conversation in English if they sat at the bar and talked to her. There was not much to say, however. The farmer occasionally made incomprehensible jibes at them or engaged in acrimonious but illogical argument with Stone, the headteacher, about government subsidies or corporal punishment for everyone under sixteen. For the most part when they spoke to her they talked about the weather or the health of a neighbour she scarcely knew.

Sometimes Mr Stone would be more talkative if he managed to free himself from his dour wife for the last half hour of drinking time.

'Stella, my dear,' he said once, 'You must find it a change from the Metropolis, coming to our little hamlet?'

Because she was attuned to requests rather than conversational gambits of this sort, she only caught the last word properly and she turned absent-mindedly to the packs of cigars on the shelf behind her. He was looking fondly at her, and she realised her mistake. She rearranged a pack or two and gave an embarrassed shrug.

'Were you brought up in London? I detect a hint of the Southeast in your intonation, do I not?'

Ray had been passing behind her and he put his hands on her waist at this point. It meant, humour him. She tried to.

'Not exactly.' She heard her own voice, which sounded so normal, and tried to compare it to the precise articulation of the headteacher. He spoke differently from the other locals, but still sounded incorrigibly Welsh to her.

'I was born in Sussex actually. I went to College in London.'

This revelation pleased him greatly and the subject of higher education was a favourite topic from then on. He never called her Stella when his wife was around though.

She did not reply to Ray's sanguine remark about the rush of trade that they should expect. He was pouring himself a glass of beer now. He sniffed at it unappreciatively. 'Doesn't keep all that well in there, you know.'

Stella shrugged. Cellar work was his department. She picked up a vinyl covered menu from the bar.

'Do you think we ought to be a bit more adventurous?' she said.

'Well, you know, a dish of the day, and perhaps a vegetarian dish of the day as well. Or something Provencale-ish ...'

'If we can't persuade anybody to eat steak pie and chips, we won't be able to persuade them to eat bloody bean casserole, will we?'

Stella knew she wasn't much of a cook, but the frozen food rep had suggested some more exotic dishes. She had thought to try a dozen lemon sole, but perhaps Ray was right. A Kids' Menu and the normal pub fare should suffice really. Nevertheless, she had her doubts about the holidaymakers in the very basic caravan park nearby spending fifteen or twenty pounds on lunch at The Hope and Anchor; two halves and a coke for the kids and back to the caravan for sandwiches was more likely.

Roy was looking up at the clock behind the bar: a minute to eleven. You could tell he was anxious about trade, not many landlords in this part of the world were this keen to open up bang on time. He timed his walk to the front door so that he could open it exactly as the second hand reached the perpendicular. There was, of course, no one waiting outside. In fact, apart from the boy who had put up the sign, who silently drank two pints on the house, no customer arrived till nearly twelve o' clock. Then two workmen came in. They had left their van outside, rather than parking it in the car park at the back of the pub. They stayed for one drink but said nothing, not even to each other. One read *The Mirror* while the other hazarded some loose change in the fruit machine, before moving over to stand by the window and gaze disconsolately out at his van.

Stella did not hover, for this might have invited the fruitless sort of conversation which bored her, though Ray was constantly urging her to chat to any new customers in order to pick up trade. She watched the younger of the two men, the one at the window. He was sipping distastefully at his lager as if it were medicine and still staring blankly out. She was reminded of the sort of British detective film that came on TV on Saturday afternoons, where the gang members wear workmen's clothes and hang around before the rendezvous with the rest of the gang, waiting for them to screech up in an old Jaguar.

No such car even passed. She walked back into the kitchen and opened the freezer. She looked glumly at the racks of individual steak pies, plaice in breadcrumbs, non-proprietary brands of frozen peas and stiff cellophane bags of frozen bread rolls. Ray was happy to eat this stuff himself as well as serve it. She felt guilty sometimes that she did not cook him something fresh more often, but where was the time? Here, her heart whispered, acres of it. She put the kettle on to make herself a coffee, to busy herself. The she heard the front door being pushed open.

A serious, sad-looking man in his late thirties had come in. He was alone in the bar, though she had not heard the workmen leaving. He looked at the pumps as if confused by the choice, then he scrutinised the coins in his hand. She examined him as he did this. He looked like an orchestral musician, she thought, noting his worn but once expensive sports jacket and faded jeans. His shirt was open-necked and his skin very white, but with a translucent quality that took her by surprise. His hair was fairly long and unkempt, but with the look of being frequently swept back from his face. She imagined him tossing this mane as he conducted a symphony.

When he spoke, the illusion was broken but she was still struck by his voice. It was not the educated drawl of the aesthete but a soft, sensual voice. His accent was neutral, but he was clearly English, not Welsh. 'Is the Guinness cold?' he said, then smiled, as if this was a stupid question.

'Freezing. '

'It's so hot out there, but I don't want lager. I don't normally drink Guinness but it's just what my body needs right now. Or what it thinks it needs, I should say.'

She listened to this little monologue with a strange interest.

'Pint?' she said, already pouring the drink. He nodded and examined the money in his hand again.

'I can sometimes guess how much I've got in change by the weight of it,' he murmured, almost to himself. 'But they keep changing the coins. I would have guessed a pound, but this is probably more than enough. These five pence coins are weightless.'

She told him the price and he dropped some silver into her outstretched hand. She wanted to talk to him, hear his voice and his strange manner of talking again, but he had already dealt with the weather. There was only one other topic.

'You're not local, are you? she said. She dropped her head to ease the last few drops into his glass from the slow pouring tap.

'Goodness me, no.' The question seemed to surprise him. 'But neither are you, I would hazard.'

'I'm from The South. I've been here, we've been here, for just over six months now.' She handed him the glass.

'It's very quiet I should imagine.'

'Yes.'

'Quiet is good. On the whole anyway.'

He spoke differently from the way people normally did. There was also a light in his eyes which you normally reserved for close friends or lovers.

'It's a strange name,' he continued.

She tilted her head slightly. Then it occurred to her that he was referring to the pub name, surely an acceptable enough one, though not so frequent in these parts perhaps.

'Landshipping? I was wondering how it used to be spelt. I thought it might have been Llanshippen, since we're in Wales. You know, Llan ...' He pronounced the first consonant accurately, something she could not manage.

'No,' she said. 'It's not that. It's to do with the quay, I think. Where they landed stuff, I suppose, coming up the estuary.'

'Oh, I see. Yes, they call Pembroke "Little England within Wales", don't they?'

She had never heard this expression.

'And you've been here just half the year?'

Again, the strange way of putting things. She smiled. 'It's quieter in the winter.'

'And less hot, doubtless.'

There was no answer to that.

'I'm looking for somewhere actually,' he began. Then he turned around as if it might be here, in this room.

'Oh, where exactly? I've sort of got to know the area, if the place you're looking for is nearby.'

'Well, it doesn't need to be, but it could be. Somewhere to stay, I mean. Just somewhere to be for a while. A short while anyway.' His voice trailed off.

'Well, there's a bed and breakfast to be had in Haverfordwest, that's about eight miles away. Probably a few places on the way out there too. Have you come very far?'

'In some ways, yes,' he said, then he smiled again. 'No, not really. Not in the way you mean. I'm looking for somewhere to live, actually. Somewhere to hang my hat, so to speak.'

The man looked at the still, creamy surface of his drink.

'Oh,' Stella said. 'I thought you meant just for a night or something. You said a short while, so I thought you meant a night or two.'

'I really don't know how long for,' he replied. 'Half a year perhaps. The other half, perchance. You see, I'm between my old life and my new one at the moment, if you can understand that.'

She could, but she did not feel that she could respond. She washed out an already clean glass, but then she looked up again. He was staring past her into the mirrored wall behind the bar.

'I lost my wife. That's what it is.'

'Oh, 1'm sorry.'

'Not to disease or disaster!' He laughed quietly. 'No, I lost her somewhere in the middle of our marriage, I should say. She sort of disappeared behind the children. I called out a few times but before she could emerge, I was gone.' He paused. 'Well, that's fanciful, isn't it? But we were as if in a wood. I'd had this quaint notion we were the same tree, you know? You branch out your different ways but you're both part of the same growing thing. It turns out we weren't, that's all.'

Stella wanted to speak. He recognised this and went on again quickly. 'Look, I'm sorry to be talking to you like this, like some sort of Ancient Mariner. Would you like a drink?'

She shook her head. He took a deep draft of his beer and wiped the foam from his upper lip.

'You're right. This stuff's freezing. I'd better go before I start getting a taste for the stuff.'

He replaced the glass carefully and pursed his lips, but he said nothing further.

Normally an encounter like this would have been mentioned to Ray. There was so little else that they could ever say to each other. But Stella decided not to say anything. He came into the bar a short while after, hoping to relieve her so that she could attend to lunch orders, but only one couple came in who showed any interest in eating, and they decided against it after a cursory glance at the menu.

'Much trade earlier on?' Ray asked, when the bar had emptied again.

'Hardly anything. Perhaps we ought to get some garden furniture.

173

Nobody wants to sit inside in weather like this.'

He grimaced. 'They've all gone to the beach. They'll be thirsty enough tonight. Perhaps we'll do some meals early evening.'

Stella nodded and hoped the soft-spoken man might come back thirsty.

He came in again late on in the evening. The room was quite full but there was an empty stool at the bar which he swung himself onto. He was fingering a twenty-pound note without ostentation. Ray was talking to a couple of the locals at the other end of the bar, and he nodded at Stella to indicate a new customer. She had not noticed him coming in and she almost blushed as she greeted him.

'Hello. Pint of Guinness? Had a good day?'

She caught a glimpse of Ray's eyebrows raised in approval at this brighter manner, for he was capable of watching everything that went on at the same time as conducting an apparently quite animated conversation with a customer.

The man was surveying the pumps. 'No, I'll have bitter please. Is it draught?'

She nodded and began pouring.

'The day was reasonably good, yes,' he said.

'Did you find somewhere to stay?'

'Uh huh. Though I don't know if this is the place I want to be yet, if you know what I mean. There's a holiday cottage not far from here that I can have from next Saturday, and for as long as I need, but I don't know if this is a place for a passer-through. I get the impression this is a tightly knit community, and they wouldn't know what to make of a stranger who was only here for a few months.'

'Does it really matter what the locals make of you then?' She handed him his drink and checked that no one else needed serving. Ray was busy laughing at the other end of the bar.

'I suppose not,' the man said. 'An intruder, doubtless. An Englishman, and therefore to be mistrusted perhaps. But no, it's not that that matters.' He swept his hair back and took a drink.

'Same for me, you know,' Stella said, in something of an undertone.

'Are you at home here?' The question bore a sudden weight.

'I'm not sure if I was ever at home anywhere, apart from when I was very young. I've sort of floated around for quite a long time, you know? But I suppose I've landed now. Made my home at last.' She laughed briefly. 'Or bed anyway'

'Home is where the hurt is.'

She looked at him in surprise at this aphorism. He had uttered the words in such a matter-of-fact way.

'In my case anyway,' he added. 'That's why I took off.'

'And where do you think you're headed?'

'Onward, I trust. But probably to the same place I started from, ultimately.'

Stella frowned.

'Do you want to come?'

The question came from so far out of the blue that it nearly made her reply honestly. He took a mouthful of beer but looked steadily at her as he did so. The room was fairly noisy, but she still felt that everyone must have heard this astonishing proposition.

'I think I've finished floating,' she managed to say. 'For some reason I thought then that you weren't just flirting with me.'

'Flirting? Goodness me, no.' he said. 'I've never been more serious. But from your expression I guess you're at anchor. Literally, in fact, I note.'

She hesitated then risked a witticism of her own: 'This is Landshipping. I've been deposited here like cargo maybe, but the estuary has dried up, you see.'

Ray approached them at this point and there was nothing more that could be said. Later, in bed, after Ray had made love to her briefly and noisily, she was glad in a way that the rest of the evening had been busy, and she had not had the chance to revive the conversation. Trade had been good after all and Ray was happy. She thought about changing the nameboard outside the pub. The Anchor would be better after all. Nothing wrong with that.

NO PROBLEMS

The old Erika typewriter I had was next to useless. I felt like I was banging in fence posts as I tried to make an impression with the keys. Word processing technology had, of course, long overtaken this East German relic of the late sixties and it was more than time for me to accept the inevitable and move up to an electronic machine, or perhaps a personal computer. I had done as much mind-numbing reading of the relevant literature as I could, but it was time to make a decision. I pretended it was still a toss-up between the Smith Corona PWP 40 and a bigger machine, but I knew what I would end up with. As long as I could try out a few things in the shop and the quality of the type was good enough I was bound to go for the Smith Corona. It was far less cumbersome than a PC. It was cheaper.

I don't know why I chose that particular office supplies shop though. When I'd first gone there, I could tell that the old guy was out of his depth once a customer started talking about bits and rom and ram. Perhaps that's why I did go back though. The whole terminological maze was a bit much for me too and I didn't want to be bulldozed into buying some IBM by a whizzkid aged about nineteen. This old man's alarmed innocence was a little touching. There was a little old lady there too, a Mrs Bellamy as it turned out, who looked as if she had done a typing course in the late thirties but not much else except a spot of light dusting since.

She looked up at me sweetly when I entered the shop. I nodded briefly at her and started examining the keyboard of a display model in an old glass cabinet which she had missed dusting. Her heart must have jumped, for she called out for the old man, Mr Howells, in a very tremulous voice. He came tottering down from his upstairs storeroom at the rate of a few hundred yards an hour. He seemed quite blasé about the prospect of a major sale, compared to his helpmate, or it might have been that he was concentrating hard on his angina at that moment. He nodded at Mrs Bellamy's telegraphed excitement and enquired if he might be of some assistance. I told him I'd just like a quick go at the machine before I finally made my already made-up mind.

'No problems,' he murmured. I watched in horror as he attempted to lift the machine out of the cabinet and onto a counter. I imagined a dying old man slumped on the floor next to a thousand bits of wire and plastic and an inconsolable Mrs Bellamy wailing his loss. He did not collapse under the weight of the lightweight machine, however, and after a few minutes rummaging behind a counter he discovered a socket and plugged in the machine. A satisfying glow hit the lift-up screen and we all admired the welcome message and company logo for some time. Then without a word the old man wandered off. I examined some of the more mysterious keys, such as those marked KBII and Reloc. Mrs Bellamy fluttered behind the counter like a teenage barmaid on her first shift. Eventually Mr Howells came back with a single sheet of A4 paper. He typed in some gibberish and tried to print it.

'I've forgotten the precise command for print for the minute,' he apologised.

'Well, it's got typewriter mode,' I said graciously. 'We could switch to that, and I'll be able to see the quality of the print at least.'

'Oh, there's no problem with quality,' he insisted.

I smiled but carried on typing the nursery rhyme I had started. I got to 'doesn't know where to find them' but was stuck on the 'doesn't'.

'I can't seem to find the apostrophe,' I said.

Mr Howells scrutinised the keyboard from about an inch distance, humming deeply to himself. He tried various options but all we got was doesn-t and doesn,t. Mrs Bellamy came round from behind the counter to help.

'I know it sounds stupid, but what's an apostrophe?' she said. 'I think I've forgotten.'

Before I could formulate a definition, Mr Howells had responded,

178

rather snappishly, 'It's a pear, an upside down pear,'

She looked totally bemused.

'It's a comma in the air,' I suggested. No good. She was really flummoxed this time. I picked up a User's Guide which someone had left lying around and looked desperately through it to find an example.

'Here,' I cried. 'See?' I pointed to the phrase 'Today's date' and showed her the pear in the air. Mr Howells had wandered off to scrutinise another keyboard. He found an apostrophe, but unfortunately it was attached to this other keyboard.

'Do you really need one?' he said, his voice quivering somewhat.

'Well, I'm a poet you see,' I said, with little real hope that it would convince. But the non-sequitur made perfect sense to them both. The panic was soon over though. That treasure, Mrs B, located the apostrophe on our keyboard. Her achievement caused a flush of pride, but she tried to modulate this with a little self-deprecation.

'I didn't have an education,' she whispered to me, 'And I only work here part-time.'

'No problems then,' Mr Howells said.

'Could I just see the handbook that goes with the machine?' I said.

He disappeared upstairs, but within a minute of his going I noticed that the User's Guide I had in my hand was, by pure chance, the one I'd asked for. Mr Howells was gone for about ten minutes, during which time Mrs B. engaged me in conversation.

'Poet, eh?'

I smiled.

'My next-door neighbour used to write things. Of course, she's dead now.' A long pause. 'And one of the people in my church. Writer, that is, she's not dead. Well, I don't think so anyway.'

I was flicking through the User's Guide the while.

'What about daisy wheels?' I said.

Mrs Bellamy looked at me as if I'd sworn, or accused her of burglary. Luckily Mr Howells chose this moment to reappear.

'Ah,' he said, 'There's the handbook. I knew it was somewhere. Good. Now, what was that about daisy wheels?'

'I was just wondering how much a spare daisy wheel would cost. I think it would be nice to have one that did italics as well as this one.'

He ransacked his mind for a few embarrassing seconds. 'I'm not entirely sure if we've got an italics in stock, but I'll go and check. It'd be upstairs. They'd be about the fifteen pounds mark.' He thought for a while. ''Plus V.A.T.'

I felt like offering to run upstairs for him as he snailed back up to his storeroom, but at that moment another potential customer came in and I was freed from the attentions of Mrs Bellamy. I turned to the keyboard again and tried to fathom how to type a circumflex, aware enough that my need for this diacritic would be pretty rare. I don't write in French. I half-listened to the conversation between Mrs Bellamy and the new customer. He was trying to explain to her that acetates were not the same thing as Letraset.

Mr Howells was only gone for about five minutes this time - barely enough time for a nap. He reappeared waggling a finger at Mrs Bellamy from the bottom of the stairs, where he was taking a breather.

'You'll have to write off to the suppliers, Mrs B, and order one,' he gasped.

She wrote something slowly in a large hand on a scrap of paper she had torn off from a stray invoice someone had left on the counter. I thought I saw a couple of attempts at 'Dazy' but I tried not to stare.

'Right then,' Mr Howells said. 'That's about it then. Was there anything else?'

'Just a couple of spare ribbons,' I said. I looked round the shop, which was littered with machines brought in for repair and discarded packaging and had a thought. 'The guarantee is in the box, I suppose? How long is it for?'

He regarded me with horror. 'Did you really want a box?

'Well, there's the cable and the tutorial disk they mention here, and there must be a written guarantee, I guess. A box would be handy to carry it all. And usually they like you to pack it all back in the original carton, if you have to send it off for repair.'

'Oh, there's no problems with repairs,' he said. 'We do our own guarantee, you see. You just bring it back to us, Twelve months. Or a year.'

I had a suspicion that there was a joke in here somewhere. I didn't smile.

'But I'll find you a box if you like.'

I smiled. 'Perhaps I could have a machine that's already packed and ready to go,' I said, though without any menace in my voice,.

'Yes, of course. Mrs Bellamy, do you know where the other Smith Corona is?'

It was like asking a dog for a light. She looked hopefully at him, awaiting further clarification.

'We had two, I'm sure. I'll just look round here, excuse me a moment.'

He tottered to the back of the shop, which was partly in darkness, and lifted various empty cases. He moved piles of acetates and packets of Letraset, and I now realised how the two could be easily confused in the dark, plus typewriter ribbons. But there was patently no other machine. Eventually he picked up a large box and examined the serial number on it. 'Read me the number on the machine, if you would, please, Mrs Bellamy.'

She peered at the keyboard for several seconds. I craned my neck over her shoulder to see if I could help, but there was no number etched, as I thought there might be, on the sides or back of the machine.

'Inside, inside,' he moaned. 'Then he tottered back, handed her the carton and pulled up a plastic flap at the front of the word processor to reveal the workings, and a silver label with a serial number.

'Read me that number,' he said to Mrs Bellamy. 'No, not this one, the one you've got on the box.'

The room fell silent for a while. 'Just the last three digits will do.'

'747,' she murmured.

'747,' he repeated. No problems.'

'Sound like an aeroplane,' the gay Mrs B. quipped.'Only smaller,' I riposted, caught up in the jollity..

Mr Howells looked at me sadly. 'Well, this is the right box. Now, what else was there?'

'The tutorial disk?' I offered, 'It does mention here that one comes with the machine.'

He attempted a look of scepticism, but his thick glasses interfered with subtle eye gestures like this, and he shook his head sadly instead.

'Well,' he said, 'I suppose I could take a look upstairs to see if there's one about, but it's usually with the book. Could you check for the customer, Mrs Bellamy?' He staggered back up to his storeroom, leaving the redoubtable Mrs B. to shake the handbook, riffle through the pages and generally go through as many searching motions as she could think of.

'We'll probably find it after you've gone,' she said confidentially. 'Perhaps we could send it on to you?'

I suppose I partly believed that they might. Partly also I knew that she would write my address on a piece of paper and leave it on the counter for some other day, when they would both stare at it in utter incomprehension.

'So, could I have your address?'

I told her and she wrote it down laboriously in her misspelled copperplate. 'You live in a nice part of town,' she said. 'Now isn't that a coincidence, we sold the other Smith Corona to somebody who lives quite near you.'

I let my eyes tell her she had been caught out. She looked at me like a bird. I knew I couldn't inform on her to her boss. She coloured a little, and busied herself with an invoice book till Mr Howells came back.

'There's nothing up there,' he said. This was pretty much as I had expected. 'But we'll send one on to you as soon as we can, will that be alright?'

I nodded. 'Could I have a plug though?'

He looked at the trailing wire from the machine as if someone had vandalised it. 'No problems,' he said. He traipsed back up the stairs but returned within three or four minutes this time.

'Could you put it on yourself when you get home?' he said. 'I could try and find a screwdriver, but I'm not sure I could lay my hands on one straight away.'

'No problems,' I said.

'Now for the difficult part,' he said. 'Paying.'

I had nearly forgotten. I wrote out a cheque and watched as they both pored over it, breathing heavily, treating it as though it was their offspring's first school report.

The disk never came. It doesn't matter. As Mr Howells insisted, there have been no problems with the machine. Apart from the blank screen, of course. Every day I sit here trying to summon up the words for a poem, but all I end up with is apostrophes and circumflexes and rows of pppppppps. I think the problem is the ease with which the keys depress. They don't give me time to think. At least with the old Erika, every letter, every word, was a plunge into unknown meaning. I wish I hadn't told Mrs Bellamy I was a poet. She's probably imagining me now, conjuring up upside down pears in the air, living in my nice part of town, flying in my grey plastic 747. She and her ancient boss are ensconced in their cocoon the while, problem-less and happy.

TRIVIA AND TRIFLE

They were supposed to be our best friends. I hated them. No, that's not true. 'Hate' is the wrong word. I found their tedious tales catastrophically boring; I found their mispronunciations of any words remotely French or Spanish appalling; I could share in none of their bigotries or unaccountable reading or viewing tastes. But I couldn't hate them, somehow, because I had befriended them in the first place, and it would be letting myself down to admit to myself the depth and enormity of my misprision.

That was, until tonight. Tonight they came round for a meal. Now I hate them as if they had molested my child, stamped on my old vinyl records, urinated on my rug. They didn't actually commit any of these atrocities, of course. My child was safe in her friend's house for a sleep-over. My records are in the attic since the acquisition of our latest CD machine. I can't speak for the rug. I didn't stop to sniff it.

They came breezing in clutching a Tesco bag of goodies. This turned out to contain a bottle of Spanish (and therefore unpronounceable) wine, three cans of lager, which Paul had brought for his own consumption, and the remains of a glutinous sherry trifle they had thought better of eating the previous day, or it may have been previous weekend.

'You shouldn't have gone to all this trouble,' Noya said, looking at the dinner table with a mixture of envy, scorn and glue in her voice.

'Well, it's midweek so we've only done a spaghetti,' we said, 'But there's some dips and some nice Italian bread to start. Now, drinks?'

I poured Paul a glass of Fitou to go with the lager he was hugging. Noya said red wine gave her a headache and could she have something lighter. She was looking at our last bottle of Sancerre on

184

the wine rack.

'I'll put this in the fridge to cool,' I said, picking up the sweet Spanish wine by the tips of my fingers like it was a soiled napkin. They smiled gaily, obnoxiously refusing to get the point.

We sat down and tried to initiate a conversation about the day's news, which had passed them by, then any interesting anecdotes from Paul's work, of which there were a large number, though none of them was of any interest whatsoever. Then talk turned to the progress of their awful son through his dismal school. Noya had recently been infuriated by his English teacher's impudence in awarding him a B grade for his spoken English skills. As far as I was aware these were non-existent, the boy being thirteen and congenitally incapable of anything more than a grunt whenever I had the misfortune to come across him. That and a strangled yelp that sometimes emanated from his bedroom when we visited their house, which made me suspect that he was discovering the sad joys of masturbatory orgasm.

At one stage I attempted to introduce a new topic: we had discovered a fabulous new Lebanese restaurant, had they seen it yet? Paul rolled his tongue over the word 'Lebanese' as if it were a Sapphic sexual practice. I added lamely that it was rather good anyway. I had forgotten that mention of restaurants would inevitably, as Friday brings the bin men, bring that tired old tale of the best meal they had ever had, in Tamworth, circa 1973. I quarter-listened as they dragged through the starters and the main meals and what the restaurateur said to them and what they said to him and how they'd never come across another place like it. If you insist, as you absolutely do, on going to the Raj Balti every time you go out, you're not likely to either, I wanted to say, but I could see my wife's expression and I refrained.

But familiarity to the point of boredom still should not be the stuff of hatred, I recognise. I have to recognise, too, that we have been going to the said Balti house for many years, and going along willingly enough oftentimes. Furthermore, we have been going to their house and inviting them back for an equal number of years.

Perhaps I have always secretly envied their rapport with the Tamworth restaurateur.

No. It was what happened after the dessert that finally fired the flames of my smouldering antipathy to these truly dreadful people tonight. The collapsed trifle was proudly installed in the centre of the table. Then my wife got out the pecan pie and double cream and we all partook of that particular delight. Then she got out the cheeses and the liqueur bottles and I prepared some coffee '. I won't have a coffee just yet,' Paul said. Noya indicated that she too would prefer to decimate out liqueur collection and pass on the coffee. 'But we've got a special treat for you: we've brought our brand new Trivial Pursuit cards,' she said.

It was five past eleven. I had work in the morning. Paul has no time for the actual board game but all the time in his miserable world to try and go through a whole card of questions and try to get a perfect six. His average score is nought. He once studied chemistry, but he can't even get the odd science question right. He is not interested in sport, the arts, politics or history. Noya once read a novel by Anna Sewell but got bored by it and stopped reading. She reads newspapers avidly, but only for offers and to cut out coupons. I knew that if they once started to try and get six consecutive questions right, we could be here for a fortnight and might even have to resort to eating their trifle.

'I'd better not tonight,' I said. 'I've got work in the morning and it's getting late.' You can't get much more direct than that. Paul read out and mispronounced the first question. He got the answer wrong. There were, in fact, only three Earp brothers at the O.K. Corral.

An hour and a half later I had removed all plates, glasses, coffee cups and even the trifle from the dinner table. I had switched off all the lights but the central one over the table. My wife had gone to bed under the pretence of going to check whether our daughter was asleep. I felt sure we had already mentioned that she was not in the house, but no one said anything. Paul ploughed through the cards with the implacability - and charm - of a JCB going up a steep hill. On about the seventeenth card he had been encouraged by getting an answer correct and he was determined now. I finally snapped.

'Well,' I said. 'We'll have to try another time. I've simply got to go to bed now. I've got to get up again in five hours.'

Paul looked up amazed. 'You're joking,' he said. He could see that I was not. I was closer to domestic violence - murder perhaps - than light-hearted banter. 'No, you're not joking,' he said. 'Well, I have to say this, though it grieves me, you're just not good company anymore. There, I've said it.'

I smiled, I think for the first time during the whole interminable night. 'Unlike you,' I said. 'But too much of a good thing, you know?'

Tomorrow I shall apologise, claim I was sickening for something, suggest we go out for a meal. The Raj Balti perhaps. It's two o' clock in the morning now. I can't sleep. I just had a mouthful of the sherry trifle. It wasn't bad, to tell the truth.

WRONG NUMBER

'Is that Daniel Stone?' the voice asked. It was a woman not young, not old, by the tone. I instantly imagined her in a light blue dress, or suit even; it was that sort of voice, the sort that went out of fashion some time ago, but that some people still have.

'Yes,' I lied. After, I wondered whether I'd just not heard properly, and that's why I'd said yes so complacently, but I know I heard the wrong name. I know I lied and I know why 1 lied.

'Thank goodness' she said. The phone went quiet, but not dead. I could tell she was still there, even though I couldn't hear her breathing. I didn't say anything because I was adding a pair of white low heeled court shoes to my image of her. As yet I couldn't picture where she was though. It wasn't a phone box, that's all I could tell so far.

'What is it?' I said. I let my voice pipe the words down the line like thick cream. I was whiskied and cigaretted into a brown huskiness anyway.

'Mr Stone. Daniel. A friend gave me your number ... '

'Fine,' I said. I didn't want to talk; I wanted to listen. I was halfway through joining up the dots of her nervy, prim accent and I wanted to know if she was a fat old red-cheeked woman who'd trained herself to sound thirty-five, and pinched into life's size 8, or whether she was really as reedy and plaintive as she sounded.

It's only happened to me a couple of times before. Once I had to argue with this telephone operator for minutes; she kept mishearing me, and then she let the clinical thing slip and her voice changed. I immediately asked her for a date, though I didn't know what she looked like - 1 imagined 23 and a redhead - and I didn't even know where she was speaking from. She might have been six hundred miles away. She iced up like a nurse and clicked off, which probably meant she was in her twenties and happily engaged. Women older than that are still charmed by propositions, even when they can't possibly be serious. It was a man anyway when I called back.

The other time I was waiting for the lift in an apartment block, and it turned out the thing was stuck between floors. There was a woman trapped inside, and she was actually only a couple of feet away from where I was standing, but we couldn't see each other of course. We talked for about five minutes till someone came and sorted it out. They sent the lift back up to the next floor and, such was the musk of that five minutes, I raced up the stairs to see who it was I'd just been talking to. She'd disappeared. I think about her quite a lot: she sounded like she had incredibly long curly hair - mid-brown I always imagine - and a body you'd chew your right arm off for. If I'd been on the floor above shouting down, we might have been married by now. Couple of kids.

This time it was Miss Blue Dress (or Miss Blue Two Piece) who'd stretched out across the air waves and wanted to talk to a namesake of mine called Daniel. The name was a couple of consonants out, but I was going to hang on to her like she was the lift, and I was suspended.

'I don't know how to put this,' she said.

'Take your time. That's what time's for,' I said. Cooler than a fridge.

'I thought I'd got the wrong number. I always remember numbers by associating them with things, you know?'

'I do that too.'

'So I didn't write your number down. I broke it up and remembered each bit with a picture. Do you know what your number looks like?'

'It doesn't look like anything to me, it just looks like numbers on the phone. Tell me what picture you've got though.'

'It's silly. It's two little ducks outside Downing Street with bad dentures.'

'Bad dentures?'

189

'They're clicking away. Clickety click?'

'I get it!' I hadn't got it because my number ends with 6,4. She'd probably remembered the number fine, then hit the wrong key on the pad. Also, I was disappointed. She seemed to be too au fait with bingo calls, which might well put her straight back in the red-cheeked old woman class.

'I know ducks don't have teeth, but well, at least, I don't think they have teeth.'

'They surely don't,' I said. 'But what would you have imagined if the last two numbers hadn't been 66? Say, if they'd been 6,4?'

'Oh, that's easy. I would have seen a bus passing the ducks. I used to catch a number 64 bus when 1 was a child, in the summer, going to the beach with my mum.'

'Just your mother?'

'Yes. My dad, well ...'

She was younger than I'd thought. Her voice had gone from sky blue courtelle to something else, something less convinced of its place in the scheme of things.

'Look'. she went on.

'I'm looking. And listening.'

'Sorry, that must have sounded silly. The reason I'm calling is my friend said you'd be able to help me.'

I wanted to find out a lot more before I admitted that she'd got a wrong number. I wanted to show her somehow that, whoever I was, I could still be someone to talk to in the dull suddenness of a November's chill evening. I decided to give of myself a little, hard though it is. 'If you're unhappy about this, I can call you back,' I said. 'I've got time, as it happens. I was going to go out to dinner, but my friends are sick, and they've just rung to cancel. Mean of them, isn't it? I don't have anything in, because I thought I was being fed tonight. Are you on your own as well?'

It wasn't much that I'd given, just a sense that I wasn't entirely sorted, that I was vulnerable to the whims of other people's sickness, or excuses for avoiding my company.

'I'm sorry to hear that,' she said. She paused. 'I am on my own actually. I'm baby-sitting for a friend.'

That changed things. As soon as I heard the word 'baby-sitting' I had a twinge of embarrassment. She was just a girl. But then when she added 'for a friend' I realised that she had to be older than that.

'Were you planning to watch TV or something?' I said. 'I don't know what's on tonight.' As soon as she mentioned a programme or a film I would have more to go on. It's a very rough rule, but I reckon nobody much under thirty-five watches documentaries, or cookery programmes. Even better, if she enthused about a Brad Pitt movie, or a Barbara Streisand film, I'd have her pinned right down, practically to her year of birth.

'I don't know,' she said. 'Is there anything on?'

'I'm a useless person to ask,' I said. 'If I ever watch TV, I tend to switch off the sound, or maybe even just listen to the words. I turn away deliberately to see what it's like without the pictures sometimes. If I can't turn away, I've even turned down the contrast. Does that sound daft?'

'A bit.' She laughed slightly. I don't think she found it funny though. Funny ha ha, anyway. 'Mary said you were a bit strange.'

I laughed this time. Then I started to wonder about this Mary person.

'Sorry,' she added quickly, 'I don't mean strange. Eccentric, I think she was trying to say.'

'We're all eccentric in the strictest sense of the word,' I said. 'Different accents, different fingerprints.' I'd hit on something here. 'For instance, if you called again I'd be able to recognise your voice. Know you out of the thousands of people I must have spoken to on the phone. That makes you a one-off too, doesn't it?'

'Yes, I suppose so. Perhaps I'd recognise your voice too, I don't know. It is strange, isn't it?'

'I couldn't picture you, of course,' I said. 'Though I already have, as a matter of fact. That's strange too, isn't it? Can I tell you how I

191

see you? Would you be offended by that?'

'Mary's already been in touch, has she? You couldn't possibly guess what I look like unless she described me. I'll have a word with her.'

'Well, do you know what I look like?'

'No … er … well, I suppose I have formed a picture in my mind. You sound quite nice, actually.'

'I am. In my eccentric way. But you sound … can you score me on this? First, I think you sound slim.'

There was a natural enough silence.

'I don't actually mean slim. I mean very slim. Slender, can I say. I don't want to say skinny.' I pressed on, gauging each utterance carefully by the absence of her breathing sounds. 'And I think you sound blue. I mean dressed in blue, but maybe I mean a little bit sad too. But only temporarily sad. I think you're thirty. No, that's too exact.'

I listened for a reaction. 'I mean over twenty-five and under thirty-five, I think you've got short hair. And I think you've probably got one hand over your mouth - in amazement, or because you want to burst out laughing because I'm way off the mark. Am I?'

She didn't laugh. 'I don't believe Mary hasn't spoken to you,' she said, after a long pause.

'She hasn't.' I decided to trump my own ace. 'I don't even know Mary. Actually, my name is David, not Daniel. Though, amazingly, my surname is Stone. My number is 221064 not 66. I'm a wrong number, but sometimes wrong numbers turn out to be the right people.'

There was a slight gasp on the other end of the line. I knew she was on the point of slamming down the receiver in shock and anger.

'Wh ...' she said. I waited. 'You're not Daniel Stone?'

'Would it be better if I was?'

Her tone sounded hurt, like I'd invaded her privacy, though all I'd actually been doing was sitting in my own house, dinnerless. That bit was true. She'd phoned me, hadn't she?

'I don't know. I think I'd better go.'

'Don't ... '

But the phone clicked off. I watched the TV with the sound off the rest of the night, but it was like the people in that bright box were watching me.

She rang back the following evening at the same time. 'I'm sorry about yesterday,' she said. 'I didn't mean to interrupt your life, but it was kind of you to be prepared to listen when I was some stranger with a wrong number ... '

'I'm a right number tonight, I see. Unless you're still trying to talk to Daniel, of course.' I laughed hollowly. 'Did you get through to him after, by the way?'

She ahemmed. 'No. I was a bit confused by what happened last night. I thought I'd better stay away from the phone. '

'Did you watch TV instead?'

This seemed to surprise her. 'No . . er . . I had a bath and an early night. Is that what you did?'

'Bath? No.'

'No, I mean, watch TV.'

'Oh, yes. No sound though.'

It wasn't going well. Somehow, she'd grabbed the handlebars of this wobbly conversation, but she wasn't happy about it. When the pause had gone on for too long, which is only about three seconds on the phone, but that's still long, I spoke again: 'This is like pen pals, isn't it? Phone pals, sort of. Have you ever rung one of those chat lines?'

'No,' She was most emphatic about this.

'Nor me.'

'They're for youngsters, aren't they?'

'I don't know. There's sex lines too, I gather. I read a book about one anyway.' There was no response for a second and I imagined her frowning and looking at the phone like it was something sticky she'd put her hand in. 'So,' I pressed on, 'Did you tell Mary about calling a wrong number and talking to me?'

'Mary?' She seemed totally blank. 'Oh! Er ... no, no.'

I suddenly realised there was no Mary. 'Well,' I said quickly. 'I don't suppose it's much of a story to tell really, is it?'

She interrupted me at this point. 'Did you manage to find something to eat last night?'

'Oh, I didn't bother in the end. How about you?'

'I had a sandwich. My friend always leaves a plate of them in the fridge when I go round to babysit.'

'Were you really babysitting?' I blurted out, without having time to consider whether it was a wise question or not.

She blurted back her answer equally quickly. 'No. How did you know?'

'Are you going to tell me your name?' I said. 'You know mine, but I don't know yours.

'That's not right for phonepals, is it?'

She must have smiled. That amount of time passed before she replied. 'I'm Mary,' she said.

'I thought there wasn't a Mary at all, but it's you!' I said, as delighted as I could sound.

'You knew there was no Mary?'

'Only tonight.' I paused and pulled out a digestive biscuit from an open packet by the phone. 'There's no Daniel Stone either, is there?'

'How do you know?'

'I guessed. I could check though. How many "D. Stone's are there in the phonebook?'

A pause. 'Three.'

'And was I number three?'

'Two, actually.'

I breathed in. 'What did number one say?'

'It was a woman.'

'Old or young?'

'I don't know. I didn't speak to her. 'Probably the same age as you, or me.'

'Can I ask? No, it doesn't matter.' I thought about it. 'Does it matter?'

'Not really. You weren't far out when you guessed last night. I was impressed, you know. And to be able to guess that you must be late thirties, forties, yourself.'

'You're not far out.' I made a snap decision. 'Is there a plate of sandwiches in the fridge tonight?'

She knew what I was going to say, and she forestalled me. 'Are there really friends who invite you to dinner then call up and say they're sick?'

'There might be. Just because it didn't happen, doesn't mean it doesn't happen.'

'No, I guess not,' she said. It was like someone had opened a back door, the draught of silence that caught us both.

'Well,' I started.

'Yeah,' she sighed.

'Doesn't mean it will happen either, does it? Is that what that silence means?'

'The fun's gone out of it,' she said. She sounded a little saddened by her realisation.

'Was that it?' I gasped. 'Fun?'

'Yeah. Or at least, that's what I thought.'

I started to tell her about the girl in the lift that time, but she stopped me. 'I'm not her,' she said.

'I know,' I said, 'But you're a person.'

'We're all persons,' she said. 'Our own voices, our own fingerprints. I know you're more than a name in a book now, at least.'

'But I still don't even know your name, or what page to look on. Are you really Mary Somebody?'

'I'm not Mary,' she said quietly. 'I'm just somebody.'

The line went dead a moment or two later, before I had a chance to say anything else. The biscuit I was holding looked drier than I could ever face.

IS THIS YOUR VEHICLE?

The toys were in a cardboard box in the back of a wardrobe. She'd taken everything else and she'd said he should throw them, they were just plastic cars with wheels off, bits of a plastic train set with the battery compartment cover missing from the loco; stuff like that. Then Charlie had written a note with her last letter - Pleas can I have my toys. Love you dad. There was a P.S. on Marcia's letter:

Charlie insisted I include his letter. If you haven't thrown them out already perhaps you could bring whatever's left. Doubtless your car will be off the road, or some such excuse and you won't be able to come up, but there, I've asked anyway.

He crumpled her letter, the rest of which was nothing but a series of demands for more money, and threw it in the kitchen bin. After a while he folded Charlie's note and placed that in the bin as well. As it happened the car was playing up; the battery was unreliable, and he had to make sure he parked on slopes in case he needed to bump start the thing. He resented the idea of having to buy a new battery though, especially since things were so tight now, but he knew he'd probably have to get one, if only to make sure he could get up to Sheffeld and deliver the box of useless broken bits of plastic. What with the cost of the petrol, it would have been more economical to send a cheque for Charlie to have a new train set, but it was a clever little piece of manipulation by Marcia. He came to this conclusion after a few minutes wondering whether, despite her scornful tone, she might actually want to see him, or whether she could actually be occasionally reasonable enough to accept that Charlie needed to see his father.

The letter came a few days before Christmas. He had tried to talk to her on the phone about arrangements for the week he had off work. She was adamant that she wasn't going to allow him to have Charlie to stay. 'You can't go trekking him up and down the country like that,' she said.

'You have!' he retorted. She ignored that and said he could come up and see the boy for an afternoon. Then they had started arguing and he had slammed down the phone before they had reached any agreement about when the visit might take place. He still half-contemplated going up on Christmas Eve, in order to demonstrate his love by leaving a bag of presents for Charlie. Then he thought he might go up after Christmas. He could make sure that Charlie knew that he would be getting presents from his father, but that it was because Marcia was so cantankerous that he hadn't got them on the right day. When it actually came to Christmas Eve, he still hadn't got a battery for the car, and it was too late to think of going. He would have to sort the car out as soon as Halfords opened after Christmas and travel up on the 27th or 28th.

On the afternoon of Christmas Eve he got drunk on his own in a dismal pub that he found in a suburb. He had been driving around and had come to this part of the city that he didn't really know, almost without realising it. He was surprised that the place was so empty on this day of all days, but plainly the locals had made their way into the city centre to carouse the afternoon and evening away in more convivial surroundings.

'Lost, are we?' the landlady said when he was looking around at the bar.

'No, I know where I am for once,' he said.

The woman frowned at his cryptic tone and gave him his beer without further word. There was a tattered silver and green garland wishing patrons 'A Happy Christmas' above the bar, but no other gesture to the festive season. He had five steady pints without further discourse with the sullen landlady and when he got back home, he drank most of a bottle of whisky in the dull, echoing house. It was enough to knock him out for most of the next day.

The roads were empty and dangerously iced with a black veneer as slick as the covering on a fairground toffee apple when he set off for Sheffeld two days later. He drove so slowly that a police car nosed up alongside, sharkily investigating this dithering minor life form. He must have looked something like a fish himself, he decided, though one in a tank not a sea-borne creature, for the demister on the car wasn't working properly and he was trapped in a grimy glass world. He peered through the smeared side window to see what the cruising car wanted. The policeman in the passenger seat glared at him and motioned him to move along. He increased his speed and the police car dropped off, to hang around and molest some other driver, he supposed. The radio in his car had been stolen several months before and there was nothing to distract his attention from thoughts about Marcia and Charlie, and oddly, much more of the time, tedious thoughts about the motorway miles ahead.

At last, the steelworks and factory chimneys of Sheffield loomed up and he began to feel his chest tighten at the thought of his meeting with his son and ex-wife. On the phone the previous day it had been agreed that he could spend a couple of hours in Marcia's house with Charlie. She said that her new partner Richard would make sure he was out between two and five. She sneered when he asked if it was possible that she could absent herself too for that time. 'It's my house,' she said. 'I'm the one doing you the favour, you know!' He was aware that it would be a lot better to be indoors than to have to drive around, or try to find a McDonald's or whatever in a strange town, but he still felt it was a very slight favour she was offering. 'I'll be there by two,' he said. It was now half past, but the roads had been icy.

The house was a small one on an estate and he felt a wave of something between panic and nausea as he pulled up outside it. Even before he saw the number on the door, he recognised his own curtains from his dining room in her front window. Marcia had left him most of their furniture, but anything of any worth she had removed, saying it was for Charlie as much as herself, and this had included this pair of curtains. At the time he had shrugged and said, 'Have it all. Why don't you see if you can get the wallpaper off?' Now, the familiarity of something he had never really noticed at home appalled him. He sat in the car for a while, even getting an AA book out of the glove compartment and pretending to study it when a pedestrian passed slowly. Then after five minutes or so he thought he saw one of the curtains move. He got out of the car quickly, wanting to confront Marcia on her own territory, rather than be caught sitting in his car like a nervous date, or a rookie policeman unsure of his rights.

'Couldn't get here on time, I see,' Marcia said. 'Charlie's been hanging around for over an hour waiting. Don't you care that you upset him?'

'I'm forty minutes late,' he said. 'I've driven over two hundred miles in a freezing car on freezing roads, with no demister even. I think that shows that I do care, don't you?'

She shrugged and held the door open wider for him to enter. Charlie was sitting on the bottom stair chewing a fingernail. He trotted forward obediently as his father put down his bag and held out his arms.

'Who's a big boy then?'

Charlie buried his head in his midriff and let his hair be tousled.

'Let's see what we've got here then.'

The boy brightened as he saw a large boxed game coming out of the bag. His eyes narrowed at the next gift: a pair of Thomas the Tank socks.

'And I brought those toys you asked for as well.' He rummaged in the bottom of the bag and brought out a red plastic Ferrari with a missing tyre and some other smaller cars. 'Though the train set was no good,' he went on. 'Half the track was missing and the loco was broken. I'll get you a new one for your birthday. How about that?'

Charlie prised a moist thumb between his teeth and sat back down on the bottom stair to open the new game.

'Well, what do you say to your father?' Marcia said, her voice brittle.

'Thank you, daddy.'

Marcia snorted. 'I was thinking more, "What the hell do you think I want with Thomas the Tank socks?" actually, but good boy for saying thank you.' She spun and walked towards the kitchen at the end of the entrance hall. 'I suppose you'd like a cup of coffee or something?' she said. 'Though you probably stopped on the way up. I won't offer you a drink because you're driving.'

He said a coffee would be fine and he turned to help Charlie get the plastic off his new game. Then, when Marcia brought his coffee, he followed the boy up to his bedroom and tried to feign interest in the fatuous board game. But Charlie soon got bored himself.

Instead of a free rolling die, there was a plastic bubble that you needed to press down on hard to spin the die trapped inside. Charlie wasn't strong enough and he started to look about at the more interesting play possibilities amongst the other toys in his bedroom. He didn't object when his father said he needed to pop downstairs and talk to mummy about things for a few minutes.

'So,' Marcia said, 'I see you really splashed out on presents for him. Have you still got your job?'

'Yes,' he replied. But I see you're doing well enough on my money too.' He motioned his head round the room they were sitting in, which was furnished if not opulently, then at least comfortably. There was a drinks cabinet and an expensive stereo in one corner.

Don't imagine that you've paid for all this,' Marcia snapped. 'Ted's a generous man. And he's got a good job.'

'Good for Ted,' he said. 'I'm thrilled.' 'But it's Charlie who benefits too.'

'And you, of course.'

Marcia did not reply this time. He put down his cup. 'Mind if I smoke?'

'Yes I do. You'll have to go outside if you want to indulge in your filthy habits.'

He put the packet back in his pocket. 'And what about your filthy habits, eh?'

There was an electric silence.

'Like sleeping with my best friend?'

201

'I don't want to go through this all over again,' Marcia shrilled. 'You'll only upset Charlie.' Charlie was upstairs, playing happily. It was Marcia who was red-faced and ready to burst into tears.

'I'll get out of here,' he said. 'I'll say goodbye to Charlie and I'll be off. I wouldn't like to bump into Ted again.'

'He wasn't your best friend,' Marcia said quietly, stifling a sob.

'You can say that again.'

He went up and tousled Charlie's hair again, not knowing what else to do. 'Got to go now,' he said. 'Look, here's some money. You can get the train set before your birthday if you like. But I don't want you to give this money to mummy, understand?'

The boy took the notes and looked utterly miserable.

'Anyway, I'll speak to you on the phone soon, okay?'

Charlie nodded and looked down at the red Ferrari he was holding.

It was dark and the roads were empty as the car slid through a huge black puddle and skidded across a junction. He realised that he had gone through a light on red. He stopped, his heart racing, and wondered how it was that he had managed to drive for minutes without seeing anything; without knowing what he was doing. He hadn't even seen the traffic lights coming up, though his eyes had been wide open.

He had pulled in just past the junction, outside a gloomy shuttered jeweller's shop. It may have been the location, or simply the fact of his sitting in a car on his own at this time of night, in an otherwise deserted street, that caught the attention of a passing patrol car. He did not notice the eerie single sweep of the blue light in his rear-view mirror, but he pulled himself together as he saw the police car pulling in a few yards ahead of him. He took a deep breath and wound down his window.

'Evening,' he said.

The policeman crouched to look inside the car. 'Any problems, sir?'

'No, no. I was just having a breather for a minute.'

'Did you know you were parked within fifteen yards of a road junction?'

'Am I? Oh, sorry. I'd better get going again.' He started the engine.

'Could you switch your engine off, sir?'

The other policeman had approached now, and the two men said something to each other that he didn't catch.

'Is this your vehicle?' the first man said.

'Of course it is.'

'Would you mind stepping out of the car for a moment, sir?'

He looked a little hurt, but he didn't want to prolong this encounter any longer than was necessary, so he decided to be totally compliant. He got out and stood away from the door as the second policeman looked inside the car.

'Could you put your vehicle in neutral and engage the handbrake for us, please?'

He did as he was told and moved round to stand on the pavement. A car had swished by and sent up a fine spray.

The first policeman went to the back of the car and leaned into it. The car moved forward a few inches. He stood up and smiled. The second policeman went to the front of the car and pushed against the bonnet. The car rolled back, further this time, and the first policeman had to step out of the way sharply.

He suddenly found it funny, watching these two men pushing at his car as if it were a friction toy. He threw his head back and laughed out loud. The damp night air caught the sound of his uncontrollable laughter and sent it reverberating round the empty street.

'I don't think this is a laughing matter, sir,' one of the policemen said.

'No,' he said, 'I don't suppose it is. Nothing to laugh about at all.'

MAN OF FEW WORDS

Sleep. Balm of hurt minds. Raveller up of something or other. Blair couldn't remember what it was for the moment; he was too tired. He had travelled overnight from London and was now sitting in a piece of Belgian rolling stock that had probably seen better days on some twisting track in the Congo. He had strong hopes, however, that any hour now the train would move off and the motion might at last ravel him up or unravel him; it was a moot point. A party of Scandinavian teenagers was gathered on the platform outside, squatting round an enormous circle of rucksacks and listening to instructions from a youth leader, or teacher, though he looked too young to be either. Blair wondered about such latter-day Norse and Viking raiding parties. Whenever he was in a large city, when he had visited Paris that one time, and indeed anywhere he had ever been in Europe, he had always run into a party of healthy, confident, precocious, ash haired teenagers from Denmark or Sweden. They were always laughing and talking loudly, unlike Blair, who often had little to say, or rather, often had nobody to say anything to. But it would all be very different soon. At least, as long as he had understood Sabine's invitation aright.

Sabine was such a difficult person to understand. Her English was fine, of course, but her general demeanour was so open, so ... Blair struggled for the right word in his own mind as if he were trying to communicate what it was about Sabine to a third party sitting opposite him on the hard upholstered bench of the compartment, agog. Well, perhaps 'undiscriminating' was the word. He weighed this choice. It was a slightly unpleasant word, and therefore not the right term for the ever-genial Sabine. The trouble was, she had the same smile for everybody. Perhaps she had invited everyone she had met in Britain back to her hometown in Germany. Blair couldn't believe it. 'Come over to Trier for New Year,' she had said to him.

You'll have a great time.' People in their right mind didn't invite all and sundry home for New Year celebrations, however. Of course, that had been back in July. She might have expected him to forget about it in due course of time. If she thought that though, she was very much mistaken about him, Blair told himself. Something like a smirk crossed his face. He was still looking out unseeingly at the platform and a blond teenager caught his expression and turned away in some alarm.

The train did not pull away till twenty past seven, by which time the refreshment stand had opened and the Scandinavians and some other early morning travellers had started to buy themselves tea and coffee. Blair had no Belgian currency, and he watched the world sipping and warming its hands on hot polystyrene beakers with an increasing sense of the unfairness of being. He was not sure he had the linguistic means to order coffee here anyway, but he tried to comfort himself with the knowledge that the train was due to stop in Luxembourg. There he hoped he might be able to make himself understood; from what he could gather the people in that tiny country spoke bad French too.

He was wrong. He found a minuscule coffee bar that looked like it was somebody's front room but, despite there being nothing much else on offer apart from hot drinks, the man who served him refused to understand Blair's request for coffee. Blair pointed at the cups and at the filter machine in despair, but the man rattled away in rapid and perfect French. When he finally deigned to understand the order, Blair asked for milk, using the proper French word. He was given a tin of condensed milk with a jagged hole in the top, apparently punched by a pocketknife. When he came to pay, the man asked for fifty francs. Blair took a step backwards and asked if 'c'etait juste.' The man dismissed him with a flip of his wrist and a grimace at the two old men who were drinking black coffee, clearly with a foreknowledge that there was no fresh milk available at the establishment. Blair paid the fifty francs in confusion and with a suspicion that he was somehow being mocked by the two old men, though they did not actually say anything out loud.

205

On the last leg of his journey to Trier Blair ran through what Sabine had said. He had had to ask for her address after she had suggested that he pay a visit to Germany, but she gave it to him readily, with an apologetic laugh. He had written twice since the summer and she had said 'Of course you must come,' when she had replied briefly to the second letter. He had tried telephoning her a couple of days before setting off but had twice not been able to get through. The third time there was only a gruff German voice.

This did not bode too well, but it only slightly tarnished the veneer of his memories of last summer with Sabine. Though it could not be said that they had had time to get really romantic, she had always been more than ready to join him for a cup of tea in the staff canteen; she had laughed a lot at the things he had talked about, and she had kissed him on the cheek on that last night, when a few of the staff had got together to say goodbye to their German visitor. She had even seemed a little sad at having to go back. 'I will always remember my English friends,' she had said, with a look aimed particularly at him, he was sure.

Blair buried his face into the rough fabric of the seat back and tried to get some sleep. He might wake with a mottled pattern impressed deep into his cheek, but he wanted to be as fresh as possible for the rencontre. It was five months since they had seen each other and he could not quite picture her face any more, try as he might. If asked to do so by a police sketch artist, he could have described her features - her rosy complexion, her short brown hair, a dimple on her left cheek - but he couldn't put these constituent features together into a snapshot. He had asked in his first letter if she would care to send him a photo, but she had obviously forgotten by the time she wrote. He hoped she would remember him.

When he awoke from a fitful half an hour's sleep, his face was red and blotchy from the moquette upholstery. He veered off to the toilet and tried to wash off the marks, then he decided to stay standing for the rest of the journey, looking out at the unremarkable scenery till it gave way to the outskirts of Tier. It was eleven o'clock when the train finally ground to a noisy stop. Blair hoped he would be able to get through to Sabine from a station call box. It was four days after Christmas; the period when she would surely have some time off work. But it didn't matter too much; he had her address and could take a cab and just turn up.

It took him a little while to get through to Sabine from a call box at the station, but he eventually succeeded. She sounded surprised when he announced that he was in Trier and waiting at the station. The line went dead for a moment, but she returned and said that he should wait where he was; she would drive there and pick him up in ten minutes. He sat on his suitcase in the middle of the concourse watching heavily overcoated families greeting each other and long-haired students returning for the Christmas holidays. No one took any notice of the duffel coated man sitting expectantly on his luggage like an overgrown schoolboy returning from boarding school, but he did not have to wait too long. About half an hour passed and then he saw Sabine approaching. Her hair was longer, and she looked older than he remembered, though he knew she was little more than twenty three or twenty four. She looked rather serious too. Blair put on his most charming smile and reached out to grasp her hands. She took one hand and shook it politely.

'This is quite a shock,' she said.

'Didn't you get my letters?' Blair asked apprehensively.

She nodded, but without conviction.

'How long were you planning on staying in Trier?' she said.

'Well, I'm free right up till the sixth of January, but I won't impose on you for too long,' Blair said gallantly. Sabine gave a half smile and looked about. as if she feared that they were being observed.

There was so much to talk about, but strangely Sabine seemed more interested in pointing out features of architectural interest, like the antiquity of the Porta Nigra, than in annotating their personal history from those intense weeks of the past summer. Blair tried reminding her of the time when they had had tea at Eynon's, and of the time when the photocopier had broken down, but these memories

207

seemed stronger in his mind than in Sabine's. Blair fell quiet, apologising after a while for his lack of conversation and offering train-lag as an excuse. Sabine seemed happy to concentrate on her driving.

Sabine's flat was on the third floor of a dowdy town house near the centre of the town. She said she shared it with an engineer called Ernst and a girl called Maria. Maria had gone back to her parents for Christmas, so there was a spare bedroom for a couple of days. Sabine thought that Maria would not mind Blair staying, though to be fair she was not certain when her flatmate would be returning. Blair declared his satisfaction with these arrangements. They were standing outside the entrance to the flat as she said this and as soon as he got through the door Blair found himself being introduced to Ernst. He was rather a frosty type, Blair realised, typically German in his rigid politeness. He did not appear to speak any English, sadly, and the introductions and translations accordingly took some time. In a way, however, Blair was glad that he did not have to chat at greater length about his journey, or the weather. He wasn't all that good at chit chat and he was dreadfully tired, and anxious to be shown where he would be sleeping. Sabine showed him an untidy box room and gestured at a mattress on the floor. 'Maria has not been with us long,' she said. 'Perhaps I should clear up some of her things.' Blair said there was no need. He picked up some underclothes from the bed and put them on a chair.

'I can sleep on top of the bedclothes,' he said brightly.

Sabine went back out with a shrug and Blair lay down gratefully on the thin mattress. He heard his hostess and her flatmate talking in low voices in German, but his eyes soon closed. He didn't wake till late evening and at first, he was alarmed at his strange surroundings, but then he heard the same voices, talking loudly and laughing now, and he recalled where he was. He ruffled his hair and appeared in the living room. Sabine and the stern looking engineer were eating pasta from plates on their laps.

'I was a little worried,' Sabine said. 'I didn't like to wake you, but you've been asleep all day. You must be hungry; I've made some pasta, if you …'

Blair smiled and inspected a saucepan on the two-ring stove in a corner of the room. 'Smells beautiful,' he said. Ernst and Sabine shared a strange look.

Blair fought his way through a plate of the lukewarm pasta and smiled a lot. Sabine smiled back once or twice but spent a good deal of time gazing down at her own meal. Ernst kept staring at him, rather rudely for a man who had seemed so polite initially, Blair felt. Eventually, Ernst spoke up, and in English, to Blair's surprise: 'Would you like to watch some TV?' he said. 'I'm afraid Sabine and I have to go out, but... '

'Please make yourself at home,' Sabine finished for him.

Blair watched an incomprehensible German drama and then an equally baffling comedy show. He tried a copy of *Stern* instead, but it was no better.

The next day he got up early, but Sabine and Ernst were nowhere to be seen. Though he did not want to be seen as taking things too much for granted, he made himself a cup of black coffee, for he couldn't even find any condensed milk. Then he wrote a note to Sabine to say when he would be back, with a message that he hoped she would have returned by that time to let him in again, and he went out and walked the streets for a few hours.

There was no answer when he rang the bell at two o' clock that afternoon, so he had to spend another few hours studying the inconsequential architecture of the suburb he accidentally wandered into. He went back to the flat again at six and this time got an answer when he rang.

'Oh, there you are,' Sabine said. 'We thought you had got lost!'

'I went for a little walk,' Blair said. Then he couldn't think of anything else to say. Ernst offered him a thin cigarette that he had just rolled. Blair shook his head politely. 'I'm afraid smoking repels me,' he said. Ernst gave a questioning look. 'Ich nicht rauchen,' he added. Sabine laughed, unaccountably.

Blair went to his room and lay down. All the walking he had done that day had exhausted him, but he did not fall asleep directly. Instead, he gazed up at the ceiling as the light began to fade outside and orange sodium lamps came on in the distance. Maria, or some previous occupant of the room, had stuck luminous little moons and stars to the ceiling and they began to give off an eerie green glow which held his attention for a long time. Eventually he got up, switched on a table lamp and took out an exercise book from his suitcase. He wrote a heading in block capitals on the first page - MY STAY IN TRIER - but then he found he had nothing to say just yet.

He was disturbed once by the sound of low voices from the room next door, which he assumed was Sabine's bedroom, but a little while later he heard the front door bang shut and he realised he was alone in the flat again. It didn't matter. The next day was New Year's Eve and Blair hoped there would be a party somewhere. He was confident Sabine would invite him to some celebration, and then he would have plenty of time to regale her with all the news from Britain.

There was indeed a party for Sylvester, as Sabine put it. She said that her friends in the flat on the ground floor of the house had invited them for drinks. Just a small gathering. Would he like to accompany Ernst and her? 'I think some of the people who will be there speak English,' she said. This was good news.

The gathering was not so small. There were forty or fifty young people crammed into the three rooms which made up the ground floor flat. The first room was a tiny kitchen full of German sausage and intense long-haired Germans. The second room was a bedroom, but the bed had been removed and replaced by a knot of less intense, rather more boisterous Germans, with hair of differing length and hue. The third room was bare of furniture but contained the machinery of the dance: an enormous complex hi-fi system and disco lights dominating one wall. Blair was unsure if he was up to dancing and he retreated back to the kitchen, where he nursed a bottle of Bitberger and a cardboard plate of kartofel salat, until such a time as he could seize a chance to talk to Sabine. Oddly, she had temporarily disappeared shortly after introducing him to a man called Harald.

Harald was not one of the people who spoke English and, after showing Blair the three rooms, he too disappeared.

Blair did his best to mill around for half an hour, then he stood next to a girl who he thought had been staring at him earlier, though her look had not been promising, being more suggestive that he had his jumper on back to front than that she was anxious to strike up a conversation. Nevertheless, he moved over to her side to allow talk to ensue, should she wish it. She looked away, then hailed a friend and went into the next room. Blair waited a few before going into the room. Sabine had shown up again, but she was in deep conversation with Ernst in a corner; Blair judged it an inopportune time to approach her. He gazed down the neck of his beer bottle and felt himself warming from the heat of the crowded room. He was lost in a quiet reverie when a voice spoke to him from close by. It was the friend of the girl he had stood next to.

'You are English, I think,' she said.

Blair nodded sadly, as if rightly accused of some childish indiscretion.

'I speak a little of the language,' the girl pursued. She was little more than seventeen, Blair realised, and was perhaps trying out her school English.

Blair nodded again. 'Me too,' he said softly.

'What is it like?' she said. 'They say the English are men of few words.'

'That's right,' Blair said. He put down his empty Bitberger bottle and smiled sadly. 'I'm afraid I have to go now.'

The girl tilted her head slightly then shrugged. Blair started to push his way back out to the front door, but there was too much of a throng for him to get through before a tight ring formed and people started chanting in unison. Blair realised they were counting down from ten. He just managed to get to the door as the countdown ended and everyone began cheering. Someone grabbed his hand and shook it firmly, then he felt a light brushing of lips on his cheek. 'Happy New Year,' he heard close to his ear. It was the girl he had just spoken to. He did not know what to say. Just over the girl's shoulder he could see Sabine and Ernst kissing warmly.

When he got up late next morning Ernst found a page torn from an exercise book taped to the television screen. He called into his bedroom, where Sabine was dressing.

'Schatze,' he said, 'There is a note from your English friend here.'

Sabine hurried out into the living room and picked up the piece of paper.

'He does not say much,' Ernst said matter-of-factly.

''No,' Sabine replied. There was one word on the piece of paper. It said, 'Sorry.'

FLAT

Mac was his best friend. He only saw him a couple of times a year now though, when he and Jenny brought the children up to London for a day out. They had been regular visitors before the children came along and had persevered at first with the baby, and even with both children, but they didn't stay overnight anymore. The flat just wasn't childproof. They sensed his tenseness. It was a shame, but he couldn't apologise for being house proud, perhaps a little set in his ways. When you live alone you get used to things being exactly where they always are, and just a flicker of alarm in his eyes was enough to alert a woman like Jenny that her children's freedom to play with any of his books and ornaments was only really a verbal gesture. But the invitation was still there, of course.

On this occasion work had taken him abroad for a couple of days, and he had been only too pleased to leave a key for Mac to use the flat. Mac had a meeting in London. Could he stay overnight to take in a show? He had not been asked this before, but he didn't think to ask what sort of meeting this might be. He was surprised that Mac had written rather than phoned, but when he called him, Mac said, 'I don't like speaking to your answering machine, John. At least when you ring, I'm either here or not here. Not disembodied.'

They were both sorry that he'd be out of the country, and they would miss seeing each other this time, but of course he could use the place. He'd leave beer in the fridge and a TV dinner or two.

'I'll only be sleeping there, John. I'll even sleep on top of the bed, so I won't rumple the sheets.'

There was a thank you note on the coffee table when he got back. He'd drunk a can of beer, but he'd more than make up for it next time when he came down, it said. He let the note flutter back down and he slumped on to the chesterfield. It was nearly nine o' clock at night, but he didn't switch on The News. Mac should have left early

213

in the morning, but he knew he'd only left minutes before. It wasn't a smell of other human beings, it was through other, more sophisticated signs that the flat yielded up the secrets of its recent occupancy. He involuntarily slipped his hand down the side of his seat, but there was nothing as obvious as a pair of briefs or a crumpled tissue. Everything was in place. The two glossy books on wine and European architecture were where they always were, on the occasional table; there was still a rolled-up piece of paper by the wicker wastepaper basket where he'd missed a couple of days ago. He picked it up and placed it in the basket. He knew that Mac had spent some considerable time here, perhaps checking that everything was in its proper place.

He got up and went into the tiny galley kitchen. There was one upturned cup on the draining board, He picked it up, ran a finger round the inner edge and it was wet. On an impulse he opened the wall cabinet and, as he knew it would be, the first cup he picked up was damp too. So, it was a woman. Mac was not the type to have two cups of coffee, carefully wash them out and then replace one cup in the cabinet. Now he wanted to know what the woman was like, so he began to search for clues.

The bed was made, but not as he had made it. The bottom sheet was folded under neatly on one side and bundled under on the other. This told him something. So did the wardrobe. His clothes had been pushed to one side. So, she (or perhaps Mac and the girl?) had made some room to hang up their clothes. This spoke of a fastidiousness he did not recognise in Mac and suggested to him that the companion was not a young girl. Didn't girls throw their clothes on the floor these days? Unlike their elders, brought up to respect the creases and folds of one's apparel. He was unable to judge in this matter.

He re-entered the living room. Several minutes of searching yielded no further clues until he noticed that a sheet had been torn from the telephone pad in the hall. There were impressions in the new top sheet, and almost without thinking he took out a propelling pencil, slid out the lead, and shaded in the marks. There was a six-figure number. He could dial it, but he didn't want to know. Anyway, it had to be a provincial number and there was no code.

He was surprised at his own lack of emotion. If he had been presented with the hypothetical case of Mac committing adultery, he would have strongly disapproved. Jenny was a lovely woman. He'd known them both nearly twenty years, since university. Faced with this flimsy but certain evidence he felt quite different. Elated almost. Then suddenly he was filled with despair. This meant he could not ask Mac and Jenny to stay any more, for Jenny would sleep in the bed where Mac and his unknown mistress had lain, drink from the cup she might have drunk from. He was used to solitude, but now he felt dreadfully alone. He looked at the stupid books on the occasional table and he wanted to throw them at something.

The flat was spoiled. Not by stains on the sheets or perfume lingering in the bathroom, but by occupancy. He realised he never touched it, never luxuriated in it, never felt anything here. He turned on the television and kept his finger pressed down hard on the remote's volume button. But no noise could drown the soft low murmur of the woman that he heard deep inside his own bones.

IN CONTROL

I wear my hair short now. It used to be a luxuriant dark brown before I got ill. Of course it's easier to manage these days; I just dye it - my hairdresser calls the shade titanium -   and I keep it cut close, like a soft silver helmet, but I do miss the sensation of movement. I could toss it around like a golden retriever emerging from a quick dip, or twiddle the ends like a coy teenager. I didn't have to solely rely on my eyes and mouth to express whatever I was feeling; I could choose to wear my hair up to suggest seriousness or professionalism, loose and flowing to stress that I was a free spirit, or styled with waves or curls to allude to my sensual nature. You can't tie ribbons in a hair helmet. Still, people seem to think this more utilitarian look suits me now. Perhaps my metallic hair conveys a sense that I'm enclosed these days, but in control. Robotic even.

Not many people know now in my new life that I have coloured contact lenses. They're steely blue. I actually have brown eyes, but when I dyed my hair blonde that time in Los Angeles Carlos said he hated blonde hair and brown eyes. He didn't actually say he hated it; he just said it was all wrong. Blonde hair, blue eyes; dark hair, brown eyes, he insisted. Then he added that, despite this rule, the sexiest combination was sapphire blue eyes and jet-black hair. I could have opted for that look now, twenty years later, when my hair grew back and I decided to dye it, and when I opted for the tinted lenses. I always think dyed black hair looks too much like paint though.

Carlos was all about physical appearance, and his own in particular. Of course, we were living in West Coast America, where tan is a state of mind as well as body and muscles are more important than morals. Or brain cells. He was an athlete, he claimed, but he was working as a waiter when we met. Calf injury, he said. Out for the season. I used to wonder why he felt the need to fabulate when it was perfectly clear that he was in great condition. The injury didn't appear to stop him running five miles every morning before breakfast anyway. I think he was probably cruising along the promenade, his muscles bulging out of his crisp white singlet, with one eye out for potential replacements for me.

The sex wasn't great, if I'm honest, but I was twenty-three and in a sparkly new country and I guess I thought I would always be twenty-three. Sex was just a topping on a wonderful confection made of new people, new music, and new sights and experiences. I was meeting famous film stars. I say 'meeting' but really it was just smiling and perhaps saying 'Hi' when they popped their heads into the costume department where I'd managed to get a job as a factotum to a very junior costume designer. I altered the odd hem on a toga or dirndl skirt, but most of the time I chatted to the proper costume people. It wasn't real work; it was a holiday from real work. The harsh reality of earning a proper living was to come later, when I moved to New York and got a job in an independent publishing house.

Klaus got me that job. He didn't work there but his sister's husband was one of the directors and he told me they were looking for a junior to train up as an editor for their non-fiction titles. I put my hair up, donned a pair of clear spectacles, and bought a flattering grey suit. and I got the job, despite having a degree in art and design, not the English degree I would have thought was what was expected. I think the interview panel, three attractive men in their early thirties, were suckered in by my deep brown eyes and quaint Welsh accent, rather than my academic background.

Klaus was another attractive thirtysomething. I met him as if it had been a scene in one of the romantic comedies the studio was churning out in the dream factory I'd just left. He came to my rescue when I slipped and fell on the sidewalk on 42nd Street. It was raining and I was wearing impossible high heels, but I'd only slightly jarred my ankle. He ran over from the shop doorway where he was standing and helped me to my feet, insisting that we go straight to the Emergency Room and have it x-ray'd. I held on to his arm for a few seconds, quickly deciding to do my coy teenager bit because he was *very* attractive, and he was wearing a suit that must have cost a small fortune. Or a small fortune in terms of the wages I'd been earning working as a junior costume designer's even more junior assistant in Los Angles.

We didn't go to a hospital: we went to a coffee shop, where I ordered a milkshake and he opted for an espresso. That sort of conformed the innocence/experience balance we were both happy to establish as the background for whatever was going to happen next.

We didn't make love that night because I was chary of letting him see the run-down hotel that I'd booked into a couple of days earlier. The next evening, we went to the cinema and then to his studio flat on the Upper East Side, where we made love, at first with incredible passion and then again with a tenderness that almost made me weep. It was very different from sex with Carlos. If I was really living in a movie, it should have been the other way round: perfunctory lovemaking with my Teutonic saviour and animal frenzy with my Latin lover. I was still twenty-three, but I felt like I'd grown up overnight.

Klaus worked in finance. I didn't know if that meant he was a teller in a bank or a hedge fund manager, but his expensive wardrobe suggested the latter. We both tacitly agreed that I did not need to know any more about what he did in the daytime, however. It was only a few days, and a lot of lovemaking later that Klaus suggested that I try for the editing job. I'd saved up enough to get me through a few weeks in the Big Apple, but I decided I was not simply a demure little thing from the Welsh valleys, I was a high-risk gambler. I blew an unseemly amount on the smart grey suit and the hairdo from Fabio's in Tribeca and strode into the publisher's surprisingly small office as if I was on a catwalk. I think Klaus had blessed me with a sense that this was my time, this was my stage.

Of course, I didn't know then that Klaus was married.

I kept the job, despite what might have been seen as an unfortunate liaison with my employer's brother-in-law. They kept me on because it transpired that I was quite good at line editing, though the texts I worked on, tomes like *A History of Lithography* and *50 New Uses for Sorghum* were hardly the stuff to invigorate the creative life I'd imagined for myself. Nevertheless, it paid enough for me to rent a room in Soho, and see the occasional off-Broadway production, and that was way beyond my aspirations as a teenager In Merthyr Tydfil. I even ate out from time to time.

And it was in a small family-run restaurant on Mulberry Street that I encountered a wonderfully single man-of-my-dreams.

His name was Alessandro, but he insisted on Sand. He said people sometimes tried to call him Al, but he didn't like it, because that sounded like a garage mechanic or a standup comedian. I baulked and tended to use his full name, because Sand sounded too much like the substance, like something that I might let slip through my fingers. When I explained this, he smiled and said I was cute.

He was working as a driver for a limousine company, he told me. It was partly true, because the car he drove was a big black Lincoln, but he drove it for one man, not a limo company, as I was to discover later. I never really found out if his employer was a gang boss or just a super-rich businessman, because Alexander wouldn't say anything about it. When I enquired, he would kiss the tip of my nose and tell me I was sweet and change the subject.

We lasted eight months, which was a record for me. It wasn't a dramatic break up, we were drifting apart anyway when he said he had to relocate to Pittsburgh. We both pretended that we would visit each other at weekends but it was me who said that work was too hectic the first few weeks. Then I heard that he'd been killed in a drive-by shooting. Perhaps he was involved in some crime syndicate after all; perhaps he was just unlucky. I was too shocked to grieve, and I only heard about his death about a week after the funeral. I don't know if I would have gone to Pittsburgh anyway. Work *was* actually very pressured. I know this seems callous, but I didn't know any of his family, and I wouldn't have wanted to be a strange outsider examined critically by various cousins and aunts. Or indeed, if he had been connected to a nefarious way of life, by burly men in Italian suits and dark glasses, as I stood at his graveside.

Life went on. I got better at my job. I earned more money. I had on/off relationships with a couple of decent men. Neither of them was ready to commit, but then again, I'm not sure I was either. I hadn't become American, you see. I wasn't hankering for my old life, but I somehow knew that New York was just a phase, an interesting chapter maybe, but not the whole book of me. I also knew that I would not be defined by my job since I might switch as easily from editing to crafts, say, as easily as I had switched from costuming to publishing. And I wouldn't allow myself to be defined by my relationship with a husband or partner either. Not that anyone had seriously offered to be a permanent figure in my life, such was my fear of being owned.

In the end I realised, surely as we all do, that it wasn't in my own hands anyway. I got ill. Couldn't afford the medical bills in New York of course. So I came back to Wales. I was in treatment for months and months, but they caught it and I was given a second chance to start a new life. Not many people get that. I realise. John, who I live with now, has been very strong and helped me in so many ways. Obviously, he didn't sweep me off my feet, as they say. He slowly built a sense that we should share our lives, brick by considerate brick. He's a thoroughly decent man. You can't have excitement every day of your life, you'd spin out of control. And I want control. Or I thought I did.

I arrived early at The Mason's Arms one Friday lunchtime. I had a book, a guide to Monet it was, and I was sitting contentedly browsing and sipping at an Americano with cold milk, when a young man sat down opposite me.

'Hope you don't mind,' he said. 'Is this seat taken?'

For some reason I didn't say anything, even though I knew John would be coming in twenty minutes or so. I just looked at him to see if he was seriously trying it on. He must have been a good ten years younger than me, though that doesn't have to count, of course. I closed my book and smiled my acquiescence.

Within a few easy manoeuvres he'd established that I'd studied art at university and worked in America. I even told him about the summer I spent in Corfu. He was very knowledgeable about art and film, though I couldn't help wondering if it was all a little glib, too practised, you might say. He was definitely reticent about his own history. The closest he got to telling me anything about himself was that he had had pretensions about becoming a poet.

The dalliance lasted less than half an hour, because John came rushing in, apologising for being late. I wasn't feeling guilty about talking to this stranger, and I don't think it would have even occurred to John that I was capable of flirting, or being flirted with. I said we'd just been chatting about a Peter Greenaway film. That wasn't something John was interested in, and he darted off to the bar to get us drinks.

There was a table free nearer the bar and John and I sat there, leaving the young man at his table. I keep thinking about this encounter, and the way he tried to control the conversation. Unlike Carlos, he wasn't a peacock, and unlike Klaus he didn't ride in to save me from some terrible fate, like falling over in the street. And he was different from Allesandro because he didn't smirk or give me a sense that he was in charge of everything. This young man was more a lost puppy seeking a new owner.

They all try to impress, and then when they think it's safe to relax, and they've trained you to be what they thought they'd desired for themselves, they pick up the reins and point you in the direction they've decided. I didn't get the impression from my nameless interlocutor in The Mason's Arms that he wanted such mastery. It felt like it was always me who was in control. Except when he gazed so earnestly into my eyes, when perhaps I felt a little more innocent. Vulnerable even. I had a terrier in my New York brownstone who looked at me like that. It was the following day that I decided to change to blue contact lenses, if I'm honest.

Still, I miss being the one not in control.

Other books by Lloyd Rees available from Cambria

Speaking Daggers ISBN 9780957245976

The Two of Us ISBN 9781838075200

Voices without parts ISBN 9781916453265